# THE RELUCTANT RAPPAREE

JIM McCOMISH

*For Scarlett*

First published in Northern Ireland in 2015
BY EXCALIBUR PRESS

This edition published in 2015
BY EXCALIBUR PRESS



ISBN-13: 978-0993501500
ISBN-10: 0993501508

Formatting & layout by
BY EXCALIBUR PRESS

**EXCALIBUR PRESS**
Belfast, Northern Ireland

excaliburbelfast@gmail.com
07982628911 | @ExcaliburPress
**www.excaliburpress.co.uk**

# 1.  A BLOODY BEGINNING

Caoilinn McGrogan had often wished to see her husband as quiet as he was on that fateful morning of 21st of February 1731, his usual early patter being a damning critique of the quality of his breakfast or a bad tempered snap at anyone inadvertently aggravating his whiskey head; but this was a time for neither silence nor inaction. This was a desperate situation, as the newcomers unravelled the tattered threads of the McGrogans' lives before their eyes with carefree abandon. Looking back and forth from the eviction scene to her husband, she nervously swept a twisted clutch of rusty hair back from her pale brow as her heart pounded in her throat.

'Patrick! Are you just going to stand there and do nothing? Where will we live? How will we eat?' One could think of a thousand questions in such a moment but Patrick McGrogan didn't have an answer for a single one of them.

What answer could there be? There was no money to pay the rent, no one to lend it to them, and no way to persuade the bailiffs to defer the debt for another week. Their little ramshackle holding in the townland of Drumgooland near Clough in County Downe was the McGrogan's world, and it was lost to them. Maybe Patrick could have tried harder, but he was never a man given to either physical exertion or reasoned argument.

Bang, bang, bang.

Every tap of the hammer driving the nail into the cottage door felt like a heavy slap on top of his balding head; but the consequences of this hammering would be much more far reaching than any chastisement Patrick had ever suffered.

'Perhaps if you wait another hour Mr Deasley, my brother in law was trying to get some money for me.' pleaded Patrick, wringing his hands together as if he were trying to remove a pair of invisible mittens. The tick man didn't answer, his head buried in his book and preoccupied with mental calculations. The wind whistled up abruptly, flicking the ledger back several pages to the recently crossed out accounts of several other bad debtors. Deasley tutted with annoyance and scraped them back roughly into place with a pointed index finger. McGrogan looked pitifully to Caoilinn, who stood clutching the shoulders of their 6 year old son Angus, and just shook his head. He looked back to the tick man, who was once again jotting up the eviction in his ledger.

It had taken the 6 heavies accompanying Hugh Deasley all of 3 minutes to empty the contents of the one room cottage onto the muddy lane. 'That's your debts settled then McGrogan, you may take what's yours and make yourself scarce. There'll be other people wanting this tenancy; they'll not want the likes of yousuns knocking about.' Deasley wasn't even trying to be cruel; he had evicted so many people over the past few years all the tears and pleading just washed over him. It was the same thing every time.

'There's been a mistake.'

'I paid that bill last quarter.'

'Give me two more weeks I'm good for the money.'

'No I'm not leaving, go get the bailiff then!'

'But what about the bairns?'

Always the same and always in that exact order; human beings were so utterly predictable, especially the poor ones. At the end of the day they all had to accept their fate because the bailiffs had the means to take whatever they wanted and the law of the land was behind them. Invariably the tenants would capitulate and wander off aimlessly, which was probably what Patrick McGrogan would do in a few minutes when he failed to come up with any effective contingency plan. He didn't look as though he had a clue let alone a plan. McGrogan looked despondently at the hastily scribbled docket which Deazley had thrust roughly into his hand. English words, English laws; it was a second language to the McGrogans, who conducted their daily business mostly in their native tongue. Patrick didn't need to understand the words on the paper to know what it meant though; first you get a piece of paper, then you get a whack with a cudgel if you don't get moving sharpish. A rough shaking of the arm from Caoilinn pulled his attention away from his pointless survey of the document and back into the real world. 'Patrick, you need to stop them!' begged Caoilinn incessantly in Irish; 'For God's sake do something man!'

'Give over will you woman!' protested Patrick, wrenching his arm away. 'There are 6 of the blaggards there, bigger than me and with guns and cudgels, what do you want me to do about it?' Caoilinn turned away contemptfully and returned to comforting their sobbing son.

Patrick McGrogan might have been a man with no appetite for a fight in him, but his two eldest sons were born for it. At 17 and 20 years of age respectively, Shane and Seamus McGrogan were two big lumps of lads who Patrick couldn't put manners on since Seamus was 14. Today however, it would be someone else who would have them to contend with. The first of the bailiffs noted their presence when they were some 100 yards from the house, when Seamus threw down the heavy load of peat he'd been carrying and the two advanced angrily up the lane, clutching their spades. The bailiffs felt a slight unease as the approaching figures seemed to get bigger and bigger.

'What the Hell's going on here?' demanded Shane angrily of Deasley.

'Were you just going to stand there and let them do this? Why didn't you come and get us?' barked Seamus to his father. Patrick said nothing but stood with his head bowed, biting his fingernails. In truth he was hoping they would be out before the boys got back; he knew well the sort of them.

'I am here to serve notice of eviction on the tenant of this property, vis-a-vis Mr Patrick McGrogan, due to non-payment of the agreed rent...'

'You want money? I can get you the money!' reasoned Shane, desperately. The truth was he couldn't and everyone there knew it. 'I can have your money by the end of the week. I have debts I can call in.'

'It's too late I'm afraid you've had your chance to pay.' replied Deasley, dismissively. 'No more chances. I want you all off the property now.'

'Who the hell are you to tell us to get off this land?' countered Seamus. 'Our family has been farming here for generations you can't just throw us of our-'

'It's not your land it is the Viscount's land.' retorted Deasley.

'To hell with the Viscount!' shouted Shane; 'He won't be happy until there isn't a catholic farmer left in the whole of the country.

Yousuns may take yourselves off, you'll get your money as soon as we've got it.'

'Ah, cursing your betters eh McGrogan? A fine lad you are, no doubt a drunkard like your oul fella there. If you can't pay your rent then you're out no matter whether you bow your head to saint or saviour, now be off with you or my men here will be putting you to rights.'

'What did you say you wee rat?' spat Shane advancing on Deasley, as Seamus gripped his shoulders and held him back; 'You talk about betters doing the job that you do? You're nothing but a wriggling maggot in the carcass of this country!'

Deasley back stepped awkwardly in the wake of the approaching McGrogan, unsure whether to run or stand his ground, and afraid to take his eyes off Shane long enough to ensure his safe passage. He stumbled backwards over a wooden bucket and tumbled haplessly into a muddy puddle in the lane. The sight of the rotund little upstart's mishap ignited a spontaneous burst of laughter from the bailiffs, but Deasley jumped instantly to his feet and after examining the back of his sodden coat, pointed frantically at Shane.

'You saw that! He pushed me over. I want that man arrested!' he called to the bailiffs, who looked to one another shaking their heads and muttering their disagreement. 'Nobody laid hands on you, you lying little shit.' retorted Seamus; 'Aye, you'd have more than a muddy arse if you received a blow from me.' added Shane.

'See!' cried Deasley; 'See how he threatens me at my work. Seize hold of him now, I want him brought before a magistrate!' The goons held back indecisively, none wanting to be first to lay hold of the fearsome pair. 'Take hold of him I tell you! Or you'll have want of a job when I report to my superior!' Fearing a loss of employment more than the possibility of a cracked skull, the first of the bailiffs grabbed hold of Shane's left arm, receiving an elbow to the mouth for his efforts. This spurred the other five into action, but Seamus was there before them and soon all 8 men were trading blows whilst Deasley stood back and Mrs McGrogan screamed at her husband take some – any – form of action. Panicked, Patrick McGrogan ran off behind the house while the fight continued. The boys acquitted themselves well but the odds were against even them, given their opponents' superior numbers and experience. Deasley meanwhile had produced a pistol which he was attempting to train on either of the pair, but as the mass of bodies swayed and tossed he was unable to get a clear shot. He pushed Caoilinn away roughly as she clawed on his arm screaming God knows what in a language he had no inclination to understand.

Three of the heavies managed to lay hold of Shane by an arm each and another round his neck. As Deasley raised his pistol to shoot, Caoilinn McGrogan threw herself into his path, hoping to knock his hand skyward and send the shot into the air, but received the full force of the blow in Shane's stead.

All assembled gasped in horror as Caoilinn McGrogan's body crumpled to the ground.

Deasley stood open mouthed at the consequences of his actions for all of 2 seconds before experiencing a searing pain across his back, and looked down to see the prongs of a pitchfork protruding from his chest, having been run through by a vengeful Patrick McGrogan. As Deasley slumped to his death another shot rang out as one of the bailiffs delivered a lead ball to the chest of Patrick McGrogan, killing him instantly. As little Angus dived behind a cartwheel in terror, a final shot rang out, this time fired skyward as a warning to all.

'All of you throw down your guns and cease your belligerence if you value your lives. These people are under the protection of Shane Crossagh O'Mullan!' Everyone stopped fighting and turned to look at the two mounted and hooded figures, who had just arrived. Shane ran to check his parents for signs of life while Seamus lifted Angus and held him close, whispering reassurances. The bailiffs stood together nervously with their hands in the air.

Shane Crossagh, the legendary rapparee from Faughanvale and Cumber, nodded to the prone corpse of Hugh Deasley; 'That one would have had his money and left with his life if yousuns had waited but one hour. I came here to pay the debt. It would appear however, that my sister and her husband's debts are now paid in full.' Michael O'Mullan added; 'We would be well served to take your lives in vengeance for our sister; but as the murderer has been dispatched, we will satisfy ourselves by taking your horses and allowing you to walk home. Mark my words however and find yourselves a new trade, for if you are seen to be collecting debt from the people of this country again, our next meeting will end in your termination.'

As the bailiffs gathered themselves and made tracks, Shane Crossagh turned to his nephews; 'Shane, Seamus, you must come with us now, you'll be proclaimed for your actions here today although you did no wrong. There is no justice for a catholic in this country.' Seamus lifted Angus onto Deasley's horse and clambered on himself. Shane lifted his mother's body gently onto another horse. He paused momentarily, surveying the blood on the cobbles, his ruined home and shattered family. For a split second, he allowed a scattering of happy childhood memories to flash through his mind before a chill wind whistled down from the

Mournes, as if to foretell of the trials which lay ahead of him. He nodded shakily and let fall a single tear, effecting to wipe his brow so that the other men and Angus wouldn't see. There would be a reckoning for this one day, of that he was sure.

'We'll bury her in the mountains of her homeland.' said Shane, with a rasp whisper. He looked back at his father's corpse. 'He can lie where he is.'

# 2. LYING IN WAIT

It is worth remembering that even in the darkest of hours, there is always the hope of a new dawn and a better future. If you keep telling yourself that you'll come to believe it, and if you believe it long enough you can make that hope a reality. Many new dawns were to break in expectation and many suns were to set in despair for Shane, Seamus and Angus McGrogan, before the day would come when Shane's great plan could begin to be brought to fruition. That day was to be today.

Archibald McClung was crouched ankle deep in mud and briers, contemplating the twists and turns his life had taken over the past year. His woollen greatcoat offered little protection against the incessant grey drizzle, having soaked through by sunrise that morning. It was some 5 or 6 hours ago that he and his comrades first set out from their mountain bolt-hole and trudged the 16 odd miserable miles from Slieve Croob to take up their sorry, soggy vigil somewhere between Banbridge and Dromore. His greyed and threadbare stockings – weren't they a brilliant white when his mother presented them to him? were now a sickly dark brown, as were the bottom half of his once fine crimson velvet breeches. Most of his apparel had long since been stained, ripped or splattered with the horrid filth of the mountain elements that seemed to berate the hapless gang of thieves who had been his friends, companions and oft time tormentors for 12 long and arduous months now. A spattering of bulbous icy raindrops from a low hanging branch hit him square on the nape of the neck and trickled cruelly down the inside of his shirt, forcing him to retreat with a shudder further into the spiky hawthorn bush which served as his somewhat poorly chosen source of shelter. The swift passage of the drops to the base of his spine recalled to Archie his want of a hat, having been relieved of his own tri-corner by the older man directly facing him in the bushes on the opposite side of the road.

Seamus Mor McGrogan was a big brute of a man, with hands like shovels and a fiery red beard to match his volatile temper; second in command of his younger brother Shane's gang, he was hated by most and feared by all. He served the purpose of keeping order in the gang, although none would thank him for it. He made a point of serving up regular beatings to the young boys to keep any of them from getting ideas above their station. Archie recalled with a wince how only 3 days into his internship with the gang, Seamus had blacked his eye when he took the hat, and wouldn't have stopped there if Seamus' younger brother Angus Og McGrogan hadn't have begged him to stop. It was at this point that Archie first realised that rather than escaping what had seemed like a life of tyranny and oppression, he had simply traded his father's well intentioned but authoritative control to become little more than an open air prisoner, a reluctant junior apprentice to this motley band of vagrant thugs.

Archie wished he had never ear-wigged so enthusiastically to the songs and tales of the catholic farmers at the market in Banbridge, the daring-do of Redmond O'Hanlon, Naiose O'Haughan and Shane Crossagh; he cursed his naivety for having paid lip service to the tall tales of righting wrongs, outwitting the authorities and leaping the six mile river in a single bound. What made him think this would be a suitable life for him, the only son of a Presbyterian minister? All hogwash. If this past year had taught him anything at all it was that there were no heroes in real life, on the road or anywhere else for that matter. Life was all about who could hit the hardest, and be grateful if there was someone weaker than yourself because then they will get picked on instead of you. He rued the day he left behind a life of comparative privilege, the son of the Reverend Alexander McClung of Ballyvalley First Presbyterian Church.

Hailing from Ayreshire where he began life as the second son of a wealthy cattle farmer, Alexander 'Sandy' McClung had applied his protestant work ethic and dedication to the Kirk at the great theological college in Edinburgh, before taking the calling of his first ministry to better edify the poor heathens of the County of Downe as to the wishes of the Lord and the errors of Rome. He mercilessly chastised the churchgoing sinners of the townland from the pulpit, sending even the most proudly bonneted heads home of an evening bowed in shame and repentance. His big bushy eyebrows made small children cry. The good Reverend was a man of great standing in the community and although the ministry wielded little wealth, he had put by enough to hopefully send young Archibald to one of the smaller theological colleges in Scotland, having failed to whip him hard enough to implant a thorough working knowledge of the holy scriptures, let alone the advanced learning necessary to secure a place at Trinity College in Dublin. The lash of his father's cane would be infinitely preferable to the fear, anxiety and pervasive threat of physical violence that he and the other youngsters in the gang felt in the presence of Seamus and the others like him on a daily basis. Archie would never forget the date, the 29th of April 1742, a year to the day, when he made a decision that would change the course of his life forever.

With young Archie having arrived home to the Rectory from fishing, late for supper and sodden with mud, the good Reverend raged at his son on the perils of sloth and the failure to honour one's father and mother. The sight of his unrepentant wastrel of a son sighing and rolling his eyes as the Reverend quoted line and verse sent brimstone flying from the old man's ears, and the swift application of an open hand to Archie's lughole had sent the youngster sprawling on the hearth. As his mother pleaded with the older man for restraint, Archie had rose up rashly and sharply glanced a nearby toby jug off the good Reverend's temple. After standing dumbstruck with horror for a few seconds as his father lay motionless and his blood poured upon the tiles, Archie pelted out of the house and down the road with his mother's screams ringing in his ears and tears streaming from his eyes.

He spent the first night sleeping up a tree for fear of being eaten by wolves – unaware that these were long since extinct in Ireland, and narrowly avoided capture by a troop of the local militia. Secreted in a patch of particularly thick heather, he had overheard the Captain saying; 'I will soon put manners on this young ruffian for striking a man of the cloth when I catch him!' Assuming himself a wanted man, Archie saw no recourse other than to ply his trade robbing on the highway.

And so McClung had ran from hearth and home and all he'd known to seek sanctuary in the lowliest and darkest places of the neighbourhood. The short coinage in his pocket hadn't got him far before a wordly wise barmaid had relieved him of his last penny for a flagon of beer, slice of stale bread and cheese and a quick feel of her devil's udders. Bereft of any further means of support, he had been sitting on a stone sobbing when the gang stumbled upon him and took him in, impressed by his ability to catch fish, light fires and read the various pamphlets and letters they had taken from the Banbridge mail coach before they wiped their arses on them.

Archie lay his short musket across his knees and drew his snot filled nose across the sleeve of his great coat, leaving a long, silver snail trail. He once had a handkerchief, but Seamus had taken that as well.

'Archie!' hissed a slight dark figure, diagonally to his right. 'You're in a fairy bush, get out of there or you'll have us all cursed.'

Although at 5'11 Barra McCann was considerably taller than most men of this age, he was also the only one of the gang lighter than Archie. Being of little use for anything other than carrying water and tall tales, McCann had taken to the road after trying to fence an army officer's coat at a flea market in Ballynahinch. He hadn't even realised it was a soldiers coat, having found it hung over a hedge whilst the owner engaged in insalubrious activity with a cowherd behind a bale of hay. When word got out the coat had gone missing every home in the area was searched with the intention of having the perpetrator shot as a spy. The coat wasn't found but several whisky stills were overturned resulting in gallons of the golden nectar finding its way to the officer's mess at the barracks in Saintfield. Taking to the road was actually a wise decision for young Barra, as the locals would have strung him up if the army didn't get him first. This slight, freckly auburn haired lanky man cut a comical figure, having neither shoes nor stockings and seeming none the worse for the want of them. His pantaloons were tailored for a man twice his size and hung down just below his calves. His frock coat was fastened securely at the waist with a piece of rope, pulled over tightly to protect his shirtless pigeon chest. It was of odd stitching and looked to Archie as if it was inside out. He thought himself to be between 19 and 24 years of age and his remaining teeth numbered slightly less than either of these figures. He didn't mourn their loss too greatly as, he explained, 'never was given anything worth chewing on anyway.' Despite his woeful physical condition and the harshness of his environment, Barra seemed inexplicably to be in an almost permanent state of happiness, which was greatly puzzling to Archie and a source of constant irritation to Seamus.

'Hold your tongue, half wit!' snapped Seamus, delivering a stinging slap to the back of Barra's shaggy head. The rest of the gang sniggered sneakily; always nice to see someone else getting it because at least then it's not you. 'And you can stop laughing too, preacher boy', grunted the brute; 'Use a handkerchief, you dirty wee bastard.'

Now Barra sniggered, halting sharply as Seamus caught him with a steely glance. 'Fairies indeed. You'll believe any oul shite wont you? Bletherin idjit.'

'He's right Seamus!' called a voice from 12 feet upwards on a branch of a massive sycamore tree, where Tomas McCafferty sat lookout. 'This is their land, we took it from them like the English and the Scottish pirates took it from us. No offence Archie.'

'None taken', replied Archie, resignedly.

'But they still live on here in the spirit' continued Tomas, airily; 'They're in the rocks and the trees, and you can hear them calling you on the wind sometimes. My Grandmother often speaks with them, she has a gift, she calls them Tuatha De Denaan, Children of Dana.'

Tomas McCafferty once prided himself on being the master cockler of the Ards peninsula, and had recounted to the boys on many occasions how he single handledly fed half the county during the famine of 1737, by carrying upwards of 2 hundred weight of shellfish on his back every day for a year from Ballyhenry bay to the needy souls of the surrounding hamlets. He claimed to have taken to the road after being falsely accused by the harbour master of being a lookout for smugglers, although Shane had remarked that the only smuggling involved was the secretion of Tomas's private member into the harbour master's wife's drawers. Cuckolding rather than cockling had been Tomas's downfall.

'Who the hell are the children of Dana?' said Seamus sharply. 'We were the first people here, we didn't take this land from anyone; the only ones who stole it were the ones who came over with fancy drawers over there', nodding at Archie.

'Keep your fairy stories to yourself Tomas. I don't want you frightening the boys'.

Archie sighed at the irony of the last sentence. He wanted to point out to Seamus that his father was a preacher who owned no land and had therefore stolen nothing from anyone. He weighed up the balance and decided the personal satisfaction that he would gain from this quip would not justify the fat lip it was likely to attract. He allowed himself a wry smile; despite the bleakness of his environment and loathsomeness of the company he had chosen, Archie had hope. He still envisioned a dazzling future; one day he'd wear fine silk stockings again. One day he'd sit by his own hearth in front of a roaring fire and smoke his pipe and sip the finest port without worrying about some big bullyboy trying to take it off him. One day he'd have a shite without getting stung on the arse by the jeggies. One day he'd have something in his pockets other than lint and holes. He didn't know how to accomplish all this but he knew it wouldn't happen while he was a member of Shane MacGrogan's gang with a price on his head. For now he needed to bide his time and make the most of it.

'Tell me more about these fairy folk, please Tomas.' called a cultured, foreign sounding voice from the darkness of the forest, making all present jump slightly at the unusual politeness of the request. Most had almost forgotten that Eugene O'Cahan was present, the interloper having so effectively concealed himself. O'Cahan, or 'the Frenchman' as the others called him, stepped slightly forward into a narrow slither of sunlight that permeated the bushes, his head bowed beneath his broad brimmed hat as he lit up his pipe; 'It will give us some light relief as we await the delivery.' Seamus scowled hatefully at the tall, elegant and markedly out of place figure, dressed in the style of a French officer. Eugene for his part nodded smugly at Seamus with a raised eyebrow and a sly grin. The Frenchman had been undermining Seamus' position in the gang ever since he arrived under cover of darkness some 3 or 4 months ago. He was a somewhat enigmatic figure, although Shane certainly seemed to have no end of stories to tell about him. As his name betrayed, Eugene wasn't a true Frenchman at all.

The O'Cahans were an ancient, princely bloodline from county Tyrone who had fought with some distinction in the Williamite wars. Eugene's grandfather had raided the Prince of Orange's encampments on a nightly basis alongside Galloping Hogan during the great retreat south, and his negotiating skills had been crucial in securing the safe passage of some 12,000 of the 'Wild Geese' to France under the Treaty of Limerick. Three generations of the family had since served as professional soldiers for hire to the various Royal houses of Europe, his father being conferred the title of 'Count' under the House of Bourbon. Eugene however disdained the use of such title, believing that a man's reputation should be built on his deeds and character rather than the circumstances of his birth. Seamus had heard plenty about Eugene's skills with a sword or a pistol, enough to know he wasn't a man to be tangled with lightly; but what really disturbed Seamus was the fact that Shane seemed to have more admiration for this pernicious dandy than he did for his own brothers!

Seamus feared that if the Frenchman joined the gang, he would likely bring others with him who would also challenge Seamus' authority and push him further down the pecking order. For Eugene's part, he had little interest in either allaying Seamus' fears or confirming them. Eugene had, at the behest of his old friend Shane with whom he had served on the continent for 8 years, agreed to 'come over and have a look' at the gang, with a view to joining up as co-leader. Being somewhat non-committal but not wishing to refuse his friend outright, Eugene had agreed to 'observe, assess, and report' to Shane on the gang's potential to be moulded into an effective fighting unit. He would not, for now, accept a position within the command structure and would neither take orders nor give them to anyone.

Eugene was as much a source of wonder to Archie as he was a source of antagonism to Seamus. No matter what the wind and rain did, Eugene was never soaked. He was never without powder. He was never without water in his bottle or bread in his satchel. His clothes were black because they were supposed to be, unlike the others with their perpetually muddy brown clobber. His shoes were always shiny, his moustache, hair and nails trimmed to precision. His brass buckles and trimmings shone like gold, and perhaps they were. His pistols, sword and equipment were always spotlessly clean and maintained to the highest standard. He could stuff his pipe and light it with a tinderbox using either hand singly without looking at what he was doing. Even when wearing the brightest of clothes he seemed to be able to become almost invisible in the deep vegetation of the forest or against the craggy rocks of the mountain face. He could trek for miles across the dirtiest, sloppiest bogland, camp in a filthy ditch and still present himself the next day dressed as if for a Sunday service. Mud just did not dare to stick to him. Some of the group wondered if he might be a sorcerer, or even a devil. The truth, if it be told, was much more mundane. For Eugene, having trained and fought with some of the elite military forces in Europe, the 'devil' was in the detail; it was all about preparation. Eugene was up and about 2 or 3 hours before the rest of the group in the morning, and he never partook of their whisky soaked evenings in the fields and taverns, seeming to prefer his own company. During this time Eugene was honing his skills, washing his clothes, cleaning his equipment and armaments, and attending to the sundry other duties which someone used to a lifetime in military encampments knew were necessary to make life bearable. Archie, like the others, had never dared to ask the Frenchman what he did during these absences, which was a shame as the reply may have proven to be quite edifying.

As it happened, Archie had a comparatively esteemed position in the gang. There were 37 of them altogether, although only 8 were sent on this mission. Of that number, Archie was one of only two dozen who were entrusted with a firearm, being familiar with the correct use and maintenance of a musket as taught to him as a boy by his father. Sandy McClung had been permitted to shoot grouse, pheasants and rabbits on Viscount Hillsborough's estates as a sop to the disestablished clergy. Archie looked down at the weapon; it made him nervous. He knew enough about guns to know that this was a shoddy piece of workmanship, cobbled together by a local blacksmith from the broken bits of 3 different guns. It had been passed to the gang by a local catholic farmer in return for the recovery of 4 of his own prize hens. The farmer was afraid of falling foul of the penal laws having only just managed to conceal the weapon from the militia in recent raids, and was planning to throw it away anyway; the gang were short on arms so everyone gained from the transaction, except for the unfortunate travellers along the Banbridge to Newry highway who found it lodged up their nostrils whilst their pockets were lightened. When Shane handed it to Archie it was as if he had been conferred some great honour. The other young lads had looked on enviously and he knew some of them hated him for it; they only had short pikes and sickles and the like. Barra for instance, had only a bill hook that had been dropped off the back of a butcher's wagon. There had been whispers about 'giving guns to one of themuns when our own people had nothing but shite.' These mutterings hurt Archie but he knew they weren't without justification. He had been the architect of his own downfall, whereas most of the others had been forced off the lands their families had held for generations by the bailiffs and goons of the ruling protestant ascendancy. As a Presbyterian of middle birth Archie was hardly an aristocrat himself, but from the perspective of some of the other lads, who when they took to the road were shoeless, starving and in a worse state than what Archie was now, he might as well have been a blue blooded prince of the Electorate of Hanover. Barra, Angus and Tomas seemed to tolerate him though.

If the truth be told the weapon was of more danger to the man holding it than to those it was pointed at. He had only ever fired it twice in practice, and estimated that its accuracy could only be counted to a range of about 4 yards. It was heavy, hung 15 degrees to the left and kicked like a mule. Lacking the requisite stock for a firearm of this size, Archie was unable to steady the weapon in the pit of his shoulder and instead had to hold it with both hands at arm's length. The shock had rung up to his funny bone when it went off and he stumbled backwards several paces before landing feet up in a mulberry bush. He greatly feared that one day the barrel would shatter and take his face off. The only benefit of the weapon was the psychological advantage it gave the owner; it was a fierce looking piece of machinery, and when you point a gun at someone they do what you tell them to do. He couldn't see that working against a fully armed troop of light dragoons but it worked fine against the lesser members of the gang and general members of the public. Archie had long since decided he would never fire the weapon in anger; he would use it to threaten and if faced with a shootout situation would simply run away.

'If it pleases your honour I can tell you about some of the terrible spectres that lurk in these here woods, sir.' Interrupted Barra with his typical enthusiasm; 'Ireland is a land full of all manner of devils and goblins sir. In these here woods alone, you can expect to see the hanging man, the grey lady and a family of human toads to name but a f-'

He was unceremoniously cut short by Seamus' massive right hand clamping itself around the back of his neck in a vice like grip.

'I swear boy I will raise up the blood in your face if I hear one more single word about ghosts or goblins or the like; any more of that shite and I'll be introducing you to the devil in person!'

He released the captive Barra with only the slightest of pushes, which was enough to make the poor fellow drop to his hands and knees.

'Perhaps we'll save our stories for the campfire tonight eh sir?' said Tomas diplomatically, winking to Eugene. The Frenchman concurred, not wanting to cause any further trouble for the boys. 'maybe instead we'd be better served were the Captain to advise on the nature of our mission?' added Tomas with a nod to Seamus. Seamus seemed to like being called Captain. Archie and some of the others thought it a ridiculous title for such a rude fellow, although none dared say it. Archie wondered also whether Seamus' insistence that the ghost stories be silenced was because he was secretly afraid of the supernatural. They had all heard the rumours about this part of the woods.

'All you need to know is this' said Seamus importantly, as if he knew something over and above the knowledge he was about to impart.

'A coach is passing through here from Newry today, it may come down this road, or more likely the usual way where Shane and the rest of the gang are positioned. We do not yet know which. On the coach there are some important passengers and a box full of jewellery, which is our intended haul. We are to procure the box and its contents and deliver it to Shane.'

'What do we want the jewellery for Captain?' asked Barra, dimly.

Seamus looked at him contemptuously; 'We've been invited to a dinner ball by the Duke of Abercorn and we all have to look our best.'

The boys giggled childishly.

'How the hell should I know what it's for? Jewellery's worth money. We're probably going to sell it and use the money to buy guns or something.'

'I hope we are sir,' replied Barra thoughtfully. 'I can't see me ever making a fortune with this here hook as my friend.'

'Barra', said Seamus, slowly and precisely so as to give maximum effect to his insult;

'the day anybody ever lets you get your hands on a gun I hope I'm standing well behind you. To be sure you're more of a danger to yourself than you are to others.'

The boys giggled again, less enthusiastically this time as Seamus' bullying became more embarrassing to witness. Barra grinned broadly, mistakenly believing there to be some well-intentioned affection in this banter. There wasn't.

'You appear to have omitted a very important part of Shane's instructions, captain.' Said Eugene haughtily, putting a sarcastic emphasis on Seamus' bogus title.

'And what would that be, you great preening peacock? Are you wanting to lay claim to the ladies' dresses for yourself?' retorted Seamus, laughing at his own joke whilst looking around for confirmation of his wit from the others, which was not forthcoming.

'You may have recalled, had you gathered the strength of character to abstain from the whisky for one night, that Shane gave very precise instructions that none of the passengers were to be harmed, and that anyone who did so would be dealt with accordingly.'

'Ah yes!' nodded Seamus, clapping his hands with mock enthusiasm. 'Don't kill anyone – or rather any of the *passengers*.' He allowed a leery stare to linger on the Frenchman as he emphasised the final word.

'The farm! Jeannie!' called a distessed voice out of nowhere. Finbarr Rafferty rose from the bush he'd been dozing in with a start. 'You're all right there Fin, just sit down there son,' called Seamus. Rafferty paused and looked around confusedly, then complied with the Captain's order. No one spoke about the incident.

'Here somebody's coming, Captain.' called Tomas from his lookout post in the sycamore tree. The boys sat up on their honkers and those that had them cocked their pistols in anticipation.

'Who is it?' asked Seamus.

'Can't make him out yet – oh hang on – it's just a carter pulling a load of hay.'

The gang let out a collective moan and settled back into their boredom.

'Working man,' Said Seamus, dismissively; 'let him pass.'

Shane had a strict policy that the ordinary people of their area were not to be harmed or harassed except in the most urgent of circumstances. He had a great affection for the common man, and he regarded it his God given task to protect and help them as far as possible. Shane had tried to instil in the gang the belief that they were brave and noble rapparees rather than lowly footpads, and that they should behave in a manner that befits their fine heritage. In this manner they should consider it their duty to serve the people, rather than for the people to serve them. This was a mutually beneficial, unspoken arrangement that the gang had with the local populace; although it was possible for the gang to subsist for extended periods in the wilds, their Spartan existence was made all the more bearable by the small donations of butter, cheese, milk, or even meat that they would receive from time to time. A night's billeting in a barn or cowshed on a cold winter's night could be as luxurious to the boys as the finest bedroom in the Viscount of Hillborough's mansion would seem to a lady or gentleman of middle rank.

The boys watched as the cart drew nearer and nearer.

'Keep well in lads, don't let him see you. We don't want people knowing we're here in case word gets back to the English before we've bagged our prize.'

A few moments later the cart rolled slowly by.

'What are you doing sitting in that bush there?' called the puzzled carter to a clearly visible Barra. 'Err... wanking sir! Heh heh...' came the reply.

The carter rolled on, shaking his head and muttering 'blethering imbecile' under his breath. The boys watched from their hideyholes as the cart trundled a couple of hundred yards up the road, before adjusting themselves into a more comfortable position. As the carter was about to round a corner, a loud altercation was heard, as six young men armed with cudgels presented themselves and began to treat the man roughly.

'Who in the name of blazes is that up there now?' shouted Seamus, angrily.

'They're not with us, Seamus', replied Angus Og McGrogan, Seamus' younger brother;

'We don't have anyone else posted on this side of the forest.'

'They'll give the game away, the impudent rascals. Angus, you and the preacher away up there and chase them off.'

Archie lit up at the opportunity of stretching his legs after Lord knows how many hours crouching in a damp thorny bush. He and Angus rose up, stretched and stamped out their pins and needles. 'C'mon Archie!' called young Angus, amiably. The two marched enthusiastically up the road, pulling their scarves across the lower half of their faces as they went. Angus was a pleasant young man of about 18 or 19 years of age. He was tall like his brothers but hadn't quite filled out yet, as much due to his poor diet and living conditions as his age. He wore a fine leather jerkin beneath a shaggy sheepskin which his brother Shane had presented him with due to his susceptibility to the rigours of the mountain elements. Shane had wanted an easier life for his bright young brother but Angus, much like Archie, had felt unfulfilled by the schooling he had received and wished to be with his brothers on the road. Such being the case Shane and Seamus had endeavoured to protect their young charge to the best of their somewhat limited ability. The rain had finally stopped but the road was littered with deep muddy potholes. The boys hopped to and fro to avoid getting their shoes any wetter.

'I'm sorry for the way Seamus treats you all' said Angus, apologetically.

'It's not your fault.' conceded Archie.

'He seems to respect the older ones more, once they've been with us a while and proved themselves. Maybe this job we're on will be your chance to show him what you can do.'

Archie nodded and smiled faintly; he wondered to himself somewhat cynically if Seamus' seemingly newfound respect for the longer term members of the gang was due to him fearing that these more hardened men may one day rise up against the bully. He wisely kept these thoughts to himself, for now though. The two drew near to the group of six youths who had been harassing the carter. Two were on the back of the wagon and two were grabbing at the horse's reins. The carter was cursing them loudly and they laughed contemptuously at his impotent anger. The other two turned to face the approaching rapparees and brandished their cudgels while frowning disdainfully; the frowns dropped when Archie and Angus drew their coats back to display the firearms in their belts.

'Problem here lads?' asked Archie as the would-be assailants looked at each other as if for leadership.

'Just messing about.' said the nearest, trying to maintain his bravado although a slight quiver in his voice betrayed his nervousness.

'What are you going to do with that?' snapped Archie, snatching a cudgel from one of the boys. 'Are you going to hit me with that?' he demanded, holding the weapon to the lad's nose.

'No sir!' came the reply, with a frantic shake of the head. Archie tossed the cudgel into the bushes, figuratively castrating the leader of the pack.

'We weren't going to steal anything off him, honest, it was only a rake.'

'Take your shoes off.' snapped Angus.

'What?' spluttered the boy, incredulously.

'Get your frigging shoes off the whole lot of you, or else I'll blow them off!'

The boys removed their shoes in double quick time.

'Now throw them down that hill into the river there.' said Angus.

'Ach please Mister, me Ma will kill me.'

'Will your Ma stick a lead ball through your forehead, because you can be sure that's what I'll do.'

The boys, some of whom were now weeping, reluctantly threw their shoes down the deep gully, never to be seen again. They turned and looked from one to the other and back to Angus and Archie, fearing what would happen next.

'What's your name and where are you from?' barked Archie.

'John Higginson, 26 Newry Street Banbridge Sir' replied the boy, obediently.

'Well John Higginson, the people going about their business in these here woods and the surrounding area are under the protection of Captain Shane McGrogan, the bold and famous rapparee, and we are his men.'

'Forgive me Sir I-'

'Shush John Higginson. I am here to tell you that if I ever here tell of you or your friends haranguing people on the highway again, I will be coming a knocking on the door of 26 Newry Street Banbridge and will be putting manners on the occupants therein with this here musket of mine, do you understand?'

'What's an occupa-'

'That's the people who live in the house John. You, your Ma, your Da, your Granny, your brothers and sisters, the cat and the dog. Do you understand?'

'We don't have a do-'

'Just nod John, just nod.' Said Archie, clamping his hand over the boy's mouth. John nodded.

'Right well off you go then, make yourselves scarce. And remember, we hear about everything. If you start acting the cod again, sooner or later we'll come looking for you.'

'Yes sir, thank you sir.' snivelled John Higginson.

The boys ran off as fast as their shoeless feet could carry them, half grateful for their lenient escape and half dreading the whipping their fathers would give them for the loss of the shoes. The carter nodded thankfully to the two rapparees and went on his way, as Archie and Angus strode proudly back to their hiding places. Archie actually felt almost as if he had done something worthwhile, like a true knight of the road from the stories he'd heard at the market that time. In any case, he felt he'd done the boys a favour. They may have regarded their tomfoolery as a bit of fun, but in the eyes of the law they were about to commit a very serious criminal act which could potentially lead to their demise at the end of a rope, or perhaps transportation to the colonies.

'We sorted it all out Captain.' announced Archie to Seamus, triumphantly.

'Did you give them a thick ear?' demanded Seamus, with a scowl.

'No we err took their shoes off them.' replied Angus, proudly.

'Shoes?' pipped Barra, brightly; 'What did you do with them?'

'We made them throw them down the gully to teach them a lesson.'

'Alas!' said Barra, slumping. 'I have want of a pair of shoes.'

'And did that make yous feel like you were big men, taking the shoes off a bunch of wee boys?' snapped Seamus, scornfully. Angus and Archie looked at each other open mouthed and then back at Seamus and then back at each other. 'I would be well minded to take my belt off to the pair of you, you cowardly wee bullies. Get back in your positions before I change my mind.'

# 3. The Carriage

Captain Richard Pilkington of the 37th North Hampshire Regiment of Foot was slouched sulkily in the horse drawn carriage thinking himself extremely hard done by. He glanced across intermittently at the two females in the seats facing him, still hoping on the off chance that the lady may deign to engage him in conversation on one of the many subjects he considered himself to be fluent upon. He wished now that he had not so gingerly acquiesced to the

Colonel's request to escort the ladies from the harbour at Newry where their ship had docked, to the newly incumbent Viscount Hillsborough's residence at Hillsborough. The fanciful fellow, whose ideas were so far above his station they could only be seen with a telescope, imagined that the mysterious Lady Isabella Murray, the second daughter to the Duke of Atholl, would be swept of her feet by his gallantry, exquisite taste and intricate knowledge of the music and art of the day, not to mention his devilishly impressive wig which he had powdered for the best part of an hour that morning. Pilkington was, in all fairness, a man of some learning, although greatly given to espousing the odd 'did you know' fact rather than possessing any great amount of knowledge on any particular subject. His father had often remarked that he was a 'mine of useless information' and should apply himself more vigorously to his studies in preparation for a career at the bar, or perhaps medicine.

Young Richard was unfortunately, the sort of hapless chap who expected the world to be handed to him on a plate and would become quite frustrated at the universe if it forgot the sauce. His friends at Eton had declared that if a selfishness competition were to be held, 'Pilkers' would probably win it, and if not he would smash the prize into a thousand pieces to prevent the winner from having possession of it. When playing cricket he was given to absenting himself from the field if neither bowling nor batting at that time, only to return when it was his turn again. Pilkington was not an evil man by any stretch of the imagination; he was, like many people, totally lacking the capacity for self analysis and was unaware of his own egotism; hence he allowed his narcissism to run unchecked. No one ever thought to instruct the young officer on the basic laws of decency, mistaking his quite impeccable manners for the presence of a properly functioning moral compass. He was, in terms of social maturity, a 14 year old boy in a 28 year old man's body.

Having failed to achieve his early potential in his studies, Pilkington's father had sent him to the military college at Woolwich to train for a commission with the army. Pilkington had barely scraped through his examinations and was, when all was said and done, an incompetent officer who had risen to his position in life courtesy of the privileges bestowed on him by his father's wealth and the predominant values of English society at that time. If it weren't for the British establishment's insistence on promoting officers in this manner rather than allowing the cream of the talent to rise naturally to the top, England could quite possibly have conquered the entire world.

Pilkington had, for the past several hours, been bursting to interject into the conversation with his carefully rehearsed musings on the writings of Voltaire; however, his initial brainwave to greet his guests in the French language, according to the custom of the day, had backfired spectacularly as the ladies conversed freely in the language for the rest of the journey. Poor Richard with his pigeon knowledge of the tongue had to strain his ears in hope of recognising a word here or there and nod in agreement from time to time as if he had a thorough understanding of the conversation. Additionally he was given to saying 'Ah yes!' intermittently very loudly much to the ladies' annoyance, although in truth this was to disguise the uncooperative behaviour of his rumbling stomach which had been protesting the quality of the mutton pie he'd had for supper last night since the early morning. He bitterly cursed the fact that on a day when he desired most wholesomely to release a long and protracted series of flavoursome farts, he had caused himself to be entrapped in a small carriage on a bumpy road in the company of a noble lady, her maid and a Minister of the Church of Ireland. As tension built of Pilkington's bowels he decided he would wait no longer before joining the conversation.

'Ah yes, news has reached me most recently, by incident, of a most amusing occurrence.'

The ladies hid their annoyance and graciously ceased their chatter to turn and face the captain.

'By all accounts, a chap was travelling through Somerset, or was it Cornwall? Yes Cornwall I believe it was, anyway the good fellow, I believe it might have been the Earl of Gloucester, or was that another joke? Anyway he was travelling I believe from Tavistock to Poundstock or the other way round in a carriage very much like this one, when he came across a local bumpkin sitting idly on a garden wall. Yes so he said to the fellow;

'Good morning my good fellow, could you advise me how far it is from here to' Tavistock or Poundstock or whatever it was and the bumpkin replied 'Please good sir it be another 6 miles if it pleases you your honour.'

So the chap thanks the bumpkin and carries on his way, and after 6 miles finds himself to be only half the way to his destination that he expected to be. So on the return journey he meets with the fellow again and remonstrates with him most uncommonly saying 'you told me that it was only 6 miles to Tavistock.' So the bumpkin replies,

'That be true sir tis 6 miles to Tavistock from my house.'

So the traveller asks 'and where, pray tell, would your house be?'

To which the bumpkin replies...'

'Another 6 miles up the road sir', interrupted the Reverend Threader without looking up from his pamphlet. 'Ah, you've heard it then.' said Pilkington, quietly. A few seconds of embarrassing silence followed before the girls nodded slowly and gave a faint smile, before returning to their conversation. Pilkers felt deflated.

'Shouldn't you be outside the carriage captain,' asked the Reverend unhelpfully, peering over his bone rimmed spectacles 'Riding in front and keeping charge of your men?'

'Ah' said Richard, trying to think of a quick explanation. 'Well you see sir, I thought that with there being such esteemed company travelling in the carriage, to wit the Lady Isabella and your good self, it would be only right and proper that in the name of proper etiquette and decency that I should accompany yourself and the good lady by acting as chaperone in order to avoid any unseemly—'

'How dare you Sir!' Raged the clergyman suddenly, making Richard and the ladies jump slightly.

'I am a man of the church am I not? You dare to accuse me of impropriety?'

'No of course not my good sir,' grovelled Pilkington 'What I meant to say was...'

'Enough of your blethering Sir! Never have I been so insulted. Mark my words your commanding officer shall here of this! Chaperone indeed.'

'I am sure' interrupted Lady Murray; 'that the good Captain intended no slight on your honour or your position, my good Reverend Threader.'

Threader held his breath for 5 seconds.

'Of course, milady.'

He flashed a quick grimace and a nod at Lady Murray and reluctantly conceded to the will of his social superior. Threader was in no position to assert himself anyway, being indebted to the ladies for allowing him to share their carriage with his own transport having cracked its axle just outside Newry. Lady Isabella had felt that no Minister of the church should be left in such straits when attending to the Lord's work. He would, however, bide his time and write a strongly worded letter of complaint to Pilkington's superiors when he eventually returned home to his own parish.

Pilkington for his part thought it would be better if he said no more for the time being. The Reverend Joseph Threader was a man of scarce humour and in truth, he had committed a serious breach of protocol by riding inside the carriage. His orders were to lead the carriage along with the four mounted horsemen who trotted sombrely ahead, however he had tethered his own horse to the back of the carriage as they left Newry harbour and sat inside to enjoy the comfort and company of his betters.

Threader returned to examining his papers and attempted to filter out the noise of the ladies' foreign whisperings, caring little for the French language or French manners. He reread the notes he had taken of the last synod meeting for the umpteenth time and shook his head despairingly at the latest directive for the reinforcement of tithe collection in the outlying regions of Ireland.

'All very well' he thought; 'in the places such as County Downe with its military garrison and militia, but who would dare enforce such a tax amongst the wilds of Galway or Mayo, where a fellow would likely find himself dragged into a hedgerow and his throat cut from ear to ear?' His misgivings were by no means borne of any sense of social injustice or concern for his fellow man, and he never would be so presumptuous as to raise his concerns with any of the Bishops. His usual tactic was to confide his opinions in the younger clergymen and let them take the risk of ruining their careers when they naively passed on his musings as their own, or if the idea was greeted positively, he would quickly move in to elaborate and claim the credit. This strategy had served him well for almost 40 years of ministry, many thinking of him as a humble and softly spoken gentleman of hidden depths. Threader had hidden depths all right, only in that his soul was a murky pothole of stagnant self-interest.

He browsed over his copy of the Belfast Newsletter and General Advertiser, and raised an eyebrow at the death notice of the Reverend Doctor Thomas Rundle, Lord Bishop of Derry.

'He'll be supping with the devil in hell before evensong tonight' thought the uncharitable clergyman with a thin smile, recalling the rumours of Rundle's youthful flirtation with Arianism (a belief that Jesus Christ the son of God was subservient to God the father.)

'A seat in the See of Derry perhaps?'

Age was no barrier to ambition in the church, and Threader was a very ambitious man. If he could only court favour more effectively with the Bishops, Deacons and senior clerics and perhaps secure a couple of nominations, such a seat could be his, a massive step up from his position as a lowly Vicar in the parish of Killeavy. He stared down at the letters he was carrying, all sealed with wax to ensure they could be viewed by the addressee only. A trivial task for such a man to be acting as a messenger boy, but hopefully his false humility in agreeing to deliver the letters on his travels would permit an opportunity to ingratiate himself to both the sender and to the recipients.

Threader's ambition was of a completely different nature to Richard Pilkington's, who yearned for an easy life of wealth and happiness but was prepared to make little effort to achieve it. Threader was a power mad workaholic who would step over his own mother's dead body to further the ends of his career. Despite having an encyclopaedic knowledge of all things theological, Threader cared precious little for the doctrines of the church and severely less so for the teachings of Christ. Had he been born in another era he would have made a fine Pharisee or inquisitor, and as it was he greatly lamented the fact that the burning of witches had recently passed into antiquity. Threader was a heartless man who recited the scriptures line and verse with neither feeling nor understanding of their true purpose. Never was a man more perfectly suited to a career in the church.

'I imagine the scenery here would be quite breathtaking milady;' observed Mademoiselle Amelie Babineax, with a submissive sigh that belied her statement; 'Where it not for the incessant rain. Is Ireland always so grey?'

'We gather that it is a most beautiful country in the summer' replied the Lady; 'although there is none in all the world to hold a candle to the magnificent views of Scotland.'

Amelie gave a faint smile which implied submission to her lady's statement rather than agreement.

'I sense that you are somewhat melancholy to be called away on this journey, Amelie. I really cannot begin to express how comforting it is to me to have you attend me on this journey. I must also convey to you the vital importance of the task that we are engaged upon, although we must be cautious of our words in the presence of strangers.'

This was of course a reference to Threader and Pilkington. The ladies had assumed that the limitations of Pilkington's grasp of the French language rendered him incapable of eavesdropping effectively, however this could be a ruse to gain their confidence. The older man on the other hand appeared highly educated and it was safest to assume he could understand every word.

'I understand that you were looking forward to us attending the ball in honour of King Augustus of Poland's visit.' Continued Lady Isabella; 'however we must be minded that the privileges which we enjoy must be earned through the conquering of trepidation and disconsolation.'

'Yes milady, of course.' replied Amelie. In truth Amelie would rather have not been asked to accompany Lady Isabella on this trip to Ireland, the circumstances of which she considered most unusual and highly improper. For a lady of the nobility to be travelling unaccompanied save for her maid through a wild country such as Ireland seemed to be a ludicrous proposition, likely to invite scandal and indeed danger. One would usually expect at least half a dozen servants and several trunks for such a journey, however as Lady Isabella had explained, it was to be nothing more than a flying visit of 3 days at the most, and the Viscount had graciously arranged for the ladies to be accompanied by a troop of soldiers from the harbour to their destination and back again. The visit, Amelie was told, was in return for the hospitality shown to the Viscount and his late father several years ago by the Duke of Atholl at Blair Castle. Isabella was at that time present in Scotland although she undertook her finishing mainly in France. She and the present Viscount William Hill – or Wills, had become close friends during the visit.

Lady Isabella herself could have easily been mistaken for a French noblewoman of the court of Versailles, although she was somewhat too waif-like to be considered a great beauty by the standards of the time. Her face was a powdery pale save for the rouge of her cheeks and her dark crimson lips, her eyes a steely blue-grey. Her light chestnut hair was piled high upon her head in an ocean of curls and was held in place by a diamond encrusted blue silk ribbon. Her tiny figure seemed to be swamped by her lace trimmed pale blue dress, which was accessorised by a gold embroidered red sash.

Amelie was a much larger woman in a smaller less ornate dress, which was somewhat plain by French standards but smart enough to be mistaken for a lady of some standing in comparison to most of those they had met since arriving in Ireland. With her pleasant oval shaped face and sturdier build she would have been considered the more comely of the two by the standards of the time. When Pilkington realised that his chances with the lady were non-existent, he had pondered the possibility of bestowing the honour of his favour upon her maid. In truth however he may as well have been contemplating the possibility of a romantic liason with Reverend Threader.

Amelie and Isabella had as close a relationship as would be reasonably possible between mistress and servant in the mid 18th Century; although Amelie held Isabella in a great deal of affection, she did not share Isabella's rather naive supposition that they were 'as close as sisters.' Such a relationship would by its very nature have to be based on some sort of parity of esteem, which was certainly not the case in this sort of domestic arrangement. Isabella had never had to hold Amelie's hair back whilst she vomited into a priceless porcelain sevres after a bottle and a half of champagne. Isabella had never had to scrub the skids marks from Amelie's bloomers or cut her toenails, pluck her eyebrows or stand lookout while she disgraced herself with a captain of the Garde Suisse behind a decorative peacock shaped hedge. Amelie had a great deal of affection for her very generous mistress who had bestowed many gifts and hand me downs over the years, and had allowed her to visit her father and even paid for his medical bills when he fell ill; but like most people of the time, Amelie knew her place and was grateful for it.

Amelie turned to Isabella with a puzzled look and asked; 'Milady... what is a bumpkin?'

The carriage slowly rumbled on and gave a heavy bump as one of the wheels rolled over a boulder in the road. The sudden jolt temporarily robbed Pilkington of his ability to hold back the torrent of expectant farts that battered impatiently against the door of his rectum. An almighty parp was let loose causing the shocked faces of Threader, Isabella and Amelie to spin towards the red faced Captain. A fart is a fart in any language.

'Pilkington!' exclaimed Threader, with an unforgiving scowl.

'Most dreadfully sorry, he he' said Pilkington, almost visibly shrinking with embarrassment.

'I'm afraid that the mutton pie seems to have disagreed with me somewhat.'

Isabella took her fan from her bag and waved vigorously, remarking to Amelie; 'I trust that answers your question.'

Pilkington wished he was outside the carriage where he was supposed to be, having left a much more capable soldier to do his job for him. Sergeant Seymour Wilkes was a pleasantly rotund fellow, who when he removed his hat was reminiscent of a happy face painted on a boiled egg. At 50 years of age it was likely that at his next examination by the regimental doctor he would be found to be unfit for service and recommended for retirement on medical grounds. Failing that he could take his pension in 6 months time when his current contract ended; either scenario pleased Seymour greatly. It wasn't so much that he hadn't enjoyed the last 30 years of soldiering, having had postings in Jersey, India, Canada, Jersey again and then finally Ireland, but he now looked forward to collecting his generous pension, easily enough to cover the rent of the cottage he'd been eyeing just outside Aldershot where he and the wife could live very comfortably. Seymour had been smiling to himself inanely at the thought of this for most of the journey even through the worst of the rain, and the rest of the troop wondered if he'd been supping from a hip flask on the sly. All Seymour wanted to do was keep out of trouble for the next few months and this easy posting in the heavily militarised, mainly protestant county of Downe was the place to do it. He'd spoken a lot more casually than he ordinarily would have to the men prior to the journey, and the younger soldiers had raised the matter of the possibility of ambush by rapparees.

Seymour had laughed off the idea, given that the available military intelligence indicated that the local rapparee gangs were badly organised and poorly equipped. When pressed on the matter, Sergeant Wilkes had advised the boys jokingly that 'If there's any more than a few of them, just surrender and they'll let us go.'

One person with no thoughts of surrender of any kind was Mr George Higginson, master butcher of Banbridge and a recently inducted Captain of the South Downe Militia. Mr Higginson was a popular man who took great pride in the quality of his wares and the cleanliness of his shop. When you bought a pound of Higginson's sausages you knew you were getting the finest minced pork produce, and it wouldn't be mixed with sawdust or corn flour or 'any of that other crap which that lot round the corner would give you.' People of a discerning palette came from miles around to buy his meat from his shop and on market day long queues would form at his stall whilst the other butchers looked on in envy. George had bored his wife silly bragging about how the local magistrate, the doctor and even the mayor had approached him after church on various occasions to compliment him on his fine cuts of meat and to place orders with him for delivery. It was through the establishment of these connections that George was able to secure his captaincy within the militia, although none begrudged him it as he was such a popular fellow. George's only worry in life was that at 53 years of age, the physical side of the job was starting to catch up with him. His lower back pained him when he helped lift the big sides of meat off their hooks in the shop and down onto the table for carving. This was a younger man's job, and he was thankful that he had a strapping son who he could eventually pass the business on to, if he could just get the boy to apply himself to the minor details of the job. There was no business being done today however; George had given young Johnny the day off to go strolling in the woods, and the customers had been given plenty of warning that the shop was closed for the day. Higginson had organised a celebration to thank his friends and allies for their support and to get to know the men in the troop a bit better for when they eventually go out on manoeuvres, whenever that may be. More than 50 people had crowded into the shop and house to enjoy the fine spread that Mrs

Higginson had put on and many had brought smalls gifts of wine, ale, whiskey and poteen. By the early afternoon many of the participants were pie-eyed, singing party songs and slapping good old George on the back in appreciation. Higginson was loving every minute of it, a pity young Johnny is missing all the fun.

George called for silence, thinking it only appropriate that he should say a few words; 'Ladies and Gentlemen, and members of the baking profession' the crowd gave a good hearted 'ooh' and chuckled politely.

'I'd like to express to you all my sincerest gratitude for joining me in this little celebration today, just a small to-do to say how happy and proud I am to be taking up my new post with the militia, and how grateful I am for this opportunity to protect the town and all the dear people who live here from the filthy robbing bandits we have lurking about the countryside.'

The crowd gave a loud cheer and a round of applause allowing George to pause briefly, beaming brightly; 'Now I know you all want to get back to your drinks, some moreso than others, eh Charles?' winking to a friendly face in the crowd, who raised his tankard in acknowledgement.

'So can I just finish by calling on you all to raise your glasses to his Glorious Majesty King George. Gentlemen, the King!'

'The King!' replied the crowd, downing their drinks in one.

'And can I also call on every man of you, to refill your glasses and give thanks once again, to his Glorious Majesty King William of Orange, who in the perilous days of our fathers, when the people of Ireland were besieged and attacked by the papish hoards, did so valiantly come to the rescue of the people of Derry and did save this beloved country from assured mayhem and destruction. My friends, His Glorious Majesty King William.'

'King William!' roared the crowd, downing another full glass in unison.

'And may I also;' added Higginson, staggering slightly. 'May I also ask you all most sincerely to raise you glasses to the Lord Protector Oliver Cromwell, who in tumul... who in tumult... who in hard times when papish hoardes were murdering the poor protestants again did come over here and give the bastards a bloody good slap, oh yes indeed... The Lord Protector!'

'The Lord Protector!' Shouted the crowd as one, downing another drink and looking increasingly riled.

'And finally, let us not forget our most esteemed and generous benificators, I mean beneficatators, I mean benefactors, without whose sponsorship the formation of the new militia would not have been possible. Gentlemen, the dearly departed former Viscount of Hillsborough, Trevor Hill, and his most worthy successor, our present landlord, Viscount Wills Hill'.

'The Viscount!' cheered the crowd, downing another.

'And it is in the spirit of these great men that I can assure you that if I catch any of themuns...' just at that minute the door burst open;

'Da! Da! Shane McGrogan the rapparee stole our shoes and threw them in the river!'

Back in the woods, Seamus was continuing to irritate and demoralise the men under his command. Despite spending most of the day insisting everyone remain as silent and motionless in their hiding place as possible, he was becoming increasingly boisterous, attempting to engage in 'a bit of craic' with a group of men who were by no means comfortable in his presence. It had become apparent that for some time Seamus had been supping from a jar of poteen which he had slipped into his sack bag of provisions that morning. Shane had very specific instructions that no man was to imbibe or be under the influence of alcohol when there was work to be done and indeed, drunkenness was a court martial offence. Seamus however resented his brother's orders and felt that due to his immense size, he could drink more than the other rapparees and still be fit for his duties. Besides which, he had only intended to take a little peck to keep out the cold, although it never worked out like that. These boys kept getting on his nerves, they were all useless apart from McCafferty and McClatchy; Rafferty was a step away from being a complete imbecile and shouldn't be out on the mission. Shane needed to get rid of them all and get some boys in who knew what they were doing. That big frigging pansy was getting on his nerves too, looking down his nose at everyone as if he was lord of the manor – he'll keep though. Seamus hated people trying to make him feel like he wasn't good enough, just like his father did all those years ago. He winced and clenched his fist to force a deep hidden, never spoken memory to the back of his head.

Seamus had tried to rile Eugene by singing a humorous ditty about the King of France; Eugene merely applauded and then politely enquired whether an Englishman had written the song. Seamus had no answer to that. He then proceeded to instruct everyone, for about the sixth time, on how the ambush was to proceed;

'Listen carefully simpletons and your uncle Seamus shall explain once again.' He smarmed, before taking another sip; 'The carriage should hopefully come along this road. The driver and his mate will probably be a couple of the usual lads, so they'll give us no trouble. I'll throw them a few shillings each when we're done. There will likely be about half a dozen soldiers, four in front of the carriage and two behind, something like that. When it reaches yonder bush where the preacher sits we all jump up at once and demand their surrender. Myself and Owen McClatchy there will both let off a shot, I want the guns trained on the Captain and the carriage. Make a lot of noise then move in and take the rifles quickly. Don't give them time to think about it. Don't shoot the carriage either. Then we get everyone out, line them up and Barra, Archie and Angus keep everyone in line while me, Tomas, McClatchy and Rafferty retrieve the goods. Feel free to help yourself to the goodies but the main thing is we get the jewellery. Do you all know what you're doing?'

Everyone nodded.

'Do you know what you're doing Barra?'

'We're robbing the coach Captain!' replied Barra.

'We're robbin the coach Cap'n' repeated Seamus, with an exaggerated impersonation of Barra's voice. 'You couldn't rob yourself, McCann, could you? You haven't a frigging clue. Have you actually ever robbed anybody since you started in this gang?'

'I can so rob people Sir!' replied Barra, indignantly. 'I'll rob the next person who comes along this road!'

The boys gave a short sharp burst of stifled laughter. Seamus stared at Barra cynically for 10 seconds. Barra dropped his head after 5.

'Right then my boy. The next person comes down that road will be relieved of his burden by Barra McCann, the brave rapparee.'

'Somebody's coming Captain!' called Tomas McCafferty from above.

Seamus was right about one thing; a clip round the ear for young John Higginson and his lackeys would have served the rapparees' purpose a lot better than robbing the boys of their shoes. A clip round the ear would have served up an edifying dose of humility to an unpleasant young man whose parents' aspirations to genteelness had resulted in him believing himself to be something more substantial than a butcher's apprentice. A clip round the ear would have sent the boys home with something to think about. As it was, John and the others had hopped home in a distressed state, anxious at the thought of how they would explain the loss of their shoes to their parents and masters. The Higginsons were a well off family by the standards of their neighbours but no one could afford to replace a pair of shoes lightly, especially not when one had travelled to Belfast with one's mother less than a month ago to have them made to measure. These boys were in deep shit.

'It was Shane the raparree I say Da! Him and all his men!'

'There were about 50 of them, with guns and knives and all!' Interrupted William Roddy.

A huge uproar ensued as the rabble of drunken militia shouted solutions to each other, each more ridiculous than the last. Mrs Higginson pushed forward through the crowd and pulled her son's sobbing head into her ample bosom.

'Just a minute now, just a minute,' pleaded Mr Higginson, his hands raised in a placatory manner. 'Now before anyone goes off and does anything silly we need to establish exactly what happened here. John, now you take a wee sip of this whiskey and tell us all exactly what happened.'

John took the tankard shakily and gulped and spattered in a dramatic manner; his accomplices were suitably impressed with the display.

'Well you see, me and the boys were having a wee stroll through the woods, thinking about the beauty of nature and contemplating the wonders of God's creation.'

'Ah my poor sweet boy' sighed Mrs Higginson, pulling John to her bosom again and patting his head.

'And then I thought to myself, we are so lucky to have all these wonderful things, we should go pluck some flowers to put on Grandmama's grave.'

'Always thinking of others, never himself!' sobbed Mrs Higginson, almost smothering the duplicitous young apprentice.

The crowd murmured in agreement.

'So then I thought to myself, where doth the prettiest flowers on the woods grow, and I thought, well of course, there are the lovely bluebells that grow in the meadow just passed the north side of the road going to Dromore – OW!'

John was interrupted with a loud clear slap to the earhole from his mother; 'How many times have I told you to stay away from the north side of that road? Didn't I tell you about the devils that live up there in those woods? Good Lord if the toad people had got you..'

'It was Shane the rapparee I tell you Ma! He threatened us! Stole our shoes and threw them in the river! He said if we tell anyone, he would come down to Banbridge and go into our house and kill everyone within!'

A roar of outrage was raised up about the house that shook the windows and rattled the doors. Mr Higginson stepped forward; 'Very well my friends let's calm down here. I can see that urgent action needs to be taken, yes. As captain of the militia, I believe that this is a matter best handled by the army. Yes the best course of action is to dispatch a messenger to Saintfield forthwit-'

'Dispatch a messenger?' cried Mrs Higginson, incredulously. 'A gang of knaves and pirates threaten these poor boys and their families and you want to waste time dispatching a messenger?'

Many nodded in agreement.

'Lord Cromwell wouldn't have dispatched a messenger!' shouted one old man at the front.

'Or King William!' called another man from the back, to a roar of approval.

'There are a lot of things to be considered here' weasled George, appealing for reason. 'We've only just formed the militia, we've no training, few arms, these are very desperate and dangerous people we're talking about here, and apart from anything else, I've to be up at 6 o'clock tomorrow morning to open the shop up.'

All but a few of the crowd were now engaged in howling Mr Higginson down; George felt like crawling under the table and curling up beside the dog, if they'd only had one. 'If you don't want to do your job husband' scowled Mrs Higginson, 'Then I bloody well will!' Mrs Higginson stepped onto a stool and balancing herself on her husband's head, stood up on to the table, taking the captain's hat from his head and placing it on her own as she went.

'So Shane the rapparee or whatever he calls himself thinks he's going to come down to Banbridge and murder us all eh? Well they tried that in Derry and by Jove we gave them a bloody nose that time. We'll show this pirate we're cut from the same cloth as roaring George Walker and the apprentice boys. There are no Lundys in Banbridge!'

The assembly were now thundering and chanting Betty Higginson's name. 'I want everyone here who has a musket, pistol, sword or a pointed stick for that matter to go home and get it, and be back here in 10 minutes time. Any horses you have bring them too. We are going up into those woods to flush those rats out of our kitchen for once and for all!'

With a final massive roar the rabble pushed at each other for the exit. The house was empty within seconds save for the Higginsons and a couple of drunken stragglers who were passed out in the corner. Mrs Higginson stepped down from the table and placed the hat sideways on the indignant Mr Higginson's head. She took down her father's pistol from the sideboard and proceeded to load it.

## 4. THE AMBUSH

Annie O'Hare shambled wearily along the mountain trail leading her two small children by the hand. They'd long since ceased to cry because they knew mother had nothing to give them. Neither child nor mother had eaten more than a piece of bread in two days. Her eyes were dead like two hollows in an oak tree. Her face was flushed of colour. Her hair was lank and brittle like an old woman's hair. At 26 years of age the harsh realities of life for a young Catholic widow with children had robbed this once lovely young woman of her youth and vitality just as it had robbed her husband of his life. She passed by the gang members in their hidey holes without looking either left of right. Whether she saw any of them, or even had the will to care if they were there, who could say. The boys watched solemnly and silently as the three pitiful figures continued a hundred yards up the road.

Seamus turned to Barra.

'Well? What are you waiting for?'

'What do you mean sir?'

'You said you would rob the next person who comes up the road, Off you go!'

'Wha? Ah c'mon captain you can't expect me to rob that wee woman!' protested Barra.

'You said you would rob the next person who came up the road. Now you get up the frigging road and get me whatever she's got.'

'But she won't have anyth-'

'Get up that road now McCann or I'll shoot you for disobeying an order!' barked Seamus, aggressively.

Reluctantly, Barra stood up, gathered himself together, and ran up the road after the young woman. The remaining rapparees looked at each other, disgusted by what was happening.

'Shane won't like this Captain'; called Tomas from his lookout post. 'No robbing of the common people, that's the rule.'

'Keep your wig on Tomas' replied Seamus with a grating chuckle. 'I only wanted to see if he was daft enough to do it. She won't have anything to give him anyway.' The boys were by no means placated by this, failing to see the humour in terrorising such an unfortunate. They watched from afar as Barra ran past the woman and jumped in front of her.

The gang were too far away to hear what was said. Half asleep with exhaustion, the girl could barely raise her head and showed no signs of surprise at the highwayman's sudden appearance. 'Hello young lady', he started; 'Don't be frightened. I am Barra McCann the famous rapparee but I don't want to rob you. My friends are hiding in the bushes back there and my Captain said I had to rob you to prove I'm a proper rapparee, so all I need you to do is to act like I'm trying to rob you and then I'll let you go without having to take anything, and we can both be on our way.'

The boys watched from afar as Annie first drew her hands to her face then pointed at the two children, then raised up her hands again in consternation, then covered her eyes as if crying. They saw Barra raise up his hands in submission, then raise his index finger as if telling the girl to wait. He ran back towards the rest of the gang, arriving at McClung's position.

'Archie!' he whispered. The rest of the boys looked on quizzically.

'What?' demanded Archie.

'Give me a few pennies or a shilling or whatever you have. I'll give you it back when I've got it.'

The rest of the boys began to chuckle.

'What for?' asked Archie.

'She's a wee widow woman. The husband died of scarlet fever last week and she's no other family. Her and the two childer haven't eaten in two days.'

'For goodness sake!' said Archie in mock annoyance pulling the money from his greatcoat pocket and placing it in Barra's open hand. 'You too Tomas, you took a load of money off the boys at cards last night. Tomas dipped into his pocket with a smile and threw down a coin. Likewise, Barra went round the rest of the gang taking donations of money and provisions. Even Seamus threw in a shilling. Finally he went to his own bag, and pulled out a large round flat loaf. He tore it in two and put the smaller piece back in the bag. He ran back up the road with his donations and handed them to the girl, who took off her thin grey shawl to serve as a bag. The boys gave a collective 'Yeooooh!' as the girl hugged Barra weakly and gave him a peck on the cheek. Annie and the children waved Barra off as he ran back to his hiding place, beaming with the warmth of true human kindness.

As he approached Seamus called out; 'Go to rob somebody and end up giving them half our wages. I knew you'd end up with nothing.'

'I did get something Captain' replied Barra, cheerfully; 'I got a kiss.'

Betty Higginson stood on the back of the horse drawn meat cart, her raven hair blowing in the wind and her steely blue eyes piercing the evening gloom with an almost supernatural fire and fury. She clasped the stock of her father's pistol, a family heirloom which purportedly saw action at Enniskillen, firmly in her right hand whilst steadying the barrel in her left. Over 100 armed men who had gathered at her bidding followed doggedly and grim faced behind the cart. She was the very image of Queen Boudicca in her chariot, leading the Britons' revolt against the Romans. Her husband George sat glumly at the reins, mulling over how his wife had stolen his moment of glory once again. In truth George owed much of his so called glory to Betty; yes when they married he was some 27 years her senior and had already set up his small butchery shop, but deep down George knew it was her diligence, her industry and her vision that grew the little shop into the Higginson 'empire.' It was she who was up an hour before him and to bed an hour after him, meticulously cleaning and sharpening the tools, and washing out the shop in an almost obsessive manner.

'There will be a name for this condition someday' George had often thought. It was she who negotiated prices with farmers for the prime cattle. It was she who inspected every cut and insisted that they outdo all their competitors for price and quality, regardless of the damage to profit margins. Betty knew there was a long term plan to consider; raise the standards now so your rivals can't compete in the future.

Everyone admired and respected Betty although not all of them liked her. Everyone knew who wore the breeches in 26 Newry Street, and despite the prevailing social norms of the time, her innate gift for leadership was infectious at times like this when people were unsure of the correct action to take.

Add to that the fact that Betty was very, very angry. Livid. Furious!

How dare anyone threaten her beloved stepson, let alone some cowardly glorified footpad who thought himself a hero for stealing a defenceless boy's shoes and making sport of him. Betty's maternal instinct made her more formidable at this moment in time than a troop of light dragoons. She intended to make sure these raparrees paid a very heavy price for meddling with her family.

The procession leading up the road from Banbridge to Dromore were more mob than militia, and George worried what might happen if they came across someone they didn't know - would he be able to restrain then from hanging an innocent man without trial? As it was, the only people they encountered on the journey were a sad looking young woman and her pauper children, who they passed by peacefully. For his part young John sat beside his father at the front of the meat cart, chomping greedily on a pig's trotter.

'John', said Mr Higginson peaceably; 'Are you sure this all happened exactly as you said it did?'

'Yes Da!' replied John, still munching; 'right hand up to God sir!'

'So they just surrounded you, then threw your shoes in the river and then threatened to kill us, and then let you go?' inquired George.

'Yes indeed sir! That's exactly what happened. I can't understand why they did it either.'

'And where exactly did this happen son?'

'Well' slopped John wiping his greasy mouth with his sleeve, you see up where that carriage is going away in the distance there? That's roundabout where it was.'

Inside the carriage, Richard Pilkington had recovered from the embarrassment of his earlier faux pas and was now engaged in boring everyone silly with the details of his short and uneventful career as a Captain in the 37th North Hampshire Regiment of Foot; 'Ah yes, and did you know my good Reverend, that the Viscount's ancestor, Sir Arthur Hill I believe? Yes built Hillsborough Fort almost a hundred years ago, as a strategic post to help secure the road from Carrickfergus to Dublin, as at that time one could expect to be waylaid by outlaws or rapparees as they call them, however we would be very unlikely to see any here nowadays, owing to...'

'Sorry, what is a... rapparee?' interrupted Amelie.

'Ah yes, well you may ask good lady. A rapparee is what the natives here call a sort of vagabond man at arms I suppose. Some of them claim to have originated from the remains of the army which was in the service of the late King James, however one must take these claims with a pinch of salt. They were at one time quite a nuisance however with the persistence of the army and the forces of law and order we've managed to reduce their number significantly, so you shouldn't be alarmed as if we were to encounter any of them on the road my men and I would be more that capable of seeing them off. I'd like to meet the rapparee who was foolish enough to cross swords with Richard Pilkington!'

The travellers jumped in unison as an almighty crack of gunfire sounded and the carriage drew to a shuddering halt. A terrifying booming voice sounding much like an ogre from a fairytale split the air; 'THROW DOWN YOUR WEAPONS AND DISMOUNT YOUR HORSES! THIS CARRIAGE AND ITS OCCUPANTS ARE PRISONERS OF CAPTAIN SEAMUS MCGROGAN!!!'

'And Barra McCann!' squeaked another.

Outside the carriage Sergeant Seymour Wilkes sat on his horse with hands raised in the air and rolled his eyes; 'You heard the man boys, put your guns down and get off your horses.'

'A wise choice Captain.' said Tomas from beneath the scarf that covered most of his face, his pistol trained on Wilkes. 'I'm not the Captain mate, the Captain's inside the carriage.'

'What's he doing in there?' asked Archie, puzzled.

'Your guess is as good as mine son.' replied Wilkes.

Far in the distance, the crowd gave a collective gasp as they heard the gunfire. The sudden shock of the bang cost many to lose their bravado and to question the wisdom of their endeavour. John Higginson jumped down off the cart. 'They're attacking the carriage!' cried Betty. After them, husband!

'Now Betty I really think this has gone quite far enough. We don't want to be rushing into a situation where – Aaaah!' with a push of her foot Betty sent her jabbering husband sprawling in the mud rather than endure any more of his procrastination. Seizing the reins with one hand and holding the pistol in the other, she let go a crack that sent the horses into a gallop. The crowd followed at varying speeds commensurate to their level of enthusiasm, a few dozen in full charge followed by some dawdlers who weren't so keen but still wanted to show their faces anyway. George Higginson picked himself up and looked after the escaping mob. 'Shouldn't we go after them Da?' asked John. 'Well son in these military operations it's always better to keep a few in reserve. We'll just hang back here and see what happens.'

The carriage door flew open and the occupants jumped back with a start. A massive arm reached in and grasped a shaking Captain Pilkington by the lapels, hauling him out on to the road with a girlish yelp. Seamus' red brutal features scoured the remaining passengers. 'You three, out to frigg! Line up beside the others over there. The group obediently stepped down from the carriage, and Archie took off his coat and laid it down for the ladies to step over a muddy puddle. The girls simply walked round it; Archie picked up his coat and put it on again. Seamus, McClatchy and Rafferty threw down the passengers' bags and began to rifle through them while the others searched the line-up of soldiers and civilians. The coachmen for their part sat perched on their seats, hands raised as a matter of course. Barra began walking along the line putting his left foot in line with each soldier's right foot in turn.

'What are you playing at?' asked Archie.

'I'm seeing if any of these fellas' shoes would fit me, I have want of a pair of shoes. Here this fella's about my size, get them off, you!'

'Do as he says, Johnston.'sighed Wilkes, defeatedly. The private duly obeyed. 'I'll have those lovely white stockings if you please too.' Wilkes nodded to Johnston.

Barra turned to Threader and whisked his pockets thoroughly, depriving him of his purse and case containing his papers. 'Brave rapparees indeed! What sort of men are you that would rob from a man of the church?' protested Threader.

'What sort of church is it that robs from the common people?' replied Archie with a barbed smile, hidden beneath his scarf. He contemplated repeating verbatim one of his father's fireside rants on the faults of the established church but decided that the urgency of the situation dictated against this course of action.

'Here this chap's got a lovely set of wooden teeth here too!' Exclaimed Barra, nodding to Threader; 'Gis them you.' He prised his fingers into Reverend Threader's mouth and extracted the coveted dentures, placing them in his own mouth with a slurp.

'For Heaven's sake Barra you're not taking the man's teeth. Give him those back.' reasoned Archie.

'Aye right enough, that's going a bit far. Here you are Mister, sorry.' He pulled the dentures from his own gob without wiping the slabbers off and popped them back in Threader's open mouth, upside down. Everyone grimaced a bit.

'Let him keep a few shillings too so he's enough money to get to his destination. We're not savages.' Barra counted out some coins and handed them to Threader.

'Didn't I tell you to put your hands in the air?' demanded Tomas McCafferty of Sergeant Wilkes. Why are you holding them over your nose like that?

'Well sir, the young Captain here appears to have besmirched his breeches.'

Tomas gave a sniff and glanced at the red faced captain. He walked round behind Pilkington and came back with a frown. 'You're right and all, this fellow's shit himself! What was it, the sound of the gunfire?'

'I had a mutton pie for supper last night and it seems to have disagreed with my stomach somewhat...' muttered Pilkington, by way of explanation.

'It most certainly has, here Barra this chap here has a pair of breeches you might be interested in. Probably cleaner than the ones you're wearing!'

Everyone laughed except for Pilkington, Threader and Barra; 'Aye very funny.'

'Let's see what you have got actually.' said Tomas, rummaging the unfortunate Pilkington whilst trying not to breathe through his nose. 'Oh, very nice pistol here, doesn't look like the standard issue. Silver handles! They'll fetch a price. Is this Dutch?' He rummaged the other side also. 'Oh and a silver snuff case! Very good. Thank you very much.'

'My Auntie gave me that as a present!' stated Pilkers, almost sobbing.

'Be sure to extend my compliments to her on her fine tastes.' replied Tomas, before relenting and handing the case back. 'Here, if it means that much to you then keep it.'

Leaving the contents of the bags and trunks scattered across the mud of the road, Seamus stormed over to the line. 'I have the box! Put this in your bag and don't lose it boy.' He said, pressing it to Barra's chest. Barra duly obeyed, stuffing the box into his sack along with his other treasures.

Glaring at the line, Seamus rounded on Lady Isabella. Stepping forward, her grasped her necklace roughly and ripped it from her violently, causing the lady to gasp in shock. His eyes dropped to her right hand. 'Take that ring off!' He barked. Isabella began struggling to loosen the ring; 'I can't get it, it's too tight. Grasping the Lady's wrist, the vicious thug began wrenching the ring from her finger causing her to shriek with pain. Amelie instinctively protective of her employer reached out and grappled at his giant's forearm but a backhanded slap sent her sprawling in the mud. As the others stood frozen with indecision, Eugene O'Cahan stepped forward and caught the savage outlaw with a glancing blow above the eye with the hand guard of his rapier. Seamus staggered back with a roar of pain and anger as blood trickled from an open wound down the front of his jerkin, before mixing in the muddy water at his feet.

'You were given very specific orders that none of the passengers were to be harmed, you great ignorant oaf; I will not stand by and tolerate a lady being misused in this way in my presence. To wit, I am hereby assuming control of this operation. Does any man here object?' said the Frenchman, turning to the remainder of the gang.

The question was met by a wall of silence.

'Very well the-' before he could finish his sentence Seamus' great hammer like fist crashed into the back of his head and sent him hurtling to the ground in a flurry of lights and pain. Not allowing O'Cahan the chance to he gather himself or rise to his feet, Seamus let loose with a barrage of savage boots and punches that rained down on the helpless Frenchman. The ladies stood back in shock at the violence of the onslaught. Angus attempted to grapple and reason with his older brother and received a wicked haymaker to the jaw for his efforts. Archie's heart was racing like never before. He wanted to help the Frenchman, but even if all the rapparees were to round on Seamus as one, they probably couldn't equal his brutish strength, especially in the midst of the psychotic rage McGrogan now found himself in. Archie decided there was only one course of action open to him. It was 29th April 1743, and Archie was about to make a decision that would change the course of his life forever.

'Captain McGrogan!' he shouted, summoning what authority he could; 'Desist immediately or I shall be forced to shoot!' He raised his short musket in both hands and pointed it directly at Seamus. McGrogan paused from his relentless beating of O'Cahan and stared in pure evil at McClung, who kept his weapon trained although visibly shaking. The hairs stood up on the backs of everyone's necks as they realised the stakes had now been raised to the highest level.

'Don't you point that gun at me.' snarled the bully. 'Nobody points a gun at me!' He marched glaringly towards Archie who back stepped in synchronisation. 'd-don't come any closer Seamus!' Seamus lurched forward to make a grab for the weapon, causing the boy to trip and fall onto his back. With a crack of thunder that could have arisen from the gates of hell itself, the short musket dispatched a heavy lead ball into the brute's stomach from almost point blank range.

Time seemed to stand still as the colour drained from Seamus' face and his eyes widened like saucers. Archie scrambled to his feet and stood at a distance as Seamus' eyes met him with a bewildered stare, almost as if pleading hopelessly for the younger man to undo the terrible wound he had inflicted. His lip quivered as first saliva and then a stream of thick black blood trickled from his open mouth. Those standing behind McGrogan gave a slight gasp as the small fist sized circle of blood widened to cover the lower half of his herculean back. For reasons best known to the dying rapparee he took a shuffling, pain filled step forward, followed by another some 3 seconds later. Archie broke the silence; 'Seamus- I'm sorry! I didn't mean to shoot it just-'

Seamus made a rasping noise much like a swine being hung up in an abattoir, the meaning of which was unclear although it offered neither acceptance nor forgiveness. Angus attempted to take his brother's arm but was weakly pushed away. Seamus took two more steps forward before his large intestines slopped from his great gut onto the muddy highway, filling the air with stench of black blood, bile and faeces. Amelie let out a scream and Barra and Pilkington deposited their breakfasts upon the road with a loud 'Heuuuggghhh!!'

Like a mighty oak tree crashing under the final swing of the axe, all 6'5 and 25 stone of the hate filled goliath gave no resistance as he smashed face first into the filthy dirge. The group remained silent for a few seconds before Archie, knowing not what else to do, stepped forward and picked up the tri-corner hat that the beast had deprived him of almost a year ago, and placed it on his own head.

'You – you've killed him!' gasped Angus, his voice trembling. Archie turned to his friend, shaking his head; 'No, no I didn't! Not on purpose anyway! The gun just went off, I didn't mean to shoot him.'

'You shot him down like a dog in cold blood!' shouted Angus; 'You're a murderer!' The younger McGrogan brother launched himself at Archie, but Tomas McCafferty seized him by the waist and held him fast whilst trying to soothe his captive. 'You're a dead man Preacher! You'll pay with your life for the blood you've spilled tonight!' He raged and spat and roared until O'Cahan delivered a sharp slap to his face. Angus fell to his knees sobbing.

'What will we do now?' asked Finbarr Rafferty, speaking for the first time that day. His query was answered quickly as a mighty crack of gunfire lit up the air, and a shot whizzed through the group missing several people, rapparees or otherwise by inches. The boys turned in horror to face the terrific spectre of matriarchal vengeance that was the approaching figure of Betty Higginson. The great white carthorses galloped in tandem as if they were one unstoppable juggernaut. The hot air of their breath looked like smoke billowing from their cavernous nostrils, and the noise of the cartwheels seemed to thunder behind them. High above the steeds stood the screaming visage, her eyes dancing with fire and a long slender window pole held above her like a javelin.

'It's a frigging Banshee! Run!' Yelled Barra as the rapparees escaped into the dark of the woodlands. All of the group went right uphill except for Angus who turned left ways and scrambled downhill to the river. Betty's Hellish chariot rumbled past the line of soldiers and passengers through the murky vile of the muddy, bloody, bile and puke filled puddles, showering Isabella and Amelie from head to toe in filth. The ladies looked down at their dresses, and then at each other before exclaiming; 'Merde!' in unison.

Betty drew the cart to a halt some 20 yards up the road and dismounted. The first of the pursuing posse arrived, and those who had firearms launched shots in the direction of the fast disappearing silhouettes of the rapparees in the darkness.

'Well don't just stand there, get after them!' squeaked Pilkington to Sergeant Wilkes.

'Well certainly sir, we'll need torches, dogs, can't really take the horses up there... perhaps you would like to lead the way?'

'Heavens no!' retorted the Captain; 'I mean, it's probably better we remain here to protect the passengers.'

'A lot of good you were to us a few minutes ago Sir!' snapped Threader. 'A fine soldier you are, soiling yourself at the first sound of gunfire. You're a disgrace to your regiment!'

Pilkers stared down at his shoes in silence.

'I wouldn't worry too much about shitting yourself sir.' mused Sergeant Wilkes; 'I remember one time in the colonies when the Indians caught us unawares...'

'Oh shut up Wilkes!' sulked Pilkington.

The rest of the militia had now arrived on scene including their fearless Captain George Higginson, who came huffing and puffing into the middle of the assembly almost five minutes after it was all over. Gathering his breath the master butcher rose to attention and saluted Captain Pilkington grandly; 'Captain George

Higginson of the South Downe Militia, at your service sir! Let me assure you you're in safe hands now.'

'Yes...' replied a somewhat mysterious Pilkers; 'could you just excuse me a minute, just need to freshen up.' He disappeared into the bushes to dispose of his underpants.

'Stand easy men!' called George to his soldiers, no one else was at attention anyway so they all just ignored him. George looked around for Betty, and saw her in conversation with Lady Isabella and Amelie. 'We are most extremely grateful for your most heroic actions Madame.' Said Isabella; 'If you hadn't have come along when you did, there would have been no telling what would have happened. If there is anything we can-'

'Wouldn't hear of it milady,' interupted Betty with a slight flash of a curtsey; 'Although if you are speaking to the Viscount you might be so kind as to mention that George Higginson's butchery of Banbridge retails the finest beef and pork produce in all of County Downe, at highly competitive prices.'

'Of course.' replied Isabella, somewhat bemused.

'Now then, let's see what we have here!' continued Betty, turning her back on the ladies in complete ignorance of protocol and sauntering over to Seamus' massive carcass. 'You men!' she called to a group of militia men who had just lit up their pipes and were standing chatting; 'C'mere over here and turn this bastard over till I get a look at him.' Three militia men ambled over compliantly and turned the still warm corpse face upwards, turning away quickly as to not be the first to look into the dead man's eyes. 'Close that monster's eyes or he'll take us all down to the devil with him!' called out one of the men. Betty tutted disparagingly and pulled the giant rapparee's eyelids shut. The men approached once more and gave a collective groan as they spied the man's guts hanging from the massive stomach wound. 'What's the matter boys, have you never seen a bit of tripe before?' said Betty, playing on the men's squeamishness; 'Many a Scotsman would be glad of this.'

John Higginson peered over his mother's shoulder; 'What do you think he died of Ma?' he asked, stupidly. 'Probably died of boredom waiting for your Da to show up.' replied Betty, in a deliberate barb at her husband; 'Aye don't think your cowardice went unnoticed George, we'll discuss that later.' George gulped.

'So is this the one who threatened you son?' asked Betty to her son.

'Don't think so,' replied the boy. 'the two I saw had masks on their faces, but they were nowhere near as big as him and they didn't have red hair.

'What do you mean two?' asked George, quizzically. 'You told me there were upwards of 50!'

'Aye – aye there were Da!' replied John sheepishly; 'I only really got a good look at two of them, that's what I meant.'

George folded his arms and raised an eyebrow at his son; 'Are you absolutely SURE that you are telling-'

'Don't you be starting on him just to take attention away from yourself!' interrupted Betty, her words punctuated a mild punch to her husband's broad arm. 'He has had a terrible day. He's been robbed, humiliated and threatened, and his own father wasn't even man enough to stand up for him! He told you he was attacked by rapparees, and then we found the same assaulting these fine people's carriage. If it wasn't for our John being brave enough to come straight home and raise the alarm, these fine people could be lying in the road with their throats cut. Were that you half the man your son is!'

George's lovely day was turning into a right shitter. He was too tired to argue. He'd been too tired to argue for the past 8 years. At times he wished for a simpler life. Why did he ever get married! It had oft times crossed his mind as to how happy he had been with his little meat stall at the market, when he had less money but more time to enjoy it. What was the point in being one of the richest men in Banbridge, outside the gentry, if you didn't get to sit by the river with a rod in your hand every so often? She was so much younger than he was too, it's not as if he would outlast her; when she took off in the cart like that after the rapparees, part of him even thought – no, forget that. He shook the malicious thought from his head and turned towards the recently deceased Seamus McGrogan again. 'Who was it that bagged this villain then Betty, was it yourself or one of the lads?'

'He was already dead when I arrived, and I was the first here. I heard a shot shortly beforehand. Whoever it was got him good, opened him right up like a mince pie.' George's nose wrinkled at the analogy. 'Actually, my good lady, it may well have been my good self who despatched the ruffian' interrupted the re-emergent Captain Pilkington. Sergeant Wilkes rolled his eyes once again and shook his head disbelievingly. 'Utter poppycock sir!' barged Threader waggling a boney finger; 'This young man- and I shall be writing to General Gervais Parker on this matter hmmm?' he paused to glower at Pilkington. 'This young man not only deserted his post at the very outset of his journey he also-'

'Yes yes my good Reverend all in good time.' Interrupted George Higginson, feeling some empathy for the young Captain; 'If we can concentrate just for now on how this highwayman met his demise, you see I need to set out a report on the incident to the Colonel.'

'Well,' said Threader, pacified to some degree; 'the gang of footpads stopped the coach, ordered us out, and then robbed us without such as an excuse me from Pilkington or his men. They took my money and several important papers in a leather satchel, all of which were the property of the church. Animals, sir!' George nodded agreeably; 'and the uh, incident?'

'Well, they argued amongst themselves over who was getting what share of their ill gotten gains, then there was a scuffle and this chap got shot by one of his own men!'

'Really?' replied George, surprised.

'Yes sir! Really sir! Shot the great brute right in the guts without a care in the world, right in front of these good ladies!'

'Er – with all due respect to the good Reverend, that would not be my exact interpretation of what happened.' injected Isabella; 'This man, the deceased here, was attempting to tear the ring from my finger and also assaulted my maid in a most despicable manner. A gentleman appeared and intervened on our behalf, and then himself fell victim to the most cowardly abuse. One of the rapparees then stepped forward and shot the felon dead. Not before time either!'

George Higginson nodded in feigned understanding and then thanked the lady for her help with his report. The militia meanwhile had been helping Amelie and the coachmen to salvage the remaining contents of the luggage from the road and to stuff them unceremoniously back into the trunks and cases. Several smaller items may have accidentally found their way into some of the militia men's pockets, and for some time after that some of their wives could be seen around town sporting some very fashionable French handkerchiefs, bloomers and hair pieces. Final goodbyes and thank yous were said and the passengers boarded their carriage for the final stretch of their journey to the Viscount's residence at Hillsborough. 'Perhaps you should travel outside the carriage for the remainder of the journey, Captain Pilkington?' suggested Isabella as Pilkers attempted to join them. He duly complied.

'So what do we do with this carcass then?' mused Betty, poking the corpse with her foot; 'I am minded to say we should just burn it or leave it for the crows.'

'Oh no that won't do at all!' protested George; 'This man is probably a proclaimed rapparee out on his keeping. We need to take his body back to town so that he can first be proclaimed dead by a physician, then we must send for the army so that he can be identified.'

'I say we hang him!' shouted one old man. 'No he must have a fair trial first, and then we'll hang him!' shouted another. 'We don't have to pay for his funeral if we hang him, do we?' asked another, concerned.

'No, no, no,' insisted George; 'I am the Captain here and I think you will find my authority has been undermined quite enough for one night.'

'A good thing too! You didn't even want us to come here!' shouted someone still drunk at the back, to muttered agreement. 'The next man here who interrupts me will be barred from my shop for life and will have to buy his sausages from McEwan's in

Edenderry! ' shouted George angrily, before adding 'No offence Bob.'

'None taken.' replied Bob McEwan. All others fell silent.

George stood for a few seconds to let his anger pass over him; 'We will load the corpse onto the back of my meat cart. We will store him at the shop until the physician can examine him.'

'You're not putting a dead body in the shop with all our stock George!' nagged Betty; 'who knows what diseases might be spread by such a practice.'

'Oh come now Betty,' smirked George; 'I suppose you'll be telling us next there are tiny little invisible creatures that pass sicknesses from the dead to the living. '

He paused and looked down at the deceased rapparee again; 'This fellow's capacity to create havoc in this world has long since passed.'

# 5. AROUND THE CAMPFIRE

The five hapless rapparees and Eugene O'Cahan had scrambled 200 yards up and over the wooded hill, thorns and nettles tearing at their shins as they went. There had been yelps and sobs from some as musket balls had whizzed past them, but Eugene had assured them they were well out of range by the time the militia had a chance to reload. They had huffed and puffed away desperately for a good mile after that, before watching from a safe vantage point as first the carriage and then the militia party had departed. They made camp in a shady copse and took stock of what had happened;

'Them proddies' gasped Barra, catching his breath; 'They've sent the devil's mother herself after us!'

'Hey-' objected Archie, with a pointed finger.

'Not you Archie' assured Barra; 'Didn't mean you mate. You're one of us.'

'One of us?' argued Owen McClatchy; 'That English bastard just shot our Captain in the belly and you're saying he's one of us?'

'I'm not English, my Da's Scottish, my Ma's from here and I was born here, so I'm as Irish as you. Get your frigging facts straight McClatchy!'

'Or what? Are you going to shoot me too the way you did poor Seamus?'

'That was an acc-'

'Enough of this!' shouted Eugene; 'All of you shut up.' Everyone calmed themselves. 'I understand you are upset McClatchy. However McClung here acted appropriately. Your sainted Captain tried to murder me without offering fair recourse. Archie gave him the opportunity to withdraw. I am commanding this mission now and I expect no more of this bickering. Do you all understand?'

Everyone nodded, some more enthusiastically than others. Turning to Archie, he added; 'Sir, I am indebted to you for my life. You will be considered my sergeant until we rendezvous with Shane in the morning.'

'Shane!' gasped Archie; 'He'll kill me for this!'

'No he will not,' contradicted Eugene; 'I will speak on your behalf and defend you with my life if necessary. Don't worry, Shane will understand.' Archie was not entirely at ease with this assurance but gave a faint smile anyway. 'Now.' said Eugene; 'We are all cold, hungry, damp and tired. We will light a fire, break bread, warm our toes and examine the fruits of our labours.'

'Shouldn't we say a prayer or something for Seamus first?' asked Barra. The boys looked at one another sheepishly. 'I suppose we should;' conceded Tomas. 'Archie's Da is a preacher there, maybe he should do it.'

'He the one who shot him in the firs-' started McClatchy, trailing off after a withering look from Eugene.

'I'm a Presbyterian anyway, we don't pray for the souls of the dead. Why don't you have a go yourself Barra?' suggested Archie.

'Oh! Right you be. Right everyone bow your heads and close your eyes.' Clearing his throat Barra began. 'Holy Mary, mother of God, am, please be merciful to the soul of our dear departed friend Seamus, er, who was good and kind, and sober – Here can you go to hell for telling lies in a prayer?' The boys sighed and tutted with annoyance, before Eugene interjected with a quick recital of Psalm 23 followed by the Lord's prayer. All crossed themselves except Archie and opened their eyes. Tomas clapped his hands together and rubbed them gingerly with a broad grin;

'Right then Sergeant Archie, get the fire lit there, who's for a game of cards?'

The fire was lit and everyone settled down to huddle in the warm glow. It was the first bit of real comfort the boys had had all day, and spirits were reasonably high despite the traumas they had all suffered. Seamus may be lying dead, but it's always better to see someone else getting it than you yourself; besides, the absence of the great brute allowed for the craic to flow more freely, with none having to fear the sudden changes in temper which characterised the former psychotic highwayman. They reflected over the day's proceedings, comparing the slight variances in their collective memories. McClatchy couldn't remember Archie giving Seamus fair warning, but Tomas and Barra reassured him this was the case. Tomas produced a flagon of whisky, took a swig and offered the others some. 'Shane said no drink allowed.' mentioned Archie, shaking his head. Tomas shrugged. 'You shot his brother, what's he going to do, kill you twice?' Archie laughed uncomfortably and took a swig, passing it on to Barra.

'I need a drink after seeing that devil earlier on there. What do you think it was?' he asked. 'Twas nought but a wild woman riding in a cart.' replied Eugene 'Your eyes were playing tricks on you Barra, as often happens in the heat of battle. When Shane and I fought together against the Austrians, over a score of men claimed to have been assailed by a two headed man. It was actually two twin brothers standing side by side. The mind deceives us with its flights of fancy.'

'It's true Barra, that lady lives in Banbridge. I've seen her about the place. I think her husband is a butcher or something, they go to the big church. My Da used to say their ideas are bigger than what God made them for' said Archie.

'I thought she was a fine looking woman myself.' grinned Tomas; 'I wouldn't want to come home to her with tuppence short of my wages though!' the boys chuckled.

'She did have a quare set of diddies on her, I must admit.' agreed Barra; 'she wasn't as pretty as my Annie though.'

The boys looked at him with mild amusement; 'YOUR Annie?' asked Eugene.

'Yes sir, my Annie! She's my sweetheart. I intend to make her my wife.' The rapparees looked at each other, bemused. 'Do you mean that wee widow woman you got the kiss off earlier?' inquired McClatchy. 'The very same!' beemed Barra proudly.

'Just get her bucked, never mind getting married. That's my advice to you young Barra' said Tomas casually, causing a ripple of laughter amongst the boys.

'Oh no I'm not like that, has to be marriage first and then all that funny business.' said Barra, haughtily.

'I was the same, sure that girl I had in Portaferry was married and that's what got me into this mess.' replied Tomas.

'Your behaviour towards the fairer sex leaves a lot to be desired Tomas' said Eugene with a joking smile; 'I hope you one day find the true love of your life the way Mr McCann here has.'

'And what about yourself sir, do you have a wife back in France?' asked Tomas.

'Me? Well there are always concubines in the camp, but mostly I prefer to keep my mind on the task at hand. Women are a distraction, and in my line of work a distraction can cost a man his life. No, the army is my wife and this-' replied Eugene, half unsheathing his rapier by way of illustration; 'is my sweetheart.'

'Do you not near cut the dick of yourself?' asked Tomas mischievously.

All of the party laughed together. All except for Finbarr Rafferty, ever the odd man out. Rafferty was a quietly spoken fellow, who fell into the life of the rapparee through no fault of his own. His story indeed was a tragic one; he had been a small tenant farmer who raised his family in honest abidance of the law of the land, paid his rent on time, was gracious to all and never had a bad word to say of anyone. But the bad winter of 1740 brought famine and ruin to the many in Ireland, and Rafferty received neither mercy nor sympathy from either his absentee landlord or the baliff. Cast out of his small holding and unable to procure work elsewhere, Finbarr Rafferty had endured the most hellish torture imaginable, as his wife and children slowly perished before his eyes. Shane had found him in the woods a near skeleton close to death, and had carried him on his back for 3 miles to one of the rapparee hideouts. The gang nursed the pitiful farmer back to physical health, but something in his mind remained broken. He was a timid fellow at the best of times, and was given to muttering to himself and going off alone to sit for hours, staring into space. Some of the boys were nervous of him, saying that he had come too close to death for a mortal man to live, and that the shadow of the grim reaper could at times be seen standing over him. He cried out in his sleep at night and some said that he could 'see into the next world.' Archie just felt dreadfully sorry for him, a good man whose life was ruined by a want of human compassion and the greed of others. Archie felt guilty because he himself had ruined his own life. The truth is Rafferty just wanted to go home, but there was no more home for him to go to. Sometimes he would appear to forget his family were dead and would talk as if he were returning home in the summer. Perhaps it would have been more merciful if Shane had allowed him to die. Even Seamus had found the little man too pathetic to bully and had sometimes attempted to joke with him, but never managed to raise more than the faintest of smiles. In truth he was something of a liability to the group but what else could they do with him?

Rafferty struggled every day to bury the horrors of his past deep down in his psyche; but the killing of Seamus before his eyes, the violence, the brutality, had brought these things back to the surface. The boys didn't know it yet but when Archie killed Seamus he also snuffed out that weak flickering light of sanity in Rafferty's mind. Rafferty stood up without speaking and began walking down hill silently. The boys looked at each other in confusion; 'Finbarr! Fin! Where are you going?' Barra and McClatchy got up and ran after him. 'Where are you going mate?' asked Barra, concerned. 'I – I have to go home, the fields need ploughing, my wife...'

'There's no farm anymore, Fin, do you remember? The English took it off you mate, your wife and children are gone.' said McClatchy, softly. 'Come on back, Finbarr, we're having a wee rest here then we're meeting up with Shane in the morning. It'll be all right.' Barra put his arm round the confused little man's shoulder and led him back to the camp. Rafferty sat down quietly and without knowing what to do for the best the boys continued their banter with no further mention of wives or sweethearts; Rafferty sat silently lost in his own thoughts.

'Let's have a look and see what's in that Minister's wee bag here.' said Tomas, cheerfully unbuckling Threader's satchel. 'Wee drop of communion wine with a bit of luck!' he emptied the contents onto the grass before him; 'Ach! Bunch of oul letters and newspapers. Not so much as a piece of cheese the stinjey oul devil!'

'Let's have a read at them anyway, there might be something useful in them.' suggested Archie.

'Quite' agreed Eugene 'one must never underestimate the benefits of military intelligence.'

'Here, you read them, I can't be arsed.' said Tomas dismissively, before tossing the papers to Archie and reclining with his pipe. Archie picked open a fine looking letter secured with an ornate red wax seal. He unfolded the thick yellow paper holding it at mid arm's length in the light of the fire. 'This is in Latin!' he said, puzzled. 'Seems to be a love letter.' He shrugged at the boys and continued; 'Carrissime Simonus Castellum – dearest Simone?'

'Dearest Simon; the feminine would be Carrissima.' Corrected Eugene; 'please continue.'

'Um, er, Te amo – I know that, it means I love you!' said Archie smiling proudly. 'Let me have a look at it Archie.' Interrupted Eugene. Archie handed the letter to the Frenchman.

'Dearest Simon, I pray that this letter finds you in the greatest of health and cheer. I love you more than words can say and wish nothing more than to scream it from the heavens. But alas a love such as ours must never be spoke of, lest the hollow hearts and wagging tongues be set against us to our demise?' said Eugene, quizzically. 'Terrible grammar,' He commented, before continuing; 'How I yearn for the long winter nights of yesteryear when we lay together in each other's arms, and I count the days that the good Lord sends us until I once again lie with you in loving harmony. Yours for ever in love, Jacobus.'

'Jacobus? That's James isn't it?' asked Archie.

'Yes.' replied Eugene, without a hint of surprise.

'So it's a love letter from a man to another man?' asked Tomas, smiling.

'Indeed!' replied Eugene.

'What!' shouted Barra; 'I don't understand- why?'

Tomas fell about laughing uncontrollably.

Archie frowned and muttered something about the holy scriptures.

'The dirty bastards!' shouted McClatchy 'They should all be shot!'

The boys reaction made Tomas laugh even harder, which in turn made Eugene laugh.

'I mean- what do they do?' asked Barra in a cloud of confusion; 'does one of them turn into a woman?'

'Read your Bible!' tutted Archie.

'Oh please stop, I think I'm going to piss myself.' laughed Tomas, straining to control himself.

'I fail to see what you two find amusing about this sort of behaviour, there was none of this sort of thing when I was a boy.' stated Owen McClatchy with unerring certainty. Eugene couldn't resist the opportunity for mischief; 'Oh come now McClatchy, these sorts of relationships between men proliferate in all sorts of social circumstances. Have you never, for instance, lain with a comrade beneath a warm blanket of a cold winter's night?'

'To share warmth, yes but that's diff-'

'And have you ever' interrupted Eugene; 'awoke to find that a hand or an arm may have strayed into another's jerkin to search out the heat of an armpit for instance, have you never warmed your digits against another man's thigh or your toes against his heels?' Tomas coughed and huffed as he struggled to contain his mirth. McClatchy at length replied; 'That is not the same thing at all, there's no point in freezing to death when you can-'

'And have you ever;' interrupted Eugene again; 'struggled to control the machinations of your hammer of the passions, as it sought out the sweet shelter between the pillows of another man's backside? Did you never long to sow your seed in the deep tract of your fellow's passage?'

Tomas exploded with laughter as Barra and Archie frowned in disgust. 'No I did not you dirty French bastard! I would like to hear you speak so of our men if our Captain yet survived, he would grind your face into the mud again like the dog that you are!' Tomas and Eugene laughed their fill while the others sat in silence. Eventually Tomas stretched his hands out saying; 'Let's talk about something else shall we? He rolled up the letter and stuffed it into his pocket. 'What are you keeping that for?' asked Barra. 'It's a fine letter.' replied Tomas; 'good paper, wax seal and all. Whoever sent this wasn't short of a penny or two.'

'And?' asked Archie.

'Well, he's not going to want people knowing about all this is he? If we can find out who he is, I dare say he'd pay a pretty penny to get this back.'

'Do you mean blackmailing someone?' asked Archie, judgementally.

'Well, I am sure this fine gentleman whoever he is will be so happy to get his letter back, he'll want to see his good Samaritan well rewarded. Not a vast fortune of course, maybe enough to get me to the colonies and enough for a small patch of land.'

'Ha!' said McClatchy 'Ireland not good enough for you eh?'

'No offence Owen, but I do not wish to spend the rest of my life sleeping in ditches and running from the militia. I never wanted to be a rapparee in the first place. A wee quiet farm will do me, somewhere to call home.'

'Home!' repeated Rafferty.

'Can I come too Tomas?' asked Barra eagerly; 'Me and Annie and the Childer?'

'You surely can Barra, if you can get together the money for your journey and enough to support the four of you. I imagine that would be no mean task though.' replied Tomas. 'Where there's a will there's a way, that's what I always say!' replied Barra, with a cheerful smile. 'I've got some money here anyway off the Minister' he said, holding out 3 s 10 d. 'I gave him the big thick goldy ones back like you said Archie.'

'What!' exclaimed McClatchy, astounded; 'Those were guineas, you silly bastard!'

The gang's little firelit shindig was the lap of luxury compared to the ordeal their erstwhile companion was enduring. Angus Og McGrogan had hopped, skipped, and dived blindly downhill in the darkness before sploshing into the little river, an offshoot of the mighty Bann which had been greatly swollen by a hard day's rain. A lone musket ball had flashed by but fortunately for Angus the militia were too interested in the main group who were escaping uphill in the opposite direction to pay him any real heed. A lack of torches and dogs prevented the mob from pursuing him across country. Angus gasped in the dark as freezing cold water filled his eyes and nose, he was forced to discard his heavy sheepskin to prevent himself from being dragged under. After a few brief seconds of panic which felt like an age to a drowning man, Angus was able to grasp at some roots and pull himself onto the far bank. He allowed himself a few minutes to catch his breath before moving on cautiously, as he could clearly hear the voices of the people above as if they were just yards away.

Angus was now soaked to the skin, had lost his provisions, hat and coat, and was bruised, disorientated, and still in shock from witnessing the death of his eldest brother at the hands of one of his closest friends. He tramped restlessly onwards, defying the flashes of pain that each step sent upwards from his gashed and swollen left ankle. He hoped against hope that he was on the right path towards the gang's Slieve Croob hideout, and that he could evade any hostile enemy forces who might fancy their chances at picking up the reward money for bringing in one of the notorious McGrogan brothers. He went over the sequence of events again and again in his head but it all came back to Archie shooting his brother through the stomach. He came to a field surrounded by a 4 foot dry stone wall, and heaved himself awkwardly over it, letting out an 'Aaaah!' as he landed his full weight on the bad ankle first. He paused for a few minutes to let the pain subside and made a mental note not to do that again. He hobbled as steadily onward across the field as was possible. The bovine occupants of the field mooed unwelcomingly as he crossed cautiously to the other side, daring to look neither right nor left for fear of making eye contact with the animals. With some 20 feet to go, he instinctively broke into a run as he heard the higher pitched mooing of a calf followed by the thumpety thump of a rampaging protective mother intent on evicting the trespasser from the midst of her herd. He jumped on to the wall on his belly and felt the jagged rocks on the top of the wall dig into his ribs. He rolled over in agony before flopping the 4 foot over the side of the wall, his fall being broken only by a huge cow pat which spattered across the back of his soaking wet jerkin. He lay for a few seconds until the smell got unbearable. He sat up and looked about him. Then he saw something which just might indicate his luck was about to change; a barn! If he could borrow a horse, he might just make it back home before he froze to death.

Back at the camp, the mirth continued; 'The colonies is it!' laughed McClatchy; 'the two of you have more chance of running into some of these fairies that young Barra is always on about than you do of making it to the Americas.' This cynicism was typical of what the gang had come to expect of Owen McClatchy, the oldest surviving member at 48 years of age. A grey, wiry man of rocky features, he carried his years well and never complained about the physical hardships of the rapparee lifestyle; it was more people that annoyed him than circumstances. He had no great love of wise cracks or story tellers, being of the belief that people who spoke too much would be the first ones to tell on their fellows to avoid the noose if they were taken. He had confided these beliefs in Seamus, who had come to view the older man as something of a mentor. Because of this McClatchy's main loyalty, if he had any, would be to Seamus rather than Shane.

'Ah yes!' interrupted Eugene, who had been quietly sharpening his rapier with a special stone he kept in his belt; 'You were going to tell us about these mysterious fairies Barra, I must say I find these little colloquial anecdotes fascinating.'

'There's nothing dirty about it sir!' protested Barra; 'these stories have been handed down for hundreds of years here in Ireland. You see in the old days, before even Saint Patrick arrived, there was a race of people who lived and breathed much as we do now. You can see the evidence of their being all around, they made huge stone idols and alters to their pagan Gods that stand until this very day.'

'There's one at Legananny near our base, 3 great big stones bigger than a horse and another laid across it. Nobody knows how they got it there, probably magic.' interrupted Tomas.

'You two would do better to put your faith in the holy scriptures instead of spreading this idle heresy.' said Archie, scornfully.

'Well how do you explain the stones the-'

'Stop interrupting, the both of you!' said Barra; 'I'm trying to tell a story. Be quiet and you might learn something. Yes they were a great race of scholars and magicians but they didn't know about Jesus so when they all died out none of them went to heaven. Or some people say they were angels thrown out of heaven when Lucifer rebelled against the Lord but I don't know either way. Anyway they died an earthly death but instead of going to heaven or hell, their spirits entered into the rocks, the trees, and the rivers and things like that. Anyway the queen of theseuns was called

Aine, she was very beautiful and bewitching and she wanted nothing more than to return to the land of the living. So at a certain time of the year when the spirits are most powerful and closest to the living, she would appear before mortal men and entice them with her dance, then she would lay with them so she could have a baby and be born as a human being again.'

'Fascinating!' remarked Eugene, smiling.

'That's a devil you are talking about there.' said Archie disparagingly; 'My Da warned me of such creatures. It's called a subuccus. They come to weak minded men in the night and steal their seed.'

Tomas laughed at the mention of seed; 'Here well she's welcome to some of mine. I've enough to go around for everyone!'

Archie tutted; 'It appears as a beautiful woman and then once it has your seed you see it as it is really, a hideous oul crone.'

'Many a fine tune played on an old fiddle!' replied Tomas, mockingly.

'and then after that your winkie shrivels away and you become an old man and die within 3 days.' finished Archie, in a matter of fact manner.

Tomas paused, raised an eyebrow and said 'you probably made that last bit up to ruin my fun.'

Doctor Jacob Cayley stared thoughtfully down at the massive carcass of the dead rapparee stretched out before him on the carving table in the back of Higginson's butchery, 26 Newry Street. He had sowed up the highwayman's guts back into his enormous stomach to the best of his ability, cramming them in like a jack in the box with one hand whilst trying to work the needle with the other in the flickering candlelight. It was awkward, smelly work but at least with the dead ones they're not gurning and shouting the whole time. The task was made no easier by the two overly curious Higginson men peering over his shoulder and casting shadows; at least the woman had stayed outside to wash down the cart.

'I've never seen a man's insides before.' Said John Higginson, idly; 'they just look the same as a pig's insides. Do you think God was turning him into a pig because he ate and drank so much Doctor?'

'Don't ask the Doctor silly questions John, go and sweep up the shop or something.' ordered George Higginson. John remained where he was and lazily pushed a broom with one hand in appeasement of his father's wishes. Doctor Cayley shook his head and wondered whether stupidity was hereditary. 'I think that will do us for now George;' said the stocky Yorkshireman, tiredly. He wiped the congealed blood from his veiny hands and tutted with annoyance at the stains to his shirt sleeves. 'That will need to go in to soak. The wife will have a fit,' he thought. Then he remembered his wife was dead. The Doctor turned to George and handed him a brief statement of his observations on the cause of death; 'This poor fellow is hardly likely to complain about the quality of my stitching. I think it's safe to say he's ready to complete his journey across the river Styx. Do you know who it was that bagged the villain?'

'Interesting story there actually Doctor, it wasn't one of us at all. Apparently he was the ringleader of the gang of thieves, but his own men mutinied against him.'

'Really?' said the Doctor, picking a sausage from the tray that young John offered him, and acknowledging with a nod before popping it in his mouth.

'Yes, one of his accomplices shot the big brute in the stomach. He had attacked two young ladies, striking one in the face with such force as he knocked her to the ground, and almost ripping the hand off another, then some of his fellows rebelled. Honour among thieves eh?' smirked George.

'Indeed! though it would have been quite a boon for the man who had brought this ruffian in. This is the notorious Seamus McGrogan, one of the leaders of the McGrogan gang. He has a substantial price on his head – twenty pounds I think? Dead or alive I understand.'

The mention of a large sum of money turned a light on in George Higginson's fat head. 'Oh! I say. Well, naturally as Captain of the militia it would be my responsibility to deliver him up to the mercy of the Assizes at Downpatrick. I will of course ensure that any reward monies are distributed appropriately. How did you er – know who he was?'

'Well.' started Doctor Cayley; 'as a Doctor I have taken a solemn oath to preserve the lives and health of all men. I have on occasion been called out to all manner of mysterious locations – under false pretences – to administer treatment to men suffering from sprains, buckshot wounds, that sort of thing. Best not to ask too many questions on those sorts of call you know.'

'Ah I see.' nodded George; 'Well if you have any further 'mysterious' requests for your services, you will see fit to inform the militia, wont you?'

'Of course, Captain Higginson, only too happy to do my duty. So will you be-'

Seamus McGrogan let out a large belch that caused George and John Higginson to jump four feet backwards and scramble for the door, pushing each other out of the way.

'Gentlemen, please!' laughed the Doctor. 'There's nowt to be afraid of, this fellow is quite dead. You see the body is filled with gaseous substances, that give it its motion. I've seen them burp, fart, groan, sometimes they even sit bolt upright and open their eyes. Changes in temperature can affect them too. But there's nothing to fear, McGrogan here is very, very dead. You can touch him if you like!' He held up Seamus' cold dead arm by way of illustration.

'Er, no thanks Doctor.' said George nervously as John cowered shakily behind him, gripping his shoulders. 'I think we'll just call it a night. Can you let yourself out when you're done Doctor?'

'Aye, appen as a can, George. Goodnight.'

'Goodnight Doctor. Oh, I don't know if I should mention it but the Minister noted you haven't been to the church yet and well, you came here quite a few years ago.'

'And what of it?' asked the Doctor, curiously. 'Well,' replied George; 'It's just that some people, not me of course, are starting to wonder if you might not be of the established church?'

Doctor Cayley sighed; 'I'm a very busy man George, folk don't stop being sick just because it's Sunday. Tell the Vicar I'll be attending with him as soon as my duties will allow it.' Higginson nodded.

George and John started up the stairs; 'I need you to open the shop yourself tomorrow son.' whispered George; 'Daddy's got an errand to run.'

Doctor Cayley wiped off his instruments and washed his hands. He put on his black greatcoat and tri-corner hat, then placed all of his instruments carefully back in his satchel before hanging it over his shoulder. He paused and took one more look at the deceased Seamus McGrogan; 'Goodbye my old friend, you fought the good fight.' with that he blew the candle out.

Kenneth and Gareth Clinton trundled slowly home along the little dirt path towards their farmhouse in a slightly rickety horse trap, pulled along by their faithful little pony Pearl. It wasn't their usual practise to be out after sundown, but they'd been foolish enough to follow Betty Higginson and the militia halfway to Dromore before deciding against it and 'accidentally' losing the rest of the group at a bend in the road, and heading for home. It was Kenneth's idea, as it was with most things, and he had reasoned that there were so many there that none would notice a couple of missing stragglers. They were both simultaneously relieved and guilt ridden to have heard the bangs but not been there to know if anyone was hit or not. 'I'm hungry,' moaned Gareth, the younger of the twins; 'can we put the kettle on and toast a wee bit of bread when we get in?'

'What!' said Kenneth; 'You near ate the Higginsons out of house and home down there, I'd to stop you from filling your plate for a third time. Don't be embarrassing me at a party like that again by the way, I didn't know where to put me face.'

'That was hours ago! Just a wee bit of toast before bed. Maybe a bit of cheese too.'

'Oh?' said Kenneth, quizzically. 'Cheese now is it? Listen I am not lighting the stove at this time of night to appease your gluttonous cravings. Straight to bed for the two of us, we've to be up in the morning early, them cows won't feed themselves or the horses either. Besides, you'll wake mother up.'

'Ach hell!' grumped Gareth. 'This is them rapparees fault, bad luck to them. I hope the boys catch them and hang the lot of them.'

'Rapparees my arse. How often do you hear of anybody getting robbed on the highway round here? They wouldn't dare, what with all the army here. You go down to Ballynahinch on a Saturday the soldiers outnumber the locals more often than not. People get a lot of drink in them and go off with all sorts of funny nonsense in their heads. Remember a few years ago it got round the town that oul Sadie O'Reilly was a witch in league with the devil? They'd have had that poor oul soul burnt at the stake if Sandy McClung hadn't have stepped in and calmed them all down. Rapparees, Ha!' he spat into the grass bank at the side of the road. Gareth had sometime wondered to himself if his brother's habit of taking the opposite view of any widely held belief was due to a superior intelligence or a contrary nature; either was it could be taxing at times. The brothers were alike neither in appearance nor in temperament. Although comparable in height, Gareth was more than a stone heavier, being want to revel in life's little enjoyments at any given opportunity. His central defining belief was that God had put man on the Earth so that he could enjoy the fruits of his labour and to deny such simple pleasures was to injure one's self pointlessly. Kenneth on the other hand was ever vigilant against his brother's profligate ways, and considered it his business to ensure that there was always enough put by for a rainy day, even if certain sacrifices of comfort had to be made. It was an odd relationship which the two had, as although they had affection one another to some extent they both secretly felt that life would be much easier with the other out of the way, or at least brought under heel.

'Well who threw wee John Higginson's shoes in the river then?' challenged Gareth.

'They've probably been messing about swimming and lost them. Why would a rapparee bother to take the shoes off a pig ignorant wee shite like John Higginson and throw them in the river? I tell you something though, it's a pity they didn't throw wee John in the river too, the impudent wee devil.'

'Aye well he is a nuisance I'll give you that,' agreed Gareth. 'Remember we caught him throwing stones at the cows and brought him to his Da? Not that anything was done about it.'

Kenneth nodded; 'Aye we all know who wears the breeches in that household; certainly not George anyway; a nice fellow yes, an honest man, true. But hen pecked! It's embarrassing to watch sometimes. And to make him a captain of the militia! She would probably have that off him as well if she could.'

'She's a fine looking woman though; she can have my sausage any time!' smiled Gareth.

Kenneth frowned. 'Enough of that coarse talk you; what would mother say if she heard you speak so?'

The conversation was broken by the loud boom of a blunderbuss followed by an approaching rapid drumming of hooves, as a familiar grey mare shot past them with a mysterious dark figure clinging fast to the reins. The brothers sat in stunned silence for a second before the familiar holler of Ma Clinton shouted rasply,

'C'mere back here with that horse ya thieving wee bugger yee!' The brothers looked one to the other and then back to their 80 year old mother who stood in the courtyard clad in nightgown and cap, cradling the heavy blunderbuss. 'He's stolen the horse!' they said incredulously.

Richard Pilkington's face was redder than a beetroot as he stood in the study of Viscount Hillsborough's country house, watching his commanding officer getting a thorough dressing down from an enraged aristocrat. He glanced briefly round at the pearly white walls where the portraits of the Viscount's ancestors seemed to frown down on him in pitiless condemnation of his abject failure. Glancing downward he briefly noted he had trod mud into the stylish and expensive Persian rug, which was probably priced in excess of a year's wages; this at least was not Pilkington's fault as he had been frogmarched into the room without being given the chance to clean up, but he prayed anyway that the Viscount wouldn't notice. The Viscount had arranged an elegant supper for his guests and this was expected to be a triumphant moment for the colonel; Pilkington would have even been asked to dine with the party had he not made such an absolutely terrible hash of a very simple job.

Circumstances offered the captain no opportunity whatsoever to limit the damage of the events or to present any sort of positive image of the facts as they occurred. Such was Wills Hill's affection for Lady Isabella, that he had personally came out into the courtyard to greet her as she alighted the carriage. As Pilkington rode out in front of his men, as he was supposed to do from the offset, he was the first to see the smile drop from the young Viscount's face as the procession entered the courtyard, noticing the unkempt state of the inept officer's uniform. Wills had dropped the beautiful bouquet of white lilies he had been holding to present to his guest and had run to the carriage to fling open the door. Pilkers had heard the Viscount gasp at the sight of his beloved childhood friend plastered with the filth of the road, her maid still clutching a blood soaked handkerchief to her nose, and a highly critical cleric making it absolutely clear who he believed was responsible for the whole sorry escapade.

The servants crowded over in a flurry of activity and soon water was being boiled and wounds attended. Fortunately Isabella's finger was not broken but still stiff and highly painful. Colonel Lambert ordered Sergeant Wilkes to change the horses and for he and his men to escort Reverend Threader for the remainder of his journey to Belfast. The colonel never even got a chance to interrogate Pilkington himself before the Viscount began his dressing down of both officers.

'I specifically asked you to ensure the safety of Lady Isabella for the length of her journey Lambert; a simple task, to escort the good Lady from the harbour at Newry to my house. And what do you do? Arrange an escort of only 5 men, led by this-' he shook his hand in Pilkington's direction; 'Officer, who not only decided he would idle his time away with his betters inside the carriage, not only surrendered at the first crack of gun fire, he also, by all accounts, made his toilet in the seat of his pants in terror at the sight of a few of the local oiks!'

'Well yes Sir, it's quite unacceptable, and I will-' started Colonel Lambert, before Pilkington interrupted; 'Might I just say in my defence m'Lord I did have a rather disagreeable mutton pie-'

'I don't give a Hell's blazes if you dined on your own entrails sir!' raged the Viscount. Pilkers stood rigidly to attention, trying to suppress a tear. Wills sat for a few seconds to gather his thoughts.

'If I may sir, I can assure you that young Pilkington here will be dealt with most appropriately.' assured Lambert, softly.

'Like you did the last time, eh Lambert? What was it again, ah yes, Captain Pilkington had been out strolling in the woods and had his coat stolen by a yokel! That was it, wasn't it?' the Viscount clapped his hands together and sat back in his fine leather wing back chair with a cynically half smile, shaking his head. Pilkington opened his mouth to offer another explanation but decided against it after a threatening glance from his colonel. 'I don't know that it would be fair to blame Pilkington for everything that has occurred in its entirety-' argued the colonel, apologetically. 'Oh no, so who would you blame then Colonel Lambert, yourself maybe? You are his commanding officer are you not?'

'Well-'

'Or perhaps it's my fault Lambert, what? Yes, that's what it is isn't it. Of course I should have stipulated quite specifically, when I asked you to escort my dear friend from Newry to Hillsborough, to ensure that she did not arrive here with a broken finger and covered in shit. How terribly remiss of me!' Wills slammed his hand down heavily on the desk to punctuate the final sentence, causing Lambert and Pilkington to jump slightly.

Colonel Lambert fell silent. 'It would seem,' stated the Viscount, condescendingly; 'That while success has many parents, failure is indeed an orphan!'

Lambert breathed deeply. It was difficult for him to maintain his composure when being spoken to so by a 25 year old civilian, even if they were of a much higher social status; 'Well yes M'Lord but be that as it may, we have to think about how this will be presented to the public. If word were to get out that a troop of our men had surrendered to – as you say – a bunch of local oiks, it could cause a great deal of damage to the reputation of the regiment, and also we have to think about public order. We don't want the locals thinking we've gone soft.'

'So what do you suggest then?' asked the Viscount, leaning forward on his desk and pressing his fingers together. 'Well sir as young Pilkington here has reported, one of the leading gang members were dispatched with and the others were driven off, albeit by the militia, so I'm sure we can come up with something to report in the paper that will throw a more complimentary light on us all.'

'Yes yes. Just get this man out of my sight and make sure that a more competent officer is designated to the task of protecting Lady Isabella on her return journey. Perhaps it would be appropriate for you to attend to the matter personally?' Lambert was about to suggest an alternative but decided against correcting his superior given the circumstances. 'It would be an honour m'Lord.'

'Yes Lambert.' said the Viscount fixing the colonel with a cold stare; 'it bloody well is.' Lambert and Pilkington clicked their heels and saluted before turning to march out of the room. Wills didn't bother to so much as raise his eyes from his papers to acknowledge them. They closed the heavy oak door behind them and walked along the corridor to a little side room which the Viscount had set aside earlier from the Officers' use. Once inside, Colonel Lambert removed his coarse wig and rubbed his eyes before trailing his hand back across his thinning grey hairline. Pilkington shifted uncomfortably; 'Well.' he said; 'I suppose it could have been worse, eh sir?' Lambert looked up at him frowning, but said nothing. 'Er- well what I mean is, no one was actually killed, what? In fact if you count that robber fellow who got shot it was actually quite a good resu-'

'Don't!' barked Lambert, pulling Pilkington nose to nose with him by the lapels. 'Just don't.' He released a gasping Pilkington and both stood silently for several more seconds. 'I don't think that this posting is quite working out for you Richard.' stated Lambert, quietly but firmly, at length. 'I know I promised your father I would look out for you, but the army is no place for this sort of – ninkompoopery!'

'Yes well if you put it like that uncle Roger, I do suppose maybe a return to accountancy might not be out of the question.'

'Accountancy is it sir? You signed a twenty year contract my boy, and I will certainly not be submitting your dear sweet mother to the indignity of having her son return home on a dishonourable discharge. No sir. I am recommending you for a transfer.'

'Oh?'

'To India!'

'Oh!'

Tomas McCafferty had cleaned all his friends out at cards and was now impressing them with all manner of clever tricks; 'And this sir, is your card!' he exclaimed, triumphantly. Archie scratched his head in wonderment and considered whether some sort of sorcery might be at work. 'A simple slight of hand my friend,' grinned Tomas, 'nothing of the night about it.'

'Here I can do magic as well, wait til you see.' said Barra enthusiastically. He produced the intricately carved jewellery box that Seamus had given him earlier and clamped it between his knees. He then picked up a page of Threader's notes and pushed it down hard against the lid of the box. Taking a piece of charcoal from the embers of the campfire, he rubbed it roughly on the paper, causing the imprint of the patterned lid to be reproduced on the paper. He then held his artwork aloft with a broad grin and a bright 'Tada!'

'That's not really a trick mate,' said Archie, dismissively; 'we can all see how you did it.'

'Aye but look at the pattern I've made.' replied Barra, undeterred. He stuffed the page into his pocket. 'Always hold on to a piece of paper lads, great for wiping your arse on. God knows why people waste it on writing.'

'The only other trick I can do is,' said Barra; 'Throwing my voice!'

The boys looked round to behind where Archie was sitting to detect the source of the speaker. 'I must say, that IS remarkable!' said Eugene, impressed; 'How do you do it?'

Barra shrugged. 'I don't know really. I just seem to be able to pick a spot where I want my voice to sound like it's coming from and it just happens. It's just a silly amusement.' He added modestly. 'You would be surprised how such a skill could come in handy.' said Eugene. 'Here fire us that box over til I have a look at it;' said Tomas. 'We may as well find out what Seamus died for.' Barra tossed the box over to Tomas, who set about working on the hinges with a little bait knife he kept in his pocket. After a few minutes the hinges popped open and the lid was removed. McCafferty dipped his hand in and fished out the glittering prize, the like of which none of them had ever seen. A jewelled necklace of 24 stones and a huge centrepiece jewel as big as a man's nose, that shimmered eerily in the firelight; the shards of reflected light seemed to dance like imps as the boys sat transfixed by its beauty. At length, Tomas spoke first; 'Holy Mary. How much do you think that's worth?' he asked, rhetorically. 'Probably enough to arm every rapparee in the country to the teeth; pistols, muskets, horse and canon maybe. We could liberate Ireland with that.' said McClatchy, with uncharacteristic optimism. 'It would certainly make some sort of difference.' Conceded Tomas; 'Get us all a few new pairs of stockings at least. You can see why Shane was so keen to get his hands on it. I'll keep it safe,' said Tomas pushing the necklace into his inside pocket whilst throwing the box onto the fire. 'Just don't be getting any ideas,' warned McClatchy; 'you wouldn't want me to have to come looking for you.' Tomas puffed carelessly at the idle threat; 'Where would you fence something like this anyway? I mean, if you broke it up Roscoe's the jewellers in Banbridge might give you something for one of the smaller jewels...'

'I'm sure Shane has his own ideas as to how to make best use of this asset,' replied Eugene; 'Tomas, I shall entrust the treasure into your capable hands for the time being. As Mr McClatchy has said however, don't have us to come looking for you.' A whistling breeze picked up causing the boys to pull their coats round them in a huddle. 'It's spooky up here in the dark,' commented Barra; 'reminds me of that story of the grey lady.'

'Do tell!' said Eugene, enthusiastically; 'I love ghost stories. I am hoping to compile a compendium of such tales when I grow too old for military service.'

'Well,' said Barra, as the boys crowded further in, intrigued; 'It was some 20 or 30 years ago. A young woman called Deidre O'Casey lived here happily with her husband and 2 children on a small farm where they raised a cow for milk, a pig to sell for bacon and a few hens for eggs. They also tended their little field and raised crops to eat. They were poor people but very much happy and grateful for that which the Lord had set aside for them. Despite being tenants they took great pride in the house and the farm and maintained them both to the highest of standards. Deirdre's hair was said to be as black as the wings of a raven, and she was known throughout the district for her comeliness. They paid their rent to their landlord who was at that time a Mr Jonah Forrester, a kind and fair man who would try to give his tenants some leeway when times were hard. When Deidre's husband died of the cholera, Mr Forrester kindly waived the rent for 3 months until the family got back on their feet again.

Anyway Jonah Forrester died and his son Jeremiah took over his lands and his duties. Jeremiah was not like his father though, he was greedy and cruel and cared for none save himself. His first act was to raise the rents of all the tenants he had, without pity for those without the means to pay. He came one day to take the rent and when he set eyes on Deirdre he was filled with passion. He demanded she lay with him in lieu of the rent. When the widow refused, he went away and returned with his bailiffs to take the rent. On the first day he came, Forrester pointed at the chickens and bade the bailiffs take them. Deidre pleaded with Forrester to leave the birds as without them the children would have no eggs, but they took them anyway. Deidre was greatly troubled by the loss of the chickens, and the health of both mother and children suffered for the want of the eggs.

The next week, Forrester returned with his goons to collect his rent again. At this time Deidre had a single grey streak through her hair, due to the worry about what Forrester might take this time. When Deidre again could not pay the rent, the cold hearted Forrester pointed to the pig and bade them take the animal too.

Deidre again pleaded with Forrester as without the pig they would have nought to sell at market and then children would go hungry again, but again the devil just laughed at her pleading. Forrester went away leaving Deidre to fret over what might happen the next time he came. The next week again Forrester came with his men, and Deidre had two streaks of grey through her hair, and she and the children were greatly wasted by the pangs of hunger. This time Forrester pointed to the cow, and they took it even though Deidre pleaded that without it there would be no milk for the children. The next week Forrester returned and found that the children had died, and that Deidre's hair was now purely grey. Caring not, he pointed to the hand plough and bade the bailiffs take it from her. Left with no means of support, Deidre was expired when next Forrester arrived at the farm. Thinking himself fortunate to be rid of such bad tenants, the miser elected that he himself would move into the farmhouse and make it his den.'

'What an unscrupulous cur this Forrester must have been!' said Eugene O'Cahan.

'Indeed sir!' agreed Barra; 'but the story doesn't end there. Forrester's first 6 days in the house passed without incident in splendid isolation, as he worked his evil in the home of the family who he had brought to ruin; but on the seventh night, as he lay in bed, he heard the creaking of footsteps up the stairs. 'Who is there?' he called out in terror, as the bedroom door creaked open. As he cowered beneath the sheets, the terrifying spectre of Deidre O'Casey, the grey lady appeared, her once beautiful face now a bony mask and her eyes as hollow as a pair of earthen milk jugs. As Forrester watched in frozen terror, the frightful visage floated above his bed, with arm outstretched and finger pointed; 'Jeremiah Forrester, I have come for your eye!' she said.

'Spare my eye, lest how shall I read my books!' cried the miser, but to no avail.

When Forrester awoke the next morning, he found himself to be completely blind in one eye. Shaken but undeterred, he put the incident behind him and continued with his work as best as his debility would allow. But on the seventh night as he lay in bed, the spectre appeared to him again entering the room much as it did before and floating at the bottom of the bed; 'What do you want of me now oh cruel wraith?' he asked in fearful anticipation.

'Jeremiah Forrester, I have come for your arm!' said the ghost of Deidre O'Casey.

'Spare me my arm, good lady, lest how shall I write my letters?' pleaded Forrester, but the spirit cared not, and showed the cruel landlord no more pity than what he himself had shown to the O'Casey family.

When Forrester awoke the next morning, he found his right arm hung lifeless at his side, and neither physician nor priest could offer him either reason or cure for his ailment. So once again Forrester tried to continue with his dirty work of robbing the farmers, despite having use of only one eye and one arm.

Another week passed, and Forrester had waited in terror and anxiety as to what would occur when next he encountered the spirit of Deidre O'Casey. His fears were well founded as this time the spirit came for Forrester's leg. 'Spare my leg!' he cried; 'lest how shall I collect the rent from my tenants?' But the spirit cared not.

He awoke the next morning to find his right leg to be limp and useless, and because he no longer had use of his arm either, he was now unable to walk even with the aid of a stick. No one could understand what had happened to him, and even his servants kept away from him, lest his condition be catching. His tenants meanwhile rejoiced that he could no longer come to terrorise them in their homes. But there was more to come for the evil Forrester. Jeremiah Forrester was now given greatly to dread and fear that he lived by day and night in the shadow of death. He could neither eat nor sleep for the fear of the horrible visitation that awaited him. The 7 days passed slowly, and again the spirit came creeping up the stairs into the bedroom.

'Mercy good lady,' said the errant Forrester 'for I fear there is nought left of my health that you might rob me off. Alas, I repent my evil deeds ne'r again shall I deprive the hard working people of their rightful earnings, I shall live out my life in deeds of kindness and generosity as my father did before me.' But it was too late for deathbed repentance, Forrester had had his chance. The frightful ghoul stood at the base of the bed, arm outstretched, and finger pointed.

A mighty crack of thunder was heard and in a flash the whole of the house was alight with a raging fire. The flames raged higher and hotter around the room, akin to the fires of hell itself. Finally, the angry spirit cried out; 'JEREMIAH FORRESTER I HAVE COME FOR YOUR SOUL!!''

Barra screamed last sentence with a clap of his long hands that made all the boys jump with a start. They gave a collective groan and slumped back. 'And that was the end of Jeremiah Forrester,' finished Barra.

Angus Og McGrogan had galloped for little over a mile before the searing pain of the buckshot in his shoulder necessitated him to slow the powerful grey mare to a canter. By any hap there was no chance of the Clinton brothers catching up to him at this point with Pearl as their only means of transport. Even at that the clip clop of the hooves aggravated the pain substantially, and the young highwayman considered getting off and walking the rest of the way, although he was well aware that an arduous journey all the way to Slieve Croob lay ahead of him. He recalled how carefully and quietly he had sneaked into the darkened barn, hoping to cause as little disruption as possible. He thought of how he had first selected a shining, brand new polished leather saddle, before changing his mind and taking an older worn out one, so as to minimise the loss to the farmer. He had even given consideration to how he could return the horse at a later date. Knocking that metal spade over on the way out wasn't a good move at all. The clang of the spade on the cobbles woke up the dog, whose barking woke up the cockerel, whose crowing woke up the old lady in the house. She was not one bit shy about coming straight out of the house, blunderbuss in hand, and aiming it straight at Angus' back as he rode down the little lane at the front of the farmhouse.

Angus' guilt at the panic stricken voice of the old dear calling after him had turned to terror as the thunderous bang filled the air. Luckily Ma Clinton had aimed high to prevent any of the shot from hitting the prizes horse, so most of the shot ended up in the air. The bang had of course panicked the horse which then took off at full speed, which was somewhat advantageous in that it expedited the rapparee's rapid escape from the Clinton demesne. Angus now wished he had taken the better saddle as the old one was cutting into his arse something shocking, and it would also have been just desserts to the oul doll rapfor the injuries he received. The warm trickle of blood running down his shoulder had reduced to a less worrying irregular drip, although he was quite shocked when he reached round to find his shirt had soaked through. The youngest McGrogan brother knew enough about gunshot wounds to realise that the shot needed to be removed as soon as possible to prevent the lead from poisoning the bloodstream. He also knew that the continued motion of the horse was serving only to aggravate the wound. Weighing up the pros and cons of the situation, Angus decided that the safest course of action would be to dismount the horse and continue the journey on foot. He carefully slowed the horse to a stop and threw his left leg over its neck, before propelling himself off the animal's back and onto the ground below. He winced with pain as he instinctively pulled his shoulders in on contact of his feet with the road. He slapped the horse's rear and bade it go home, to which the animal acquiesced with a casual saunter back towards the farmhouse, blissfully unaware of the gravity of the events that had just occurred.

Catching his breath and setting his bearings, Angus continued on down the beaten track, no longer possessing the energy or agility to vault the dry stone walls and thick hedges that lined the green fields. Both his breathing and his footsteps became increasingly heavy as he traipsed steadily onwards. He found himself to be occasionally staggering and felt like he was carrying a heavy bag of peat on his back, the weight of which was increasing by a pound with every step. He saw a tree ahead which became two trees and then one again. He felt the colour drain from his face and as a mounted man honed into view at a crossroads, he was unable to either evade or resist the stranger as he collapsed on the ground. He was just about to drift into unconsciousness as a familiar voice said; 'I thought I might find you out here.'

'These stories are all a load of oul hogwash if you ask me, all this about fairies and ghosts and the like. I mean, has anyone even actually seen a ghost? There's no mention of any of that nonsense in the Bible.' stated Archie, with great certainty. 'But you believe in the immortal soul of man do you not, and you believe in the Lord, his son Jesus Christ, the angels and the devil?' countered Eugene. 'There are other realms besides this mortal coil to which a human soul may travel after the death of the physical body. Who is to say that a spirit with unfinished business might not become trapped between this world and the next?'

'Aye Archie you just think you know it all cause your Da was a preacher, but I know about loads of other terrible reports of the ghostly goings on round here, things that would make you shake with terror.'

'Like what?' challenged Archie. 'Well,' said Barra; 'there's the story of the hanging man, for a start.'

'Right, let's hear it then.' sighed Archie, patronisingly.

'Well, there was once in the County of Downe a magistrate who went by the name of Judge John Armour. He was known throughout the district as being a very harsh judge, and whenever he held court both the guilty and the innocent would tremble in anticipation of their fate. He would hang people for stealing, for kidnap rape and murder, but he would also hang a man for petty offences such as forgetting to close a gate behind him.'

'That's a load of balleeks!' protested Archie; 'Nobody ever got hanged just for something as trivial as leaving a gate open.'

'No protestant maybe.' interrupted Owen McClatchy; 'Although you'll probably get away with murdering Seamus.'

McClatchy barely saw the flash of the blade before it was an inch from his throat. He gulped in terror. 'I will issue no further warning to you, Mr McClatchy, as I do not care to repeat myself. No further mention of that incident, do you understand?'

McClatchy nodded nervously as Eugene sheathed his rapier. 'Do pray continue, Barra.' He said with polite calmness.

'Well – yes as I was saying this man delighted in hanging all sorts of people with no recourse to their age or sex, and would even hang a man where there was doubt as to the fellow's guilt. Armour lived in a splendid house near the road from Banbridge to Dromore, and so much did he love his work, that he ordered the bodies of the people he had murdered to be suspended from the trees that lined the avenue to his mansion. One day an aged woman of the old race knocked on the door of his house to beg alms and to give a gift of the lucky heather as those people are known to do. The servants asked the lady of the house if a small piece of bread might be given up to the woman, as to refuse hospitality to one of the old race was known to bring very bad luck to everyone in the household. So the lady asked the Judge to wit he replied; 'away with this foul beggar, let none come here in search of succour!' and with that he took up a leather switch and drove the old crone from the door.

Now the ancient ones care little for the status of our own race and will put manners on a Lord or a King as quickly as they would a beggar or a serf if you enrage them, and enrage them John Armour did. 'Arrah!' said the old crone. 'You are a cruel and unjust man Judge John Armour, and many have suffered from your wrath where a better man might have shown mercy and kindness. Of all of those poor souls that you have sent to the gallows, not but one were given fair chance to repay you for your spitefulness. Well no longer will this be the case. In three days time you will know the pain that you have inflicted on others by the hands of those whom you have persecuted.'

Now of course Armour just laughed, as he knew that those he had deprived of life were now beyond this realm and incapable of seeking him out. He continued about his business of the courts and on the third day he returned home from work on his horse as he was want to do. He looked up the hill at his fine house and the narrow avenue of trees that led up to the dwelling. He admired the trees and the bodies of the sinners who hung from them. As he started up the hill on his great white horse, he thought only of his supper and a warm fire. As he went on a few feet, he felt something touch his ear, like an icy finger. He looked round about him, but saw none but the dead who hung from the trees. Thinking it to be maybe a raindrop, he continued onwards unabated. But before many yards had passed, he felt it again. Once again he looked around him but saw nothing but the suspended corpses of his victims. Onward he went, and was then alarmed to notice that the hat had been lifted from his head from above.

'Who is there?' called out the evil Armour, greatly taken with fright. He looked all around to ascertain what had become of his hat and when he looked above, he was shocked to see that the hat now resided atop the skull of a grinning ghoul which Armour himself had hanged but a month before!

Stricken with terror, Armour spurred the horse to gallop towards the house but as he went, the bony fingers of his many victims ripped at his hair and his clothes, as if trying to pry him from his steed. He galloped and galloped but with only yards to go before the house, the old crone appeared before him in the road, causing the horse to rear up and throw the scoundrel to the ground. But old John Armour never touched the ground again in this life, as the hands and arms of the victims of the heartless judge bore him up into a high tree and placed a noose tightly around his neck, so that the life ebbed out of him and he met his fate.'

Once again, the boys give a little shiver. 'What say you to that then Archie?' asked Tomas. 'Well,' replied Archie; 'I do notice something about both these stories that Barra here has told us tonight.'

'What's that then?' quizzed Barra. 'In both cases, there were no witnesses to either the sight or the sound of the spectres, ghouls whatever you like to call them, except for the main characters in the story, and they were all killed.' stated Archie, showing his hands and looking to all there gathered for acknowledgement of his reason. 'So what are you trying to say?' asked Tomas. 'Well if no one actually saw it, how do we know the story is actually true? Where is the evidence that any of these events that you described here tonight actually took place?'

'Granny O'Reilly told me!' protested Barra; 'what are you trying to say Archie, are you calling Granny O'Reilly a liar?'

'Well not exactly all I'm saying is-'

'Aye Granny O'Reilly toul me that too,' agreed Tomas, nodding to Barra; 'So what about that then, two of us hearing exactly the same story. What are the odds against that, a thousand to one?'

'Hang on a minute.' said Archie, intrigued; 'Are you two related?'

'Aye sort of. Barra's great granny on his Ma's side is my granny on my Da's side I think, or is it the other way round?' said Tomas, confused; 'Anyway yes me and young Barra here are kith and kin, cut from the same sod so to speak. It was me who got young Barra into the gang, wasn't it Barra?'

'It was indeed Tomas, and I am eternally grateful to you for giving me this opportunity as well!' The distant cousins hugged each other affectionately. 'This explains a lot.' thought Archie.

'I would quite like to meet this grandmother of yours, she sounds like a fascinating lady.' said Eugene. 'That she is sir, that she is.' nodded Tomas. 'And she lives but a stone's throw away from here, over yonder hill there.' continued Barra. 'Although I wouldn't want to go knocking her up at this time of night.' said Tomas, pointedly. 'Oh no, of course not,' said Eugene; 'I would have no wish to alarm an elderly lady.'

'Oh you don't have to worry about that sir,' reassured Barra; 'If we were to visit her, she would know about it before we did, you see. She has the gift of foresight.'

'Really?' smiled Eugene indulgently, with a sly wink to Archie. 'Yes sir, she told me when I was 12 if you don't stop messing about on top of that wall, you'll end up falling off and losing half your teeth. And do you know what happened?'

'You fell off the wall and lost half your teeth.' said Archie, dryly. 'No that was from when our Brendan hit me up the face with a spade. But I did lose my teeth and I didn't stop messing about on the wall. So she was more or less right.'

## 6. Serious Consequences

Joseph Threader felt more confused than anxious as he sat in the plush office of the Bishop of Down and Connor in a sumptuous 3 storey building in the town of Belfast. Bishop Peter Castle had not taken the loss of the papers lightly and had been animatedly pacing the room for half an hour whilst questioning Threader over and over again. Threader had thought twice about claiming that the rapparees had taken the 50 guineas, but the Bishop had never even asked twice about the money; it was of no concern to him at all. The loss of the letters had troubled the Bishop very much, but why? What was so important about them? 'As I've said your eminence, I am perfectly happy to revisit all those who entrusted me with their correspondence and if they would indulge me in rewriting them, I will not rest until each one is safely delivered to its destination, should I have to endure the persecutions of a thousand footpads.' whined Threader.

The Bishop stopped pacing and planted both hands on his writing desk, leaning over and talking straight into Threader's face more in a pleading manner than a threatening one; 'I appreciate that Joseph, however the matter is not so simple as that. I must have the original letters back. There is information contained therein which could cause very severe damage to the careers of some very good men within the church, not to mention the reputation of the church itself. Good grief, if the King were to hear of this, we could be looking at – disestablishment!' he plopped down into his seat and momentarily covered his head with his hands, before looking skyward in hope of divine inspiration. 'I am deeply sorry for my failure, however they were particularly villainous rascals who treated myself and my travelling companions most viciously. The armed guard that we travelled with offered no resistance, and yet still they beat the young ladies most horrendously. If I myself had not stepped forth to defend them, they may well have been most heinously used and murdered. As it was they tore the bag from my hands and laughed at my pleading, going so far as to mock the church itself!'

Lies came easily to Threader, easily and quickly they flowed like water from his mouth. He could speak 10 lies in the time it would take an honest man to speak the truth, and every word of it fully believable to even the most inquisitive cynic. Threader never worried about his foul deeds because he thought he would be able to lie to Saint Peter at the gates of heaven and gain access to the Kingdom that way. He wasn't alone in this thinking either. The truth was, if Threader had thought to ask for the return of the papers, the rapparees would have duly complied, as Tomas McCafferty did with Captain Pilkington's silver snuff box. They were not in the business of depriving people of their property for the sake of it. That was more the church's business.

'Did these men say anything, anything at all, which might give us a clue as to their identity or whereabouts? Think Joseph, think!' Threader thought at length, then clicked his fingers; 'Their leader proclaimed his own name at the initiation of the assault, called himself a captain would you believe – Captain Seamus Magoran? No McGrogan, that was it!' The Bishop clapped his hands together and started pacing again; 'Well done Joseph that's a start anyway.' He went back, forth, and back again quickly, then stood looking at his desk momentarily. He sat down, and lifted a piece of parchment. He took his pen from the inkwell and started scribbling furiously. Threader sat uncomfortably for several minutes as neither man spoke, not wanting to break the Bishop's concentration. The Bishop held his wax seal over a candle for a few seconds to soften it up before pressing it into the letter and sitting back to admire his work. 'This might just allow us a small glimmer of hope, God willing...' said the Bishop. '...and I would suggest that you pray very deeply that he is willing Joseph!' He looked at the clock on the mantle.

'Good, there's still time. Are you familiar with Arthur's Tavern?'

'I am indeed your eminence, may I enquire what you have in mind?' asked Threader. 'I need you to convey this letter to Arthur's Tavern, where you will ask to speak to either a Mr Daniel Phillips or a Mr John Hawkins. Both are habitually resident in the tavern when they're in Belfast, which I pray that they are. There are no finer men in all of Ireland for apprehending all manner of rogues and scoundrels. Have a care though, these are not the sort of men to be interfered with lightly. I have no doubt they will wish to interrogate you thoroughly to ascertain as many of the relevant facts as may be divulged, in order facilitate their investigations.' As the Bishop talked he opened a large jewelled box which sat beside his writing utensils on the table and removed several little leather bags. He tossed 5 of the bags onto the table each with a little clink. 'Take this money to them too Joseph.'

'Isn't this a little bit excessive sir?' quizzed Threader; 'I mean there must be upwards of fifty pounds here!'

'This is merely a down payment Joseph!' exclaimed the Bishop; 'Have I not made apparent the seriousness of what is at stake here? Not only for my career, but for your own as well!'

'Forgive me your eminence I don't quite follow...'

'Come along Joseph, haven't you read of the death of Rundell, the vacant seat at Derry? Yours was one of the names going into the hat sir, you have the support of at least two of the Bishops. But if the contents of this letter – which you were responsible for delivering – were to get out- well...'

The Bishop sat back in his chair; 'There are plenty of other parishes in Ireland that could make use of your particular skills as a minister. Parishes in Galway, Mayo, Donegal even. Places filled with heathens where barely a law abiding man may set foot, where even a man of the church may find himself set upon whilst out on his rounds or sat in his own parlour. Ours is not to question why Joseph. Ours is to go and do the Lord's work, wherever that may take us.' Threader's mind raced. This was not good news, not good at all. Threader considered most people beneath him, and although he feigned affection for his parishioners in Killeavy, he hated even them with a passion. But Killeavy was a reasonably well off district, with land owners, strong tenant farmers, artisans and even gentry. The people he was likely to encounter in the God forsaken hovels of the west coast of Ireland, these would be mostly poor people!

'I will leave immediately sir, and fear not, I shall procure for you the services of the said Messrs Phillips and Hawkins at the earliest possible juncture.' He rose and bowed to the Bishop. 'Very good Joseph, please do. Here is the money and here are the letters, and Joseph, please try not to lose them.' Threader gritted his wooden teeth with a vulture like smile and taking the bags and the letter, he departed the house and hailed a cab to Arthur's.

'Here fire us over the Belfast Newsletter there, to we see what sort of shite they're going on about this time.' said Tomas to Archie. Archie duly tossed the newspaper to his friend and continued with cleaning and reloading his firearm. 'Oh I say, fame at last eh young Archibald?' crowed Tomas. 'What are you on about?' asked Archie without looking up from his task. 'It appears we are now a man of some notoriety, a fugitive with a price on his head, no less!' Archie stopped what he was doing and looked up; 'What does it say about me?' Tomas cleared his throat; 'Whereas Archibald McClung, son of the Reverend Alexander McClung late of the Rectory, Ballyvally in the County of Downe, did formerly absent himself from his habitual residence in the 29th Day of April in the year of our Lord 1742, This is to give notice, that if any person shall apprehend the said Archibald McClung and bring him onto Captain George Higginson of Newry Street in the town of Banbridge, that person shall be rewarded onto the sum of ten guineas.' The boys gave a group exclamation of surprise at the substantial amount offered for Archie, which was greater than the price on the heads of some of the gangs most hardened rapparees. Tomas continued; 'Or if any person shall provide information which shall lead to the discovery or apprehension of said Archibald McClung, he shall be duly rewarded at a rate commensurate to the value of the information which he provides. The said Archibald McClung is about 5 foot and 10 inches high with a light complexion and fair hair. He is known to sometimes walk with a jarring gait and has a pointed nose.' Tomas burst out laughing and pointed at Archie as he read the last sentence. 'You made that last bit up, let me see that!' shouted Archie. He snatched the paper and confirmed with his own eyes what McCafferty had read aloud; 'I don't walk with a jarring gait! What is that supposed to mean?'

Barra laughed; 'It's whenever you've done something and you think you're the big man, like when you catch a load of fish or earlier on the day when you threw that wee lad's shoes in the river.'

'That wasn't even me that done that, it was Angus. Here I wonder where Angus is now?'

'I would guess,' said Eugene, 'that he has returned to Shane's camp to report to him on the earlier incident.' Archie shrugged, his initial anxiety of Shane's reaction having to some degree subsided. 'I wonder why there is such a large reward being offered for your location?' asked Eugene, puzzled.

'I'll tell you why;' interrupted Owen McClatchy. 'When we first found the preacher here, he was sitting on a rock halfway up Slieve Croob crying his eyes out. His own lot had been out chasing him and he couldn't go home, because he'd smashed his own father's skull in with a toby jug. Beat the old man's brains out in front of his weeping mother and left him for dead. This-' snarled McClatchy, snatching the paper; 'this is a rich man's proclamation. They're not going to proclaim the son of a protestant minister, even one of the Scottish church. Mark my words Preacher, you're just as doomed as the rest of us. Oh they might not pull your entrails out in front of a hundred baying ghouls the way they would with me or any of the rest of the lads, but as sure as the fires of hell they'll take you to a quiet place where no one can see and they'll stretch your neck for you.'

No one offered any words of comfort for as objectionable a fellow as McClatchy was, his words had a ring of truth to them. After a brief silence Eugene offered; 'Of course, they have to catch you first.' Tomas rolled up the paper and threw it on the grass. 'Don't listen to big Owen there, he's just jealous because they only put 3 pounds on his head. Isn't that right McClatchy?' joked Tomas.

'They'll hang you for one pound as quick as they'll hang you for a hundred Tomas.' replied McClatchy. Tomas gave a slight nod of agreement. 'Sometimes they print the proclamations in the newspaper. Give us another look there Tomas.' said McClatchy. McCafferty duly complied.

McClatchy unfurled the paper and flicked over a few pages; 'I think this is it here...' he said, unsurely. 'Yes, be it enacted in the name of his most Royal and Glorious Majesty King George the Second of the Kingdoms of England, Scotland and Ireland...'

'Boo!'

'Hiss!'

'Never!' cried the boys. McClatchy continued;

' At the court assizes for the County of Downe of the Kingdom of Ireland, at the general Quarter Sessions of the Peace held for the said county at Downpatrick the 16th of April 1743. It is hereby presented that the following procal – procla-'

'Proclamation.' corrected Eugene.

'The following proclamation is made that persons named below are notorious rogues and robbers out upon their keeping and not amenable to the law and refuse to be brought to justice.'

McClatchy scanned down the list; 'there are at least 2 dozen of our gang named here, plus others I know to be in other gangs in the district. Half of these people aren't even rapparees. There are women, children, even a priest in here!' He looked up at the boys angrily, changing the mood. 'There's more. 'and it be here proclaimed that if any of the person here so named do present to the assizes or the goal of Downpatrick any other of the person here so named, whether they be quick or dead, then that person making the presentment may be so pardoned by the court as to be considered a free man.'

The boys looked at each other in disgust but not in actual surprise. 'So in other words, they can try a man and find him guilty in his absence, and then pardon him for betraying another who was also tried in his absence?' asked Eugene. 'That would be correct sir.' confirmed Barra. 'But it's just a trick, they'll just hang you anyway. There's no way they're just going to let you go home.'

'Home.' repeated Rafferty.

Shane McGrogan tied his 18 hands high chestnut brown stallion to the post at the back yard of Doctor Cayley's country house as was his usual practice, and knocked loudly on the back door with uncommon anxiety. The tall caped and hooded figure could from a distance have been mistaken for the grim reaper, and given the critical state of the patient who lay therein, such a visit may well have taken place before the night was out. He barely nodded as the maid answered the door but pushed past her into the small kitchen, where the good doctor's daughter Mary mopped his injured brother's sodden brow whilst cradling his head softly in front of a burning stove.

'Shane,' said Jacob Cayley, standing up from the small bench where the family normally ate their meals and stretching out his hand; 'the boy I sent did well to find you so quickly. I've removed the shot that can be readily accessed and have patched up the wounds to the best of my abilities. Fortunately the blood loss although significant, is not critical. I've seen many a man live a long year after worse injuries.'

Shane gave a heavy sigh of relief and reflected once more on the events of the day. He weighed up the terrible price that he and his men had paid for the quarry they had sought. Shane had taken 12 of the gang to stake out the road from Newry to Banbridge and were supposed to intercept the coach before it got anywhere near Seamus' group, who were further up the road from Banbridge to Dromore as a failsafe in the unlikely event that the coach should take the longer route through the woods, circumventing the town. Countless hours he had spent sitting in a bush in the pissing rain for nothing, although hopefully the other group had managed to complete the mission and would be even now in possession of the prized jewellery box which contained something of incalculable value, the nature of which he had disclosed to no other. He had also envisaged that with his unpredictable brother Seamus placed in charge of the second group, he would be safely out of the way and present less of a risk to the main mission. 'Thank you for what you have done here today Doctor.' said Shane at length, shaking Cayley's hand; 'The boy told me about Seamus. It would be too cruel a blow to have lost both of my brothers in the one night.'

'Well,' sighed Doctor Cayley; 'We're not out of the woods yet. Fingers crossed that wound doesn't turn septic. If it does, well he could lose the use of his arm.' Shane gritted his teeth and tried to hide all emotion. This had been a stressful day even for a hardened rapparee. The Doctor continued; 'He also suffers from a hotness of the skin and in some way from the vapour of the lungs; as you know he was never really a man made for the rough living. He won't be able to be moved from here until the fever passes, two, maybe three days to be safe? Don't worry, there is a hidden room where we can keep him from prying eyes and wagging tongues; neither the army or the militia would ever dare to search here, they have no inkling of my sympathies to your cause.'

This was true; unbeknownst to the locals, Doctor Cayley was actually a catholic and his Yorkshire family were broadly sympathetic to the Jacobite cause. Their ancestors had fought with the Royalists against Oliver Cromwell's new model army. Cayley himself abhorred violence, and had dedicated his career to the preservation of human life. His late wife had been a County

Downe woman and it was at her recommendation that he had relocated to Ireland, where there was a want of good Doctors. The local people had assumed him to be a protestant, being an Englishman of good education, and it did the Doctor's career no harm for him to allow them to continue in this delusion. Not being particularly pious, he had thought it sufficient to absent himself from any place of worship, a practice which was easily explainable by his busy workload. Cayley had great affection for the local people but he despised the injustice and inequality he saw all around him. He had witnessed at first hand the degradation and want amongst the poor and the extravagance and pomposity in the homes of the rich. It was impossible to ignore the fact that many of his patients of the Catholic disposition had fallen into extreme poverty due to the machinations of absentee landlords and their manipulation of the penal laws. To this end, he saw it as his way of redressing the balance by overcharging his more well off patients by a few shillings now and then so that he could afford to treat his less fortunate patients for free or for next to nothing. He had seen Shane's work as having some parallels to his own and had endeavoured to assist the gang wherever possible. That said, Cayley was by no means a yes man; he had debated with Shane on many occasions with regards to his methods and had also protested to him of his treatment of his own men.

Shane rubbed his beard before removing his cape, kneeling briefly to warm his hands at the stove; 'Did Angus say anything about what had happened, with Seamus?'

'From what I can gather, both from the boy here and from the Captain of the Militia, some sort of mutiny took place.'

'Mutiny?' said Shane, looking up in surprise. He hadn't even considered the possibility that any of the men would possess the wherewithal to rise up against his giant brother. 'It appears that he attacked two young ladies who were in the coach, causing grievous harm to both. Then two of the men rose up and one of them shot him in the stomach. I stitched the wound myself and I can tell you it is the worst I have ever seen. No man could have survived such a blow.' Shane struggled to make sense of what he was hearing; 'So they just shot him? Did they say who it was who done it?'

Doctor Cayley breathed in and exhaled slowly; 'The boy was ranting and not in care of his words, but he did mention the preacher and the Frenchman, if that means anything to you.'

Shane's jaw dropped. He could not believe what the good Doctor was telling him, even though he knew the man addressing him would not lie on such matters. He had armed Archie himself, given him that short musket as he wished him to feel that he was fully accepted in the gang despite his being of a foreign creed. He had personally asked Eugene to come to Ireland to help him, and O'Cahan himself had sworn he would not interfere in the gang's business. These two trusted companions had murdered his brother? Surely not!

'In fairness;' continued the Doctor;'You know as well as I do what Seamus was like. I fear there is a great deal more to tell than is immediately apparent from the information available. The group that Seamus was leading seemed to have been out of control from what I heard. Do you know that people are going around Banbridge saying you have been stealing the shoes off children and threatening to burn the town?'

'I said no such thing, I know not from whence anyone would contrive such a notion.' protested Shane; 'the wagging tongues of idle women at work no doubt.'

'I believe you my friend, I doubt the men of the town will though. Apparently they are all lining up to join the militia now because you are seen as such a danger to the common man. Every man who joins that militia is one more man against you Shane. Whatever happened, it appears Seamus lost his temper and in the heat of the moment he beat the two females. No one likes to hear of such cruelty against the weaker sex. I should say also a half empty bottle of poteen was found in his bag.' The Doctor shook his head; 'You know he had been getting worse and worse. I spent more time tending the wounds of the boys he had injured himself than I did tending those injured by the soldiers. You should have reined him in a long time ago Shane!'

Shane nodded. There was no arguing with that; 'He wasn't always so, you know. Our father always railed on him the hardest as he was the biggest of the three. He was a generous soul once. He used to at times take the blame for the mischief me and Angus wrought so as he would be punished in our place.'

Cayley concurred; 'Well, I know that on occasion he was given to acts of kindness, although these had grown less and less of late. I expect that a life such as that of the rapparee would change a man, perhaps he even thought he was preparing the boys for the hardships of life. No one is born to evil, in my opinion. We can only pray that he finds the peace in his immortal rest which escaped him in this world.'

Shane nodded, before running his hands through his long black greasy hair and tying it in a bow behind his head. He lifted a bowl from the sideboard without invitation, as he was want to do, before scooping two full ladles of broth from the great pot above the stove and pouring it in with a satisfying plop. He picked up a spoon and sat down at the rough wooden table. He supped several spoonfuls before he spoke again. 'The injuries to the young ladies- where they significant?' asked Shane. Cayley shrugged; 'Well they were able to travel onward to their destination; no one sent for me to come to the scene to give relief. I believe some of their goods were taken or destroyed, one of them was injured in the face, and the other in the hand.'

Shane nodded and finishing his broth, he licked the bowl and put it back on the sideboard. The maid immediately lifted it and took it away to wash. He paused, as if about to speak, delivered a loud belch, and gathered up his cape; 'I must go now.'

'What will you do about what has occurred tonight? I mean, the mutiny?' asked the Doctor. Shane paused; 'You know how I work Doctor, the less I tell you, the less of a danger it is to you. But I shall reserve judgement until I have spoken to my men and ascertained what has happened. There may yet be an end to this. However, if I am dissatisfied with their explanation, they shall be joining Seamus in the hereafter. But now, I have other business to attend to, there are matters of such import that they transcend the fate of Seamus or of any other man. Goodbye Doctor, and thank you.' With that, Shane exited via the back door.

'I suppose we may all turn in for the night then, we've to be up early the marra to get back to the hideout afore any of them militia are out of their beds.' declared Archie. 'Somebody will have to keep watch. We can take it in two hourly shifts. Who has a watch?' Eugene produced an ornate golden timepiece from his belt; 'Tools of the trade, my men. You should all have one of these.' He tossed it over to Archie who nodded thankfully. 'What about me and you together Archie, then Finn and Owen and then

Tomas and the Captain? That way we can keep an eye on each other and make sure the other one doesn't doze off.' suggested Barra.

'Excellent idea young sir. The rest of you can get your heads down, we'll keep an eye out and make sure the fire doesn't go out.' agreed Archie. Barra grinned at the rare praise; 'You'll make a fine sergeant Archie if Shane doesn't shoot you. We do need to keep an eye out up here though, there's all manner of devilment going on. That family of human toads for one thing.'

Eugene, who had just bedded down for the night, rolled over and sat up on one elbow with a broad grin; 'Oh I have to here this one. A family of human toads you say?'

'He's wasting your time with more of his codswallop sir. It's an old story that's been going around the district for years, a fairytale with no basis in reality. I'd save yourself the disappointment and get some sleep if I were you.' said Archie, dismissively.

'It is not indeed a story sir,' contested Barra 'I've seen these creatures with my own two eyes and so has Tomas there, isn't that right Tomas?'

'Leave me out of this, I'm going to sleep.' said Tomas.

Barra continued undeterred; 'They're normal looking people from the neck down and they have the head of a toad sir, or some of them have fangs or a gigantic eye or a hump on their back. They're all different but they're all of the same family and they have one thing in common. They all eat people.'

'So how did this all come to be?' asked Eugene, amused.

'Well as you are aware sir, about 200 years ago the English Queen was a good and pious lady called Mary, but then she died and was replaced by her sister Elizabeth who was evil and cruel and hated catholics.' stated Barra.

'It was the other way round!' protested Archie; 'Elizabeth was a great queen. Mary was evil and cruel and used to burn innocent protestants at the stake.'

'She only burnt a couple of them and they were probably up to no good anyway. Ignore Archie sir, themuns is always trying to make out they got it worse than we did. Anyway there lived in these woods at that time a family of good and wholesome God fearing Catholics called the O'Tuathails, which is nowadays pronounced Toal due to the great many ignorant foreigners that reside here today. The head of the family was Cormac O'Tuathail, a great bard which in yonder days would have been a storyteller something akin to my good self.'

'I can think of a few other words to describe you.' butted in Archie.

'Well,' continued Barra, unabated; 'As I previously described this was at the time of the power of the English Queen Elizabeth, a red haired white faced witch who hated us Irish and our refined ways. Elizabeth was very jealous of Ireland and wanted to subdue the people, but in them days we had mighty heroes like Red Hugh O'Donnell from Tyrconnell and Hugh O'Neill who were more than a match for the English. Anyway as we all know the oul witch sent over her fancyman the Earl of Sussex with a great army in an attempt to capure Red Hugh and destroy his kingdom, however Sussex's men knew nothing of the land and how our bogs and marshes can produce strange and ghostly sounds and sights that beguile the senses and confuse the mind. Red Hugh knew the land of his ancestors well and used these secrets to lead the English round and round in the mists until the troops were scattered and disorientated, whereafter our brave men would attack them quickly, picking them off in ones and twos and spreading fear and disorder amongst them.'

Eugene nodded; 'That is a very effective military tactic when facing a larger and better equipped force. Knowledge of the local terrain can give a huge advantage when you are unable to engage the enemy in the conventional manner.'

'Well quite Sir, Granny O'Reilly used to tell us the stories of CuChullain, the Hound of Ulster and how he defended his lands single handedly against the forces of Queen Maeve with sneak attacks. Isn't that right Tomas?'

Tomas lay snoozing with the brim of his hat across his eyes and made no attempt to reply.

'Well anyway several of these fellows were so taken with fear in this alien landscape that they resolved to desert their masters and escape back to England by travelling south eastwards across country. This group of 4 crazed Englishmen had stumbled across Irish countryside for days eating grass roots and drinking from puddles, before they came across the home of the righteous Toal family. Now if these animals had but knocked on the door of the house and asked for hospitality they would have received their fill of food and drink as the family had to spare, as is the given custom of the people of this land. But being the cowards and marauders they were, they fell upon the sleeping family like a pack of wolves, murdering all who lay inside the house. All except Cormac O'Tuathall's only daughter Brigid, who was-'

'Don't tell me-' interrupted Archie; 'Known throughout the district for her comeliness?'

'Shut up you, you're ruining my story!' barged Barra.

'Sorry sir I shall continue. Yes, the villainous rogues used the lovely Toal daughter most hideously and left her as for dead before burning the house to the ground and continuing on their way. But survive the lady did, and in the fullness of time, she grew heavy with child. Now Brigid Toal had oft times been given to sitting on the banks of a fairy wishing pond-'

'Fairy wishing pond? Seriously?' winced Archie, looking first from Barra to Eugene sceptically.

'Try to remain silent until you're in full possession of all the facts, Archie.' said Eugene.

'Quite right sir.' said Barra. 'Yes she used to sit on the banks of a pond which was a home to all sorts of sprites and fairies as well as the usual creatures such as frogs and toads. Now before the terrible events which I have just described had occurred, Brigid's wishes as she sat on the banks of the pond were of a fanciful nature, true love and handsome princes and the like. But her harrowing experiences had changed her mind forever and as she sat on the banks of the pond for hours upon hours, days upon days, she would stare into the water and wish for only one thing; that the child in her belly would carry none of the blood of an Englishman, and that it would in no way resemble the foul brigands who had brought her to that state. The fairy folk as you can imagine are well used to people coming to their special places and wishing for all sorts of silly things, so generally they ignore such goings on. But Brigid's wishes were so intense that they could not be ignored, and the fairy queen decided that the wishes must be acquiesced to. Now the fairy folk despite their great unearthly powers are not wise to the ways of men, and they knew not what to replace the blood of the Englishmen with. They therefore resolved that in the stead of the blood and likenesses of the Englishmen, there would be the blood and likenesses of those creatures which dwelt within the fairy pond into which Brigid Toal had concentrated her hatred and bitterness.'

'Good grief!' exclaimed Eugene; 'and this is how the toad people came to be?'

'Well there's more still sir. As you know, a toad gives birth to little swimming creatures that then become toads and this happens at a much faster rate than what human people do. Within a few days, Brigid had given birth to no less than 4 children, who grew to adulthood again within just a few days. There were 3 great fearsome sons, strong of limb and great in size, but each and every one of them had hideous toad like features. One had a great bulging mouth and throat like a toad, another still the great and terrible mesmerising eyes of a toad, and another the flashing whip like tongue of a toad. The other child was a daughter, a fair and graceful girl in every way the measure of her mother for poise and beauty, excepting that she had powerful jumping legs of a toad.

But it wasn't just in their appearance that the Toals differed from us humans, their appetites were greatly dissimilar to our own also. As we all know sir, the toad is one of those rare animals especially despised amongst the animal kingdom due to its preference for feasting on the flesh of its own kind. Well these ones were the same as any other toad in that manner, excepting that they also ate ravenously of the flesh of man.'

Even Eugene gave a shiver at the last revelation; 'You mean cannibals?'

'That's right sir, cannon balls they were!' nodded Barra

'How chilling! So what became of them?'

'Well sir, they built themselves a house near the site of the one that was lately burnt and lived sometimes in the pond and sometime in the house with their mother, as they had want of the comfort of both habitats. One night when they were at the pond, the 4 Englishmen again came that way, having lost their bearings and their wits on their great expedition across Ireland. These 4 resolved once more to make visitation upon the occupants of the house and to use and murder those within most horribly. However on entering, they were surprised to find therein the lady whom they had previously left for dead. They plotted to complete the murder, but the lady swore that if they did not hence forth depart and n'er return, she would summon forth her children to put manners on them.

The Englishmen laughed at her scornfully and bade her bring forth her children, and they would make sport of them as they had done with her family before. So at their bidding, the lady called forth the 4 toad children, who quickly entered the house through the rear door. First to enter was the daughter, and not seeing what lay beneath her skirts they desired to make use of her; but as the first of them approached she gave him a great kick with her toad leg and sent him into the fireplace where he burnt to death. The others turned to run but with a great leap the toad lady bounded over them and stood before the door. Imprisoned, they turned in terror, and one of them then saw the toad monster with the great bulbous eyes. Transfixed by the creature and unable to avert its gaze, his heart gave out from him although he was but a young man and he thereby fell dead. Another ran and cowered in a corner, but another of the monsters shot forth its great toad tongue and pulling him close, he restricted the Englishman's throat until he could breathe no more and his life left him. Finally the remaining Englishman tried to make good his escape through a window, but he was seized by the greatest of the beasts, who had the throat and mouth of a toad, and with one great gulp, he swallowed the Englishman whole.

And from that day, these woods have been awash with living toad people who desire nothing more than to feast on the flesh of human beings.

# 7. A Fish Out Of Water

Joseph Threader tried to hide his nerves as he stepped down from the hackney coach onto a muddy side street adjacent to the river Lagan. He was relieved that he was at least able to persuade the driver to wait for him by offering him a couple of the gold sovereigns that were supposedly stolen from him by the rapparees. He sidestepped quickly as a passing red nosed drunk whose breeches had fallen halfway down his ample backside deposited the contents of his bloated stomach onto the road before him, mumbling 'sorry Father' as he tumbled in a heap into his own muddy mess.

He eased passed a clatter of buxom prostitutes too immodestly dressed for their advancing years; 'Spare us a penny your honour!' shouted one. 'Suck you off for a shilling sir!' called another, causing a wave of scornful, cackling laughter amongst the remainder. He rounded the corner to be faced with a trio of rough looking sailors playing pitch against the whitewashed walls of his destination, Arthur's Tavern. He pulled back the latch of the heavy oaken door to be hit with a wave of smoke and chatter, and as he pushed himself inside he didn't know whether to feel safer within or without. The vicious looking ruffians who frequented the drinking den were a far cry from the genteel folk of Killeavy who Threader so despised, and he began to doubt the wisdom of carrying a heavy bag of gold sovereigns into an establishment such as this full of footpads, cheats, gamblers, whores and scroungers. The patrons within were mostly in the full flow of merriment, except for those who were passed out drunk and those without the means to buy any more drink. Threader pushed up to the bar and hailed the bar keep, who sauntered idly over at his own pace, only slightly curious at the presence of this most obvious fish out of water. 'Good evening my good man;' weasled Threader with a tip of his hat, sensing that this was no place to assume his usual airs and graces, 'I am seeking to meet with a couple of gentlemen whom I believe are known to frequent this establishment, a Mr Phillips and a Mr Hawkins?' He smiled his hopelessly insincere, vulture smile. The great hulking bar keep towered over the skinny clergyman; he rested his huge hands on the bar and leaned forward into the old fellow's face. Threader glanced nervously at the man's massive tree trunk arms, which were a mass of indistinct fading tattoos and thicker than Threader's thighs. He looked back up into the bar keep's frowning visage, unable to maintain the false smile for any great length of time.

'Friends of yours, are they?' demanded the glowering giant. 'Merely business associates, my friend. The Lord's work you know.' replied Threader. He gulped as the big man remained silent with a fixed stare for more seconds than he desired to count. Finally, the barkeep raised a thick sausage like finger and pointed to the back of the room. 'Those two down there. Tell them I said no more drink until they settle their slate. You better have brought plenty of money.'

Threader nodded ingratiatingly and proceeded to a back table were sat a group of five war weary, bedraggled looking roughs, stern faced as they concentrated on their games of cards. Clutching his hat and bag like an old lady awaiting a carriage, Threader cleared his throat loudly but did not speak. No one looked up. Changing tack, he announced in a loud voice; 'Good evening gentlemen allow me to introduce myself, I am the Reverend Joseph Thr-'

'Ssshh!!' said a younger man who was sat nearby spectating, a dark haired boy with a ruddy complexion, holding a stump of an index finger to his pursed lips. 'The boss is trying to play cards. There's 12 guineas riding on this.' He explained in a rough Dublin brogue. 'Pull up a chair there and you can talk to him when he's done. Aggie!' The boy whistled to the nearest barmaid. 'No more tick for you lot, young Michael, the bosses orders.' said the barmaid, without waiting to hear what he had to say.

'Six whiskies for us there Aggie. The big lad there's paying.' said Michael with a cheeky smile, pointing to Threader. Aggie looked at the cleric with a raised eyebrow, to which Threader nodded his acquiescence. Aggie went off to fetch the drinks while Michael engaged with Threader.

'I'm Michael Darroch, I'm an apprentice with Mr Phillips and Mr Hawkins here. I take it you're wanting somebody done over right? Somebody owe you money? Somebody doing your wife? Or maybe you're doing their wife sir!' the boy paused to laugh at his own joke, which Threader found repugnant although he was able to muster a slight, mechanical chuckle. 'Don't worry we're not here to judge, that's the Lord's job as you well know. Anyway, if you're wanting somebody sorting out or putting out of the way, you've come to the right place sir. You'll not find better workers or better rates in the whole of Belfast. The whole of Ireland maybe. See these two here?' rabbited Michael, pointing to the two eldest men; 'Daniel Phillips and John Hawkins. These are the men who brought in Shane O'Haughan and Naiose O'Haughan 25 years ago. Frigging Naiose O'Haughan! Man, the whole English army and the militia couldn't get anywhere near that fella, but these two caught him and brought him to the gallows. That's us. No job too big, no job too small.'

Aggie brought the tray of drinks and Michael lifted his and downed it in one. 'Thank you Aggie same again please my love. Will you have one yourself Father? Sure you may as well, you're paying for them?'

'No thank you. It's Reverend rather than Father, or even Threader will suffice. The matter really is quite pressing, do you think it would be possible for the gentlemen to suspend their game until business is attended to-' Michael shook his head vigourously and put his drink down on the table; 'No sir I'm afraid that won't be possible at all, as I say there is a lot of money running on this game and also there is the matter of honour. The people in this here tavern take their cards very seriously sir. If you were to interfere in the game – well, yonder there sits the last fella who stuck his nose in.'

Threader looked over to where Michael was pointing to see a man with a red, gaping hole in his face where his nose used to be, a wound that had grown over some years ago. The sight made Threader shudder; 'Perhaps I shall wait.'

'Yes indeed sir that would be the advisable course of action, besides the night is young, the craic is good, the drink is flowing – and I'd get my head under the table now if I were you sir.'

'I beg your pard-'

'Under the table sir, now!'

 Threader heard the thunderous crash of a flying chair meeting its target just as Michael forced his head beneath the heavy wooden bench. He lost no time in squeezing the rest of his lanky body into the space beneath its legs. From this position of immediate safety he was able to espy Phillips and Hawkins trading blows with their erstwhile gaming companions. Their 3 opponents not only outstripped them in numbers, they were twice the size and half their age, but what the two men lacked in brute strength and nimbleness they more than made up for in experience. Young Michael tried to assist his employers by throwing a bottle at the back of one thug's gargantuan, shaven head, but in his inebriated state he only managed to hit Daniel Phillips square on the shoulder, preventing him from dodging a searing uppercut to the jaw that sparked him flat out. Hawkins battled on nobly but was starting to wane under the weight of the unfair odds until the bar keep presented all 3 of his opponents with a blow to the back of the head from a heavy cudgel, knocking each one in turn unconscious. As Phillips and Hawkins were regulars with a burgeoning bar tab which they had fairly good record of settling every few months, the establishment had a vested interest in preserving their health and their ability to earn money. The bar keep was quickly joined by the cellar man who assisted him in carrying the 3 trouble makers to the door and throwing them unceremoniously into the gutter. 'Do come again!' quipped the giant as he slammed the door shut.

Phillips had come to and was rubbing his balding head and looking around himself in some confusion; 'Where's the pot?' he demanded of Hawkins, concerned. 'Danny!' called the bar keep, holding up the 12 guineas in his bucket like hand; 'That's you two more or less clear now.'

'Frigg sake!' gasped Hawkins; 'Let us keep some!' The bar keep made no reply but popped the money into his apron pocket with a smile and retook his position behind the bar. Hawkins turned to Phillips and shrugged. 'Now what are we going to do? I haven't even enough to get the horses out of the stables!'

'Perhaps I could be of assistance gentlemen.' said an unfamiliar creaky voice from beneath the table. 'Or more to the point, perhaps we could help each other.' Phillips and Hawkins looked at each other and then back at the emergent Threader. 'If it's a boy you're after then you're barking up the wrong tree with us old timer.' quipped Hawkins. 'Have you tried round in White's Tavern? They're more your type round there.' added Phillips.

'No no, good sirs you misconstrue. I have need of the services of some men to aid me in the recovery of certain items, being the property of the church, that have fallen into the hands of certain criminals.' corrected Threader; 'There would of course be significant remuneration for the task?' he added, holding up the bag of sovereigns temptingly.

'Pull a chair over there old timer, you've come to the right place,' said Hawkins, intrigued.

'Aggie!' called Michael; 'four more whiskies here, our friend here is paying.'

The four men settled themselves and Threader related the events as they had occurred, presenting the letter which the Bishop had given him which was an assurance of payment for any expenses incurred in the pursuance of their goal.

'Shane McGrogan?' said Phillips, glancing to Hawkins for reference. 'Aye I know of him, he's a tuppenny ha'penny bandit operating out of Slieve Croob on the edge of the Mournes. I believe his gang has had the odd skirmish with the army down there but from what I've heard they usually come off the worse.'

Hawkins nodded; 'He's small change all right, half of his men don't even have weapons. I heard he'd been away a while fighting in France, would have been better off staying there. The only reason the army hasn't flushed him out before now is he isn't really capable of doing any real damage up there, robs the odd coach that's about it.'

Threader nodded; 'A craven bully from what I can ascertain, his men assaulted two young women in my party also.'

Phillips shook his head disapprovingly; 'Naiose O'Haughan would never have done a thing like that.'

Hawkins nodded. 'Naiose was a true rapparee. They don't make them like that anymore.'

Phillips nodded; 'If any of Naiose's men had treated a female so he'd have strung them up himself.'

Hawkins agreed; 'A brave warrior and a true gentleman of the road. It broke my heart when he had to bring him in.'

'Naiose O'Haughan' shouted Phillips, his glass raised aloft. 'Naiose O'Haughan!' replied Hawkins and Michael Darroch, raising theirs. All three looked at Threader expectantly, who reluctantly raised his glass to theirs and said; 'Naiose O'Haughan.' All four of them sunk their whiskies and Threader grimaced as the unfamiliar malt seared his throat. 'Aggie!' called Michael; '4 more whiskies on the big fella here please.'

Hawkins slapped the table; 'Now down to business Mr Threader. I'm going to need to hire at least three score and ten men skilled in the use of the musket and the riding of a horse. I'll probably need to hire the horses, also provisions and perhaps a couple of days board down there as making camp would seriously increase the amount of equipment we need to carry, which would in turn increase expenses and impede our progress. We'll need to hire a couple of trackers as we'll be combing the area in small groups, flushing out any hidden miscreants who may be lurking in the bushes.'

Phillips continued; 'it's a common tack amongst the rapparees that they'll travel in ones or twos to avoid suspicion, but will converge together at given times and places like a swarm of bees.'

Hawkins nodded; 'Cunning devils. So we will need to lay hands on those we find wandering the country in the first instance, then quickly ascertain their guilt or innocence before letting the innocent go free.'

'We bind the guilty and commit them to goal at the earliest possible station, we will perhaps take them to Downpatrick?' suggested Phillips.

Hawkins concurred; 'it's a very effective process sir but it takes a great deal of skill on our part.'

Threader nodded; 'Yes this is all very good my dear sirs but what of the letter? None of this shall be of any benefit to me if the object remains dislocated.'

'Well,'said Phillips, sighing; 'In my experience when a man who lives in the rough gets his hands on a piece of paper, he'll either use it to light a fire or wipe his arse. It's an uncommon luxury to one such as a rapparee.'

Hawkins nodded; 'It's not the glamorous lifestyle that some would have you believe it to be. If half of them knew what they were in for, they'd never bother in the first place.'

'But the letter-' interrupted Threader, losing tact.

'Don't worry about the letter sir. We will interrogate every one of them that we find and will thereby learn what became of the letter or if it yet survives. If any of them know of the contents of the correspondence, you can rest assured that we shall ensure that the necessary steps are taken to protect your confidence.' said Phillips, tapping his pistol handle.

'Very well then my good sirs, I leave the matter in your very capable hands and I shall bid you good night.' Said Threader, rising to leave.

'Michael, see the gentleman out will you.' ordered Hawkins.

Michael, who had been dozing with his elbow on the table rose up and fell straight ways to the floor.

'I'll see myself out.' said Threader, feeling slightly more confident in his surroundings. When the aged cleric had exited the building and boarded his waiting Hackney, Phillips leaned over to Hawkins; 'So what do you think? I mean I am 58 years of age now John, you're 2 and threescore years. We should be rested in front of a warm hearth at our age, not out scouring the Mournes for bloodthirsty rapparees.'

Hawkins sucked on his pipe thoughtfully; 'I've been in this game 40 odd years Danny, and I haven't a penny to show for it. Whatever's in that letter, the Bishop is prepared to pay a hell of a lot of money for it. We get that letter, we're set up for the rest of our lives. This is our pot of gold at the end of the rainbow.'

'Maybe.' Nodded Phillips; 'Let's just hope the pot of gold doesn't turn out to be a crock of shit like it usually does!' Hawkins laughed then choked on his pipe smoke a bit and then coughed. Catching his breath, he nodded in the direction of the unconscious Michael Darroch. 'We may get wee Mickey boy here a bed for the night, his head'll be poundin in the morning and it's a long ride down to Banbridge. Bit of luck this job'll get us enough money in to give him a decent start in life once we're gone.'

Phillips stared at the boy thoughtfully; 'There are some debts in this life that can never be repaid John, he's one of them.'

'Right Owen, yours and Finn's turn to keep look out,' said Archie shaking the sleeping McClatchy's shoulder; 'You too Finn, up you get.' McClatchy stirred slowly and as usual the first words from his mouth were a winge; 'Not that we got any sleep with yousuns natterin on like a couple of oul women.'

'We only talked about 10 minutes and we added that on to your sleepin time anyway. Give us your blanket there.' said Barra, planting himself down beside the fire. Archie reclined on the patch of grass which had been dried by the glow of the fire, placing his short musket carefully at his side. Finnbar Rafferty stood anxiously looking from one group member to the other to the musket. No one thought much of this behaviour, being well used by now to his peculiarities. Suddenly, he lunged at the unguarded weapon and snatching it upwards, he shakily pointed it with both hands at Owen McClatchy.

'Whoa there!' said Barra, raising his hands.

'What the frigg do you think you're doing here?' demanded McClatchy.

'Hang on there a moment Finn,' reasoned Archie; 'Tomas, Eugene, wake up.'

The other two rapparees roused slowly in a state of confusion, but the Frenchman lost no time in taking control of the situation. 'Mr Rafferty,' he said softly and calmly; 'You seem to have a weapon pointed at your friend and comrade here. Is there something you would like to talk to us about?'

'You're coming with me.' said Rafferty in a trembling voice, staring straight at McClatchy and ignoring the others.

'What are you talking about? I'm going nowhere with you, put the gun down Finn before you hurt yourself.' said McClatchy, angrily.

'Where do you want Owen to go with you Finn?' asked Eugene, trying to initiate some sort of reasoning process in the unfortunate Rafferty's tortured mind.

'I'm bringing you in! It said in that paper if I bring in a proclaimed man, I can go home to Jeannie and the childer.' cried Rafferty, his eyeballs bulging like a cow going to slaughter.

'So you're going to hang your mates to get yourself off the hook? After all we did for you? I always thought you were a spineless wee weasel. Shane should have left you to starve to death!' raged McClatchy.

'You're coming with me McClatchy! You start walking or I'll shoot you were you stand!'

'Finn, Jeannie and the childer are gone mate, remember? You lost the farm and they all perished, we are your family now.' pleaded Barra.

'You shut up! I'm sick of yousuns lying to me, you've kept me prisoner here and now I'm going home to my family and he's coming with me!' shrieked the deranged Rafferty.

'The only way you'll see your childer again is if you see them in hell, you lunatic.' growled McClatchy, spitefully; 'Your wife and childer died out before you cause you never provided for them. They're gone and they're not coming back. Give me that gun.'

'McClatchy, that is not helping let me deal-' started Eugene, before McClatchy interrupted; 'Give me that gun or so help me I'll ram it down your weasel neck, you frigging imbecile. You think I'm afraid of the likes of you, who can't even keep his wife and childer in board and bread? A Pity your Jeannie's a corpse, I'd have showed her a-'

BANG!!!

For the second time that day, that awkward, heavy, unpredictable engine of destruction let loose a thunderous crack that sent a heavy lead ball cannoning through the cranium of a deeply unpleasant rapparee. This would be the last time the weapon would fire a charge, as at the same time as it sent Owen McClatchy tumbling end over end downhill minus half his head, it split its barrel into vicious shards of iron, straight up into the face of Finnbar Rafferty. The boys in unison stood back aghast, each in turn presenting their hands to their eyes, mouths and ears like the proverbial monkeys. At length Barra turned his back as the other three looked to each other in consultation. Eugene was the first to speak, examining McClatchy's still warm corpse; 'He's definitely dead all right, nothing to be done here.'

Archie slowly and cautiously approached Rafferty, bracing himself for the site of more horrible injuries. Grasping the forehead he closed his eyes, took a deep breath and looked into the face. One eye was dislocated from the socket and hung by a red, stringy membrane halfway down his cheek. Most of the flesh was torn away revealing sinews and bone which would n'er be seen in those days by anyone outside the medical profession. Archie wondered would he be haunted forever by all he had seen that day. With a gulp he looked up to Eugene to speak, but before he could  a hand shot up and grasped his wrist, sending every hair in his body standing to attention.

'Aaarggh!!' cried the rapparee Sergeant, recoiling away and crawling quickly backwards. The hand dropped once more. 'He breathes still.' said Eugene; 'But he won't survive; not for more than a few hours anyway. And with those injuries, I'm not sure he would want to.'

Archie looked again at the wretched, grotesque little man who lay dying at his feet. 'We need to get going. Somebody might have heard that shot, the militia may even still be patrolling.' He looked up at Eugene; 'We can't just leave him though, can we? Not like this!'

'No.' agreed Eugene, shaking his head; 'No we can't. We need to finish him off. This won't be easy. Killing a man in the heat of battle is one thing, this is quite another. We can't use a pistol either as it may further alert our enemies. I'm not going to order anyone to do it; this isn't war, but it isn't murder either.'

Tomas nodded; 'If anything it's mercy. He wanted to go home anyway. Perhaps we should draw lots?'

'Yes, that's a good idea.' said Eugene. Tomas pulled up 4 pieces of grass, snapping 3 to the same length and one slightly shorter. The four rapparees stood in a circle, and one by one Tomas offered his 3 companions a straw each. When compared, Barra McCann was found to be in possession of the shorter. Eugene handed him a large boulder. 'Don't waste time, just do it quickly and don't think, and remember, it's mercy, not murder.'

Barra stood for several seconds breathing heavily in shock at what had just occurred and in trepidation of the task that had fallen to him. 'You must not hesitate Barra, Rafferty is in terrible suffering.' said Eugene, softly. Barra looked to the Frenchman and then back to Rafferty.

'Here, give me that, I'll do it for you.' said Tomas, reaching for the Boulder.

'No!' snapped Barra, pulling the stone away; 'I can't ask you to do that.'

Gripping the large, flat boulder in both hands, Barra crept nervously over to the mess that was once a happy, cheerful family man and sitting astride his chest, brought the boulder down on his friend's head again and again and again. Tears and snot flowed down the young rapparee's face as he blubbered and cried with each whack of the boulder, before Tomas reached out and grabbed his arm; 'Barra, that's enough son. He's gone, you've done your job.'

Barra pulled away and stood at a distance, refusing to be consoled by the others. Archie felt for him. Killing a man changes something in you, even if you don't want to do it or it's an accident, you can never quite be the same person again. Eugene handed McClatchy's pistol to Archie; 'No use to him anymore.'

'So where to now?' asked Tomas.

'Well seeing as we're in the vicinity, perhaps we should pay your Grandmother a visit.' replied Eugene.

Less than a couple of miles away, the noise of the shot had travelled from the hill across the calm still night air to become a faint but easily recognisable crack in the ears of Jacob Cayley, who was out drawing water from the well at the side of his house, as the maid had retired for the evening. He stared up at the faraway hillside in apprehension, silently hoping that no further bloodshed had occurred that night. It was, of course, a forlorn hope. He turned towards the house where he had detected a low moan from his patient and hauling the bucket carefully over the wall of the well, he proceeded inside to attend to his charge. Angus McGrogan had awoken and was shouting the name of his deceased brother Seamus, however after a few minutes of assurance from Mary and Doctor Cayley he was able to speak in a more coherent manner.

'Angus, can you remember what really happened up there?' queried Doctor Cayley; 'You said something about a Frenchman and a Preacher killing your brother. Shane has gone off to look for these men. I don't know what he might do, so it's important we get this right. No one else should lose their life without reason Angus!'

Angus breathed heavily and sipped from a cup of water; 'Seamus had been drinking and had been riling everyone all day. When the coach came along, we did the job well and got what we were after without having to hurt anyone. But Seamus got greedy, demanded things off the passengers and when he couldn't get them he lost his temper, and hit one of the women.'

He leaned forward and coughed heavily for several seconds. Doctor Cayley slapped the young rapparee's back carefully avoiding his injured shoulder and offered more water.

'So then what happened?'

Angus took another deep breath; 'The Frenchman stepped in and tried to take over the mission, he struck Seamus in the face. Not a good idea, I doubt any man would be a match for Seamus for fist fighting, drunk or not. He was in a rage. He pounded on the Frenchman, crushed him into the ground. I thought he was going to kill him and tried to get him to stop, but I couldn't.'

He paused briefly; 'That's when Archie McClung pulled the gun on him. Now that I think of it, he gave Seamus fair warning, told him to stop or he would fire. But that was the wrong tack with Seamus, it just made him more angry. McClung said the gun went off accidentally; I don't know if he was telling the truth or not.'

Jacob Cayley stood up and looked out the kitchen window, pondering the possibilities of what might have happened. This information put quite a different complexion on things. He wondered as to where Shane had headed when he left earlier, and hoped that he would be true to his word to consult with his men before deciding on his course of action.

Tomas led Eugene and Archie through the woods to the outskirts of the clearing where Sadie O'Reilly's cabin lay, with Barra dawdling absent mindedly behind. Archie hadn't known his friend to be so quiet for so long since the day he met him, except when asleep. The sudden deaths of their two companions had lowered the mood for all the rapparees, but Barra was particularly affected. Owen McClatchy, despite his obnoxious attitude to almost everyone, was by no means the bully that Seamus was, and no one felt him deserving of death. Finbarr Rafferty presented a paradox in that he carried such a cloud over him, his death could at least be seen as something of a release. That said, the ghastly way in which he saw out the last few moments of his life was now etched permanently on the psyche of Tomas, Barra, and Archie. These three were no strangers to the hard realities of life, having known their fair share of bloody noses, black eyes, empty stomachs and cold feet in the winter. They had fought skirmishes with soldiers and militiamen, and had traded punches with each other over whose turn it was to get the firewood or who owed who a slug of whiskey or a pinch of snout. They had even seen men killed before, but nothing quite so horrific as the events of the day. Eugene had offered a few placatory anecdotes of how his early experiences of battle had affected him and how he had learned to push such memories from his mind, but after a short while he had sensed that his advice was badly timed and poorly received. The boys had spent the rest of the journey in near silence. Tomas paused and looked back at the others. 'That's the cabin there, yousuns wait here I'll go tell her we're here.'

'I thought you said she'd know we were coming?' asked Archie. Tomas looked at him and shook his head dismissively before heading off, not yet ready to engage in further repartee. The boys watched from the bushes as Tomas approached the cabin. It was a fair sized, reasonably well made wooden building by the standards of the time, constructed in the main part from logs reinforced with clay and greening here and there from moss. It sported a single 4 pane window, 2 of which were covered with boards, and a stone chimney and fireplace at it's heart. Although living in complete isolation in the midst of the forest, Sadie O'Reilly was regularly visited by her huge brood of 8 surviving children, 27 grandchildren and uncountable great grandchildren, ensuring that the property was maintained to an acceptable standard.

He knocked gently but sharply on the door 3 times; 'Granny! It's me here, Tomas!'

A small yappy dog barked angrily from inside. 'Who is that at the door? Go away whoever you are, there's nothing here for you!'

'It's me Granny! It's Tomas!' called McCafferty.

'Tomas who?' called the shaky voice from inside.

'Your grandson Tomas! Muireann's boy!'

The latch drew back from within and the door opened slowly. Tomas slipped inside closing the door behind him momentarily, to lay the ground for the visit. 'I heard a crack of gunfire there earlier on young Tomas, I hope you had nothing to do with it.'

'No nothing to do with me at all Granny, somebody messing about with guns no doubt. I'm still at the cockling and the fishing.' He grinned self righteously. 'You're a wee liar, I heard there was people out looking for you because of some business with a harbour master's wife. Have ye no sense boy? Gettin yourself in between man and wife? Young Barra McCann is no better either, not that I've seen hide nor hair of him in nigh on a year.' scolded Mrs O'Reilly.

'Barra's here with me, he's waiting outside. We just need somewhere to put our head down for a couple of hours and we were hereabouts so we thought that we would come and look in on you Granny. We've a couple of friends with us too, a gentleman from France no less and our wee friend Archie whose father is a protestant priest would you believe.' announced Tomas, trying to sell the imposition as best he could. Granny O'Reilly sighed the put upon sigh that mothers and grandmothers do just before admitting defeat; 'Bring them in then. There's a bit of soup left over although its not the thickest, you'll have to take turns with the bowl.'

Tomas stuck his head out the door and bade the boys come forth. The 3 rapparees tramped forward one by one and entered through the little door, stooping slightly to avoid hitting their heads off the top of the frame. Once inside all were able to stand up straight. Archie looked about the place, and was quietly impressed with his surroundings given his low expectations. The house was divided into two rooms, the second of which was hidden behind a heavy red curtain. Furniture was sparse, consisting of a single wooden rocking chair, and a large cupboard containing various half empty jars and bottles. Both had been painted white at some point but the paint was now flaky and off colour. The floor was boarded rather than earthen as one would expect in a rural domicile. A large black iron cooking pot hung above the fireplace, where a few dimming embers were giving out their last offerings of heat. Granny O'Reilly herself was slight figure of a little under 5 foot, whose stooping posture gave her the appearance of being even smaller. Her eyes were a blue grey and the pupil of the left had a milky tinge to it, being rendered near useless by a cataract. Her shrivelled mouth contained but 8 teeth, which wasn't a bad count considering her 89 years of age. Her hands were gnarled and clawed like the roots of an old oak tree. She was dressed in a white night cap and grey shift accessorised with a navy shawl. Barra stepped forward and gave his grandmother a peck on the cheek; 'Hello Granny it's lovely to see you again. These here are my mates, this is Captain Eugene O'Cahan,' Eugene gave a low stooping bow announcing grandly; 'at your service Madam.'

'And this is Sergeant Archie McClung.' Archie smiled and held his hand up, uttering a faint 'Hello.'

Sadie O'Riley smiled and nodded at both of them. 'You're both very welcome. McClung you say – I knew a Sandy McClung once, a protestant Minister- Know you of him?' Archie nodded humbly; 'That was my father Mrs O'Reilly, he passed away a year ago.' He thought it appropriate to omit the details of his father's death.

 She nodded sympathetically; 'I am sorry to hear that son. He was a good brave man who did what was right when it would have been easier to do what others bade him; stood in front of a baying mob who would have burnt down this house with me in it and sent them on their way. I heard there were many still who avoided his church for his actions. If you are half the man your father was, you will do well.'

Archie was surprised at this news, having never known of his father's bravery and sacrifice. It brought forth suppressed thoughts of how he missed his family and how he wished he could return home.

All four rapparees took off their shoes and overcoats or whatever passed for them and positioned themselves in a half crescent in front of the fire. Barra fetched another log at Mrs O'Reilly's bidding, and placed it on the fire where it crackled musically. All four refused supper, not wishing to deprive the old lady any more than was absolutely necessary. After a short while the boys engaged in conversation and Tomas was able to raise a few laughs with some anecdotes of his and Barra's childhood adventures. Barra was soon joining in and began to sound a bit more like his old self again, much to Archie's relief. Sadie O'Reilly meanwhile had expertly picked the boy's brains by the use of open ended questions until both confessed, to no surprise at all, that they were both rapparees out on their keeping and fugitive to the law. Whilst Mrs O'Reilly expressed her concerns for the boy's safety and told them to look out for each other, she was not at all shocked or ashamed to learn that both were rapparees; on the contrary. It was a source of great pride to learn that two of her grandsires stood shoulder to shoulder with other wanted men who risked their lives on a daily basis to defend others from tyranny and oppression, even if they hadn't washed their socks in 6 months.

The confession however had naturally led on to further inquisition regarding the gunfire that had been heard shortly before the boys' arrival, and hence the events of the day were recounted including the killings of Seamus McGrogan, Owen McClatchy and Finbarr Rafferty. Granny O'Reilly listened thoughtfully and at length, shook her head gravely; 'This may well not be the last that you see and hear of those 3 lost souls this night. These woods where your friends met their ends- they are a place like no other, or rather I know of but one other. It is a place of resurrection, where a man's body may die but his soul may not easily leave. And this night is like no other night, being known as the feast of Beltane amongst those who walked this land before our people arrived and now walk abroad in the spirit. This was a sacred place and a sacred time to them and the spilling of blood in the time of the festival of rebirth is a desecration that the old ones will not tolerate.'

The four sat in quiet contemplation; the cynical amusement which Eugene and Archie had displayed to Barra's tall tales was quite absent when Sadie O'Reilly delivered this news. There was something so believable about her, as if she held such power that just by willing something to be true it could be made to be a fact. Granny O'Reilly wasn't telling fairy tales. She was stating quite lucidly and correctly what she knew to be true of the world.

Finally Archie spoke; 'So what will the outcome be then, if a man's body can be killed but his spirit cannot pass to the other world?'

Mrs O'Reilly breathed out slowly and looked upwards, before returning her gaze to meet Archie's; 'The spirit cannot leave this world, until the wrong that was done to it has been righted. It will travel afar, resting neither day nor night, seeking out he who caused it to be cast out of this mortal plain. Only when it has laid hands on the killer, and has bound him and taken him back to the place where the deed was done, will the spirit be able to complete its journey into the next world, and the murderer must stay in this world in his stead.'

Archie felt a shiver at this information, but after some time decided he would put it from his mind. Mrs O'Reilly seemed an honest woman and freely believed the things she told Archie to be the truth; however, these beliefs originated from the ignorance of primitive man, prior to the coming of Christianity to Ireland and as such, were incompatible with the teachings of the Kirk and all he believed to be right and true. He wondered as to why his father would have fought so earnestly to preserve the safety of one whose beliefs were so contrary to his own.

'Mrs O'Reilly, can you tell me about how you came to know my father – you said he prevented your house from being burnt?' Granny O'Reilly nodded in agreement. 'twas some 25 odd summers ago, before Barra and yourself were born, and young Tomas there himself would have been but a bairn. The winter of the year of seventeen hundred and seventeen had been a mercilessly harsh one, and the spectres of famine and cholera stalked the land. I had for a long while made a living as a midwife and a purveyor of herbal remedies for those in need of a cure, both human and animal. Your father had for a few years hence been the dissenter preacher to the people of Ballyvalley townland and for some miles surrounding. But there lately came a new preacher, one of the established church, answering to the name of Joseph Threader.'

'Arrah!' proclaimed Barra, with a smile; 'That's the oul fella we took the bag off earlier on. His name is on the side of it!' He held up the initialled leather satchel by way of illustration. 'Anything belonging to that to that scoundrel could only have bad luck attached to it.' said Granny O'Reilly, grimly.

'Yes Threader was sent here at the bidding of the protestant church and he brought with him unease and disharmony which he sowed amongst the people of the locality, protestant and catholic alike. Where Sandy McClung had preached that a man should practice humility and look to the beam in his own eye rather than his neighbour's, Threader attracted people in droves by appealing to their vanity, boasting that his church was attended by the gentry and charging the foolish dearly for the privilege of sitting in its pews, the most expensive seats being those located closest to those of their social betters. But Threader wasn't the only one out to extract an easy shilling from the working man. There was also at that time in the village a man called Hector Strawbridge, whose trade was as a doctor of horses, which in itself is no bad thing excepting that he was given to compel his customers to pay through the nose for all manner of lotions and potions being of little effect and oft times of some detriment to the animal.

Given this man's bad practices the local people were obliged to avail of my services and it was no secret that the animals flourished under my care. Now Strawbridge was greatly put out by his loss of business and contrived to remedy the situation by complaining to the clergy that I was practicing witchcraft and should be tried and burned. He went first ways to your father, who being a man of great learning in matters of the church and the bible was of the opinion that witchcraft, as defined under the law, did not exist and therefore no one could be tried for it. Strawbridge was frustrated at this view and went thence to Threader, who believed firmly in witchcraft and espoused the burning of all who practiced it. It is my belief that Threader intimated to Strawbridge that in order to prove a charge of witchcraft against me, that evidence thereof must first be identified and where none was present, it should be manufactured.'

'So they set you up Granny,' said Tomas, firmly; 'just like that harbour master with his false charges against me of aiding the smugglers.'

'Well quite young Thomas, excepting for the fact that in my case, I was actually innocent.'

replied Granny O'Reilly, to the boys' amusement.

'I digress,' continued Sadie O'Reilly; 'this pair of false knaves were aware that lately there was in the district a horse which I had treated, quite successfully, for a lameness. I had presently been called to visit the animal again, and this time I found the beast to be suffering from distemper and it's remedy to be beyond my means. I told the owner that I could do nothing for the animal and departed without demanding payment. The owner then in desperation sent for Mr Strawbridge. Marks were found to be on the animal that were supposedly made by me as a tribute to the devil, but they were no sign that I had ever recognised, and I suspect them to be meaningless daubs put there by Strawbridge in order to accuse me falsely. Strawbridge gave report of this to Threader who thence bade his congregation go forth and lay hold of me, but your father got word of this and barred the passage of the mob. He warned all gathered there that in their anger they would be party to a murder and likened their actions to the mob who stoned Mary Magdelene. He said that the first to lift a hand in anger would likewise damn themselves to the eternal fires of hell. Reverend McClung also sent a boy to summon the established priest of a neighbouring parish, who came forth and put manners on Threader. I believe Joseph Threader was shortly after sent by the Bishop to the parish of Killeavy. As for Mr Strawbridge, he died of a malady sometime later – I believe he ate something that disagreed with him.'

Archie thought he saw Granny O'Reilly punctuate the last sentence of the dialogue with a sly wink to Barra and Tomas, but considered it apt to ask no further questions on the matter.

'So Archie's Da saved Granny O'Reilly!' said Barra, cheerfully. 'That probably makes us family or something.' said Tomas, slapping a hand on Archie's shoulder; 'I wish I'd known that earlier about yer man Threader, I'd have stuck a ball through him.'

'I shall retire for the night boys now if you don't mind, these long nights don't agree with me.' said Granny O'Reilly, sleepily. 'Indeed,' said Eugene; 'We have imposed enough on your kindness Madame. We should all try to get a couple of hours sleep before we set out again. Woe betide us should those militia men be taken by a sudden burst of industry and desire to continue their pursuit.' Archie settled down to sleep on the floor, quietly regretting his decision to refuse supper. The death of Seamus had affected his appetite at the camp earlier and he hadn't had adequate nourishment in quite a while. He scanned the many jars and bottles and considered whether any of it would suffice as a midnight snack.

'I think we'll be fine Captain,' said Barra, in a knowledgeable manner; 'most of those do gooders are just farmers and shop keepers with their own work to be getting on with. They won't bother looking for us unless the Viscount of Hillsborough himself appears and gives them a pat on the head.'


## 8. THE PLOT REVEALED


'I myself will lead the hunt for these barbarous scoundrels on the morrow' said Wills Hill to Isabella, who had been sitting quietly beside the roaring fire in the magnificent living room of the

Viscount's country Demesne, her hand bandaged and slung across her shoulder. 'I'm sure that won't be necessary Wills; I am only here for a short visit and would not wish for the events of today to overshadow the remainder of my time here.' she replied in a dissuading manner; 'Perhaps we could go hunting or you could show me round the estate?'

Wills stopped pacing and sat down opposite her; tapping nervously on the arm of his chair; 'But these people who abused you so must be brought to justice, Isabella! One simply cannot tolerate a situation where a lady may be set upon by ruffians whilst going about her business.'

'Surely it can wait, Wills? We haven't seen each other in many a year, let's just put this matter to the side for the time being and allow the matter of these – criminals to be resolved in the fullness of time.' Wills bit on his thumbnail and then nodded reluctantly. 'As soon as your visit concludes I shall have satisfaction on these fellows mark my words. For now we shall put it aside and concentrate on enjoying the ball tomorrow. Should be quite a do if I say so myself.' He finally managed a slight grin. 'That's more like the Wills I know.' said Isabella, affectionately. 'Now I really should retire for the evening. Good night Wills.'

'Good night Isabella.' said the Viscount, as Isabella and Amelie took their leave. Shortly after Wills retired for the night, Isabella crept back into the living room and clumsily opened the large French style windows with her good hand. She shuffled quietly out on to the veranda and sat herself down on the terrace wall, breathing deeply of the night air and counting the stars in the clear patches of sky.

'Don't turn around; it's me.' said a low deep voice from behind. Isabella rolled her eyes upwards and sighed with slight annoyance; 'Why would I not turn around, I already know what you look like?'

Shane McGrogan stepped forward out of the shadows. 'Why on Earth did you come here, you're endangering the mission!' hissed Isabella, scornfully. 'I heard that you were injured and I had to come to make sure you were all right.' replied Shane. 'Oh so you're a doctor now are you sir? Don't worry about me I'm fine. Your men graciously put pay to that madman who you saw fit to put in charge.'

'That was my brother.' said Shane despondently.

Isabella lightened her tone; 'I am sorry for your loss Shane. However I can confirm that the mission was a success. The object is in the possession of your men, who I would expect are preparing to rendezvous with you for the handover.'

Shane nodded approvingly. 'So this is it then; the first step on the road towards freedom for Ireland.'

'And the true King of Scotland back on his rightful throne.' added Isabella.

'What? Oh aye, that too.' said Shane, lighting up his pipe.

'Give me a puff of that, I'm bloody gasping.' said the Lady. 'I couldn't light up the whole journey with that priest and that little pipsqueak of a captain in the carriage.' She took a long draw and blew out slowly. Shane looked up at the house. 'So this is how a viscount lives? Little wonder the rest of us are starving. We'll have to hit this place some time.' He said, teasingly. 'You dream, sir, you would be better off beating a retreat. Wills was talking about leading a party out after you on the morrow, I had to talk him out of it.'

Shane shrugged; 'Which room is he in? I could steal up now and knock that idea out of him.'

'No you will not, he is a good friend of mine and you will not be accosting him in his bed. Besides, he's an excellent shot and swordsman, more than the match for the likes of you.' replied Isabella, walking round to stand within the French windows. Shane laughed at the ridiculous notion that he could be bested by a pampered aristocrat, and eventually Isabella laughed too. 'You're right though I'd better go. I timed that the guards make their rounds of the estate every 12 minutes. But first, sweet lady, a kiss from those ruby lips.' Isabella looked Shane up and down with a scowl. 'You overreach yourself Sir! you also stink of shit.' she said, and closed the window. 'Worth a try.' thought Shane, as he disappeared into the night. Neither Shane nor Isabella were aware of a second shadowy figure listening in the darkness.

Archie awoke in the near total darkness to the great epiphany of the connectivity of all things within and without the material universe. He looked at his hands and saw how the blood pulsed through his veins. He heard a scratching, tapping along the floor, and looked across the room to see a tiny woodlouse scurrying along. He was amazed at how greatly heightened his awareness was. He looked to the chair, the cupboard, the walls and the burning embers of the fire and knew that all of them were alive and connected and had been since the beginning of time itself. He smiled at the rocking chair, it smiled back at him and nodded approvingly. 'Yes.' He thought; 'Suddenly everything makes sense now.' He heard the drip drop of the raindrops and marvelled at the glorious symphony of life. He wondered as to whether a dog should wear trousers and a cat a dress, or vice versa. He laughed at the notion. He struggled to contain his laughter and spluttered as he fought to hold it in. 'This is too good.' He thought to himself; 'I have to tell Barra.' He reached over and shook his sleeping friend's shoulder; 'Barra!' he whispered, not wanting to wake the other two, this was a special treat he was saving for his best friend. 'Barra!' he hissed, shaking McCann's shoulder a little harder. 'Wha-? What is it?' answered the half conscious rapparee. 'I just had the most spectacular notion. What if the King was a dog and the Pope was a cat right, and they had to wear clothes and hats like humans so nobody would notice, and the King wanted a bone, so he-'

'What the frigg are you on about you silly bastard? Go to sleep.' Barra turned over and pulled his coat over his head. Archie sat for a few seconds in disbelief that anyone would not be interested in his incredible revelations. Then he understood; these things were only of interest to those who had the understanding. Special people, like him. Archie felt very humbled that he had been chosen by God to carry the great knowledge of all things, and was almost crying with happiness. Then he saw her; dressed in a shimmering chiffon gown and floating in a cloud of lavender energy, her golden hair seemed to be woven with stars as it's 12 foot long tresses waved and soared around the room. Her movements were slow yet flowing as if time itself bended to her will. Archie knew no one in the room could see her except him. The others were asleep, but if they were awake they would neither see nor sense this vision from another plain of existence. Aine, the fairy queen had come to visit him, and no other. As Archie sat in wide eyed anticipation, the ethereal figure extended a hand and bade him come hither. As Archie rose they embraced as one in the lavender cloud and danced a slow and graceful dance to music only he could hear, music no mortal man had heard in a thousand years. Their dance raged blissfully for a period of time that could not be measured in hours or minutes, before finally the spirit pulled away from him. He stood for several seconds as the figure floated gracefully towards the curtain at the back of the room, before disappearing behind it with an enticing smile.

Archie stood indecisively for a moment before deducing the fairy queen wished him to follow. Stealing himself, he crept nervously behind the curtain in the hope of even greater ecstasy. He entered the little back room and scanned eagerly around, detecting a sole being slumbering quietly on a bed of hay, beneath a heavy blanket. Slowly Archie crawled and snuggled in behind the sleeping woman, who now seemed to be fully materialised into human form. He gently rubbed her shoulder and as she turned to face him he closed his eyes to deliver his first kiss. And instantly opened them again in terror to the face of a screaming banshee!

Captain Pilkington waited just long enough to ensure that Shane McGrogan was too far away to engage him before launching into action. He rushed into the room and threw open the French doors, pushing a startled Isabella out of the way. He pointed his pistol into the darkness and let loose a shot which connected successfully with a nearby tree. He cared not as his actions were for effect only. 'Guards! Guards! There is treachery afoot! He cried at the top of his shrill voice, ringing a small bell which the Viscount used to summon the servants. Everyone in the house rushed excitedly into the room, including the Viscount, Colonel Lambert, and Sergeant Wilkes and his men, who had not long ago returned from Belfast. 'Wilkes! Arrest this woman immediately on a charge of treachery against the King!'

Isabella and Amelie gasped theatrically.

'What in the name of blazes is going on here?' demanded the furious Viscount, tying his night coat at the waist. 'Well you may ask your grace!' replied Pilkers, with unusual impertinence; 'I have just seen off Shane McGrogan the rapparee, who had come hence to murder you in your bed. This – lady was plotting with him against the King no less! They intend somehow, by what means I know not, to overthrow the natural ruler of the three kingdoms and put in his place the Pretender sir!'

'Wilkes, have your men search the grounds.' commanded the Colonel of the Sergeant, who clicked his heels obediently and led his troops out. 'These are very serious allegations you are making here Captain,' continued the Colonel; 'if they are found to be false you will suffer-'

'Found to be false?!' repeated the Viscount, disbelievingly; 'Are you seriously entertaining the idea that my dear friend, a guest in my house, is plotting to destabalise the entire kingdom? Forbes bring me my gloves!' he addressed the second sentence to a nearby lackey, who duly went off to fetch them.

'Are you aware sir,' asked Pilkington, excitedly; 'That the good Lady Murray's father, the present Duke of Atholl, is indeed the Duke only by default?'

'Of course I know that you blethering imbecile! Isabella's uncle was attainted for his participation in the rebellion of 1715. He lives in exile in France now.' spat the Viscount.

Forbes returned with a pair of fine silk white gloves on a silver platter. 'No, no, not those ones, bring me my leather mit that I use for falconry.' Forbes bowed and went off again.

'And where sir,' asked Pilkers, 'Has the lady just returned from?'

'Well from France of course-'replied Wills Hill, trailing off to look at Isabella who was being comforted by Amelie. 'For

Heaven's sake, France is a large country. I was attending finishing school, I know nothing of any such plot!' she pleaded to Wills, who nodded reassuringly although he himself didn't quite know what to believe.

Sergeant Wilkes re-entered addressing the Colonel; 'Beg your pardon sirs, the men saw an unidentified person making haste from the house on a horse, we gave pursuit but he had quite a start and managed to elude us.' In truth Wilkes had made little effort to catch up to the escaping intruder, he was too close to retirement to start being a hero now.

The Colonel turned to the Viscount; 'I'm afraid sir given the seriousness of the allegations being made here, it would be appropriate that we transport the Lady and her maid to the barracks at Saintfield until we can ascertain-'

'The devil with that man!' spat the Viscount; 'I will not hear of a guest in my house being placed under arrest like a common criminal.'

The Colonel sighed; 'Then I am afraid sir, the Lady will have to remain here on the estate until I've consulted with General Parker himself on the matter. We have to look at the bigger picture here sir, I mean, these are matters of national security sir! The King himself may be in danger.'

Wills bit his thumbnail again and nodded angrily. 'Very well then. I shall ensure that my guest does not leave the estate under any circumstances until such times as she has been exonerated in the face of these incredulous allegations.'

Forbes appeared with a heavy leather falconry mit on a silver tray. 'Thank you Forbes.' muttered the Viscount as he lifted the glove and inspected it carefully, as everyone looked on in puzzlement. Fronting Captain Pilkington, he raised the glove and brought a mighty slap across the incompetent officer's face, almost knocking him over. Pilkers gathered himself and stood firmly, the powder from his wig partially enveloping him in a dusty white cloud. 'You sir;' said the Viscount, 'Shall meet me on the lawn tomorrow when I shall have satisfaction for the imposition you have placed on my guest and myself here tonight. Colonel Lambert, you may be my second.' With that, he strode off to bed without a second word to anyone. Isabella and Amelie then also departed to bed, followed by the servants. 'Wilkes, you can second for young Pilkington here.' said the Colonel as he left; 'I would get some sleep if I were you Richard.'

Pilkington stood in the middle of the room trying to think what to do for several seconds. In an uncharacteristic attempt to muster some fighting spirit, he turned to Wilkes; 'Well Wilkes, we'll show these toffs what? Can't imagine the Viscount would know one end of a sword from another eh?'

Wilkes blew a puff of air out pessimistically; 'Pardon my contrariness sir, but in my experience some of these young gentlemen would put you to shame! Very skilful some of them, they have the finest tutors and nothing better to do all day but practice the art! Come to think of it you know, I seem to remember there was a fete down in Ballynahinch a few years ago and the young Viscount, before he was a Viscount, sportingly gave us a splendid display of his skills. Threw an apple into the air and cut it into four equal segments before it hit the ground. The boys couldn't believe it! Never even saw the blade move. He was the talk of the barracks for weeks after, very fast indeed, and I expect he could only have improved since then.'

Pilkers pulled his wig from his head and gazed at the ground despondently; 'Oh Wilkes, what am I to do? I only ever had four lessons with the blade, I do so hate the sight of blood! I used to nip off and play cricket with the juniors instead!'

'Well I know what I would do sir.' said Wilkes, knowledgeably.

'What's that?' asked the Captain, desperately.

'Surrender sir! I swear by it, it's a very underrated military tactic. I've fought in 12 battles and led the surrender in all but three of them, and I'm still here! You must surrender at the first given opportunity.'

## 9. DEADLY PURSUIT

For a woman of advanced years Granny O'Reilly could deliver a fair whallop with a walking stick, in the highly unlikely event of a delusional young rapparee making unwanted advances. Archie stumbled back in horror at the screaming, spitting, striking vision, trying to find some path of logical thought through all the panic and confusion. Then it hit him; the subbucus! What else could it be? He pushed through the curtain and bounded past his comrades, straight out the front door of the cottage with a speed unmatched since he ran from his own home the previous year. As he bolted down the lane he could just hear Tomas's voice crying; 'After him Barra! He's tried to couple me granny!' He glanced over his shoulder to see the two outraged highwaymen closely followed by a hesitant Eugene, desperately trying to impart some form of reason to Sadie O'Reilly's grandsons. 'I'm doomed!' he thought; 'I've lay with a subbucus and now my John Thomas will shrivel to the size of a tadpole and I'll be as aged as Methusla in three days time! Just like my father warned me! I must make my way to the church and beg the Lord for forgiveness, that's as if these three cutthroats don't murder me first!' he dived and wriggled through the mud and the long grass before finally concealing himself in a thickly overgrown copse of knotweed, some 18 feet distant from where the lane met the track crossing the hill. He watched in silent terror as the three rapparees jogged down the lane and stood at the track, looking round in either direction. 'Archie!' called Barra; 'Preacher! Come back here, fear not, we have no umbrage with you.' added Tomas. Both turned to Eugene for deference.

'We need to locate him as quickly as is possible, he is endangering the mission. I will go and check up the track to the left here, the two of you may go to the right. We shall meet back here in ten minutes time whether we find him or not.' ordered Eugene.

'Oh I'll bloody find him all right, don't you worry about that.' replied Tomas, and all duly went off searching in their designated direction. Archie glanced about to assess his surroundings; he found the whispering of the knotweed in the wind unnerving, perceiving all manner of chuckling and groaning in the darkness. He tried to pull himself further into his greatcoat to avoid the stares of a thousand unseen eyes that glared at him from the ancient forest. So much of what had been said and what had happened that night, things that he had given precious little heed to or dismissed as superstitious bunkum seemed real and alive to him now. The wind WAS talking to him, chiding him for his part in the horrible events of the day; why did he take part in the robbery, why did he kill Seamus, why did he take the boys' shoes, why didn't he stop Rafferty, why did he go into Mrs O'Reilly's bedroom, why why why all the way back to the killing of his father and his lack of reverence and application which had brought that situation about. The wind called to him to answer for all of his crimes, but it wasn't just the wind that was his enemy. The knotweed seemed intent on pulling him down into the earth where the dead lay buried, or was it the dead rising up from the ground to meet him? In a sudden panic he pulled forward violently, ripping up the knotweed which clawed at him like the shrivelled talons of decaying corpses rising up from below. The knotweed released him with unexpected ease sending the confused young man lurching forward without balance, prostrating himself at the roots of an ancient oak tree. His knee hurt and was bleeding slightly; he heard the blood trickle.

'Did it sting or did it sing? Imagine a man with a smiling knee, or perhaps two. A face on each one with holes in his breeches for the nose to poke through. What a to do!'

He momentarily forgot his fear and pain and praised his immense humour; that he could compose such a ditty with such ease must make him a wordsmith the equal of Dean Swift himself, or at least Alexander Pope. Suddenly he was overjoyed to think that he possessed such enormous intelligence and talent, surely his fortune was made! 'If only Barra were here that I could share my rhyme with him, how he would rejoice and laud me for my greatness' he thought. 'No!' cried a dissenting voice from the back of his head. 'Barra means to murder you for your insult to his Grandmother!'

'Angus then. Angus will laugh aloud when I tell him. I shall be the toast of the rapparee camp when I return victorious with the rhymes that I write, they will make me their bard like that chap from the Robin Hood stories!' He paused for a moment to try to recall the name of Robin Hood's bard.

'Fool!' said the voice in his head again; 'You murdered Angus' brother before his eyes did you not, he intends to put an end to you when next you meet. You must flee from this place, flee and hide!'

Archie was scared again. The eyes of the night were boring into his back once more and the black heavy blanket of the sky seemed to gather itself to pounce on him as a barn owl pounces on a field mouse. He looked up at the veiny, knotted oak tree and pondered what ancient secrets it may be privy to, what wonders or horrors it may have witnessed in its immense life span. Staring at its snarls and branches, he was able to discern at length the shape of a face, two black spots for eyes, a stubby branch for a nose and a jagged gash for a mouth. 'Looks like Seamus a bit.' He thought. No sooner had this thought entered his head than the face appeared to change shape, twisting and cracking with a ghastly agonised groaning slowness until at last the snarling visage of Seamus McGrogan could be seen quite clearly, not a shape on a tree that looked like Seamus, but Seamus' actual face was emerging from the tree! Archie crouched paralysed with fear as the bark split open and McGrogan's shoulders, torso, and finally arms and legs freed themselves from the other world. Seamus McGrogan was risen again! Slowly, the giant resurrected rapparee paced shakily towards the prone McClung to stand inches from the boy's face. Seamus' ghost crouched down so that his face was level with Archie's; 'Hello preacher,' he said, flatly; 'Did you miss me?'

'I – I – you were dead!' stuttered Archie, terrified.

'Is that so?' replied Seamus; 'Well that's what happens when you go about shooting people in the guts you little turd.'

'I'm sorry! I didn't mean to do it, I was just trying to stop you from killing the Frenchman-'

'You mutinied against your captain you little ingrate,' said Seamus sharply, pointing a huge finger in the cowering McClung's face 'we took you in when you had nothing and you do this to me!'

'You had but to relent and none need have lost their life. It was your own fault that you died not mine!' blurted Archie, instantly regretting his choice of words. Seamus raised an eyebrow then gave a cynical chuckle. 'So you stand by your actions then eh Preacher? Good, good. It makes what will come next all the easier. You see it is not by any Christian doing that I am returned here tonight to you McClung, it turns out all those stories that you and I thought were mere amusement, all of them- all of them were real Preacher. The other people that McCafferty and McCann spoke of, they do indeed live on here in spirit. You took my life on their sacred ground at a time sacred to them and hence-' said Seamus, holding his palms out in mockery of the resurrection; 'I am reborn.'

Archie was unable to muster any form of reply to this new revelation; Seamus McGrogan, the basest ape of a man it had ever been his displeasure to cross the path of, reborn even as Christ himself. Archie felt sick to the stomach at this blasphemous notion, his heart seemed to pound in his very throat. Seamus raised his finger again; 'But not to an earthly life Preacher, oh no. For this time, I may pass only as ether, for the next three days in the thin veil between this world- your world – and the world beyond. If at the expiry of that time I have not resolved the issues which were left undone at the time of my parting, I will be stuck here between night and day for all eternity. And this is where you must put right the harm that you have done to me. In order that I can pass through the gates of Heaven to my eternal rest, you-Archibald McClung, my murderer must become as I am and remain here in my stead.'

'Never!' shouted Archie, grabbing a round, flat stone from the earth and hurling it into the face of his ghostly tormentor. The stone passed harmlessly through the deceased McGrogan striking the tree behind him. Archie turned and hurried, leaping and diving through the undergrowth to elude the horrific vision, stumbling awkwardly as the sadistic, clangy laughter echoed through the forest about him. 'Run Preacher!' called McGrogan; 'Run as far and fast as you may but no man may run from his day of reckoning. Mark my words well McClung, before 3 days and 3 nights have expired you will become like me.'

'I'll never be like you!' called back Archie as he huffed and puffed his way desperately through the pitch black forest. Eugene, Barra and Tomas had meanwhile ran back to the point where the track meets the lane, their initial search having proved fruitless. 'I thought I heard someone cry out.' Said Eugene; 'was it you?'

'No sir we heard the same cry and came back here to help.' answered Barra. 'I dearly hope he has not been injured, the journey before us in the morning will be strenuous enough without a cripple to carry.' said Eugene, pensively. 'Don't worry sir, the Preacher is quite familiar with the hardships of life having lived in our camp for nigh on a year now. He's a tough little fellow despite his somewhat comical appearance.' said Tomas.

'Bastard!' thought Archie, who was hiding in the bushes within earshot. 'There he goes mocking my personal appearance once again, and behind my back to boot. I have good mind to take revenge on the ill mannered cur. However, I need be silent for the time being. This may be a ruse to draw me out into the open.' The boys moved further away resuming their search. 'Aha!' thought McClung to himself; 'I have it. I will satirise the fool with a carefully composed ditty.' He crawled a little higher uphill and was able to observe McCafferty from some 50 yards distance. Rising up and cupping his hands to his mouth for amplification, Archie cried out; 'Tomas McCafferty is a big fat shite!' before running and diving once again through the dense forest undergrowth, stifling his laughter as his heart pounded at his act of daring do. The three turned and looked northward to the source of the insult. 'Did you hear that?' asked Eugene. 'I heard it all right!' replied Tomas, infuriated; 'He called me fat! He'll eat those words when I have hold of him!'

'Easy there Tomas, he's in the grip of madness don't you know.' advised Barra, calmly. 'He shall give account of his actions sooner or later, you mark my words.' replied Tomas. 'He appeared to be travelling in an eastern direction. I shall head Northwards to where his voice originated from, you two go Northeast and try to cut him off. We shall then work towards each other and try to entrap him.' ordered Eugene. Barra and Tomas stumbled off into the woods. After 6 seconds Barra called; 'Captain! Which way is Northeast?'

'There!' shouted Eugene, pointing. The boys took off like a couple of labradors after a stick whilst Eugene clambered uphill, shaking his head sceptically. Archie was meanwhile crawling on his hands and knees downhill, still overly amused at his insult to Tomas and trying to contain his mirth as he watched the boys' ineffective attempts at hunting him. Rapparees were typically well attuned to the art of concealments and camouflage, being as their life depended on it. Archie had been employing these skills for over a year, when circumstances had necessitated that he evade the army, militia, and Seamus whenever he had been on the hard stuff. 'See how I escape from these murderers like a shadow in the night.' he thought; 'They are no match for my superior intellect. I shall pass by them and through them all night like a spirit, until they are exhausted. Then I shall fall on them as the Holy spirit fell on the first born sons of Egypt!' He nodded to himself in agreement with this excellent plan.

Then he saw her; ahead of him in a small clearing, he perceived the head and shoulders of a young woman, fair in complexion as far as he could make out although her hair seemed to shine like a silvery grey in the moonlight. She was turned slightly to the side of him and her hair hung down over most of her face. Her hands were to her eyes and she sobbed gently. Archie was struck with a great feeling of pity towards this sad young woman, not wholly unlike the young widow who Barra had helped on the road earlier on that day. Despite the urgency of his own situation, he resolved that he would assist the lady in any way he could. Pushing his way through the brambles, Archie came to stand in the clearing alongside the unfortunate woman.

'Good evening young lady, my name is Archibald McClung. I couldn't help but notice that you appear to be in some sort of straights and I was hoping I could assist-'

The girl made no answer but continued to sob as if unaware of Archie's presence. He fumbled through his pockets and drew out a shilling, holding it towards in his outstretched hand with a smile. 'If it's money you have want of then I am able to aid you; see here a shilling, there is no call to pay me back.' She turned further away and continued to sob. Archie searched through his pockets again; 'Unfortunately my provisions have expired otherwise I would be pleased to offer you some bread. Perhaps we could pick some blackberries by way of sustinence, or on the morrow I could catch us a fish from the river?' Still no reply. Archie let the smile drop from his face and shifted awkwardly, then his face lit up with an idea; 'Perhaps prayer could be our remedy! Come let us pray to the Lord that a resolution to our woes may present itself; come.' Archie put his hand gently on the lady's arm, to which she instantly whirled round to show her face for the first time. But there was no face there, rather two dim red coals glowered fiercely from the hollow eye sockets of a bony skull; the frightful visage was picked clean of all living tissue save the long silvery hair that flew wildly about it. Archie realised at once that he had encountered the ghost of Deirdre O'Casey, otherwise known as the grey lady. As the jaw of the skull dropped open with a spine tingling, tortured scream, the wraith rose up four feet into the air and pointed its bony finger at the horror stricken rapparee. 'Archie McClung, I have come for your soul!' screamed the menacing phantom, as the wind whistled eerily about. McClung let loose a scream of his own and took off once again at his full pelt, with little regard of what lay before him. He stumbled over a root and tumbled head over heels downhill, finding himself on the track some 100 yards to the left from the point where it met the lane.

'Eugene! Did you hear that?' called Barra to the Frenchman. 'I heard another cry, but know not from whence it came.' Called back Eugene O'Cahan; 'The sound was unintelligible, either young McClung has come to some sort of error or he is now in the full flow of madness. Either way we must uncover him with all haste.'

'I think it came from further down the hill. We should make our way southwards towards the track sir.' suggested Tomas. 'Yes I would be inclined to agree with you; I will meet the two of you on the road.'

Archie had meanwhile gathered himself together and resolved to make his escape from the God-forsaken forest by whatever means necessary. 'A track,' he reasoned; 'well it has to lead somewhere.' He jogged off cautiously with a slight limp, hoping to avoid any further injurious mishaps in the darkness. After travelling some five minutes up the road he found himself at a crossroads, where the little track met the Banbridge to Dromore road; 'Good grief!' he thought 'I have travelled almost entirely back to the place where we carried out that ill advised robbery earlier in the day. I would hope that none of the militia yet remain, and that no further trepidations await me.'

Scanning around as carefully as possible given the almost total lack of light, his attention was taken by a large dark shadowy object hanging from a tree. Approaching with caution, he was able to discern the object as being a partially rotten corpse of a young man suspended from a thick chain and held fast inside a rusting, iron cage. The corpse was almost entirely fully clothed except that someone had bent the lower bars of the cage to relieve the poor wretch of his shoes. The face was partially skeletal and the eyes yet remained, giving it the appearance of a grizzly grinning ghoul. Archie by this time had seen such horror that the sight of a mere corpse was no longer a cause for distress to him. Staring up at the figure contemplatively, McClung said aloud; 'Alas my poor fellow, I wonder at what crimes you could have committed to warrant such harsh punishment.'

'Robbing on the highway sir!' called back a shrill, chirpy little voice. Archie jumped back aghast; 'You spoke! I'm sorry, you spoke did you not?'

'That I did sir, that I did. All of us deaduns can speak with the living in these here woods sir, if they but speak with us first;' the cheeriness of the voice was quite at odds with the corpse's macabre appearance, however despite his shock McClung felt himself to be in no imminent danger; 'Oh! Yes well, you have my very deepest sympathies my friend, I mean as serious as robbing is, there's no call for them to, well, you know-'

'Oh it's quite all right sir; I have quite a peaceful time of it here except for when those boys from earlier on came to poke me with their sticks. Thank you for throwing their shoes in the river by the way sir! It gave me quite a cheer.' Archie noticed that the cadaver's mouth did not move when it spoke, and thought he had heard a stifled giggling in the bushes. He wondered if someone might be making sport of him and resolved to keep the hanging man talking until he could discover the true source of the voice.

'So...' started McClung, trying to edge closer to the bushes where he suspected his prankster had concealed himself; 'You were hung for robbing on the highway, and were then taken to this place to serve as an example to others I presume? And can you tell me as to who pilfered your brogues then?'

'Well sir,' replied the voice ''twas the devil himself who took my shoes to prevent me from making my way to the gates of either his own kingdom or that of the heavenly father. He said that I must remain here to pass conversation with all who come hither and may tell them their fortune. But if anyone comes here to speak to me, they must first throw a shilling into that bush behind you there; and if any refuse me, I must pull them up here into the cage with me and hold them fast until the imps come to carry him away to the next world.'

Archie nodded in mock agreement; 'Do you mean,' asked the rapparee edging further back 'This bush?' and with that he thrust his hand deep into the bush, laying hold of the shirt sleeve of a stubby little arm. 'Aha! I have you now you little rogue!' he declared triumphantly pulling the small hand upwards by the wrist. However, McClung's victory was short lived as when the hidden figure rose, he discerned not the mischievous face of an innocent child, but the grotesque and bulbous features of a human toad! McClung instinctively let go the wrist and recoiled in horror, stumbling backwards and knocking his head on the dangling feet of the hanging man. Falling to his hands and knees, McClung watched in horror as three other hideous toad creatures emerged from the bushes, all pointing in a fit of giggling as he clambered in the mud. Letting out another scream he took off through the bushes once again bounding downhill towards the little river where Angus had earlier bade young John Higginson and his friends throw their shoes. He scrambled onto the river bank and bounced carelessly onto the stepping stones in the shallow place. The stones were wet and slippery and McClung's balance not being what it usually was, he soon found himself lying sideways on in the path of the slow rolling stream. The water was only 6 inches deep at this point but a man without his wits about him could drowned in less than that. Above him on the slope leading down to the river he could hear the whooping and chattering of his pursuers, but was now struggling with an unusual exhaustion. 'This is it. They're going to get me now!' thought the disconsolate McClung. However, he was soon relieved to feel a pair of unfamiliar but not unfriendly hands under his armpits, and was able to make out a second dark figure laying hold of his ankles.

'Quickly Ignatius!' said a rough but seemingly benevolent voice; 'we need to get him inside before he freezes.'

Up on the track, Barra had gained some pace on his fellows and had witnessed McClung's disappearance into the bushes; 'Quickly sir! Hurry Tomas! I have spotted McClung. He's being chased into the bushes by the Toad children!'

'What!' gasped Eugene, halting momentarily; 'Do you mean to tell me that these toad people actually exist then?'

'Of course they exist sir, do you think I have nothing better to do with my time than to go about making up silly stories? We must hurry sir, there's no telling what might become of Archie in his current state.'

Eugene unsheathed his rapier and ran after Barra. Running alongside the Frenchman Tomas puffed; 'I would request that you put that away sir, might be best to let me and Barra deal with this one.' O'Cahan duly complied, sensing there was more to this situation than what was currently apparent.

The sky was spinning above Archie as his two mysterious rescuers bore his aching body haphazardly through the bushes, down a narrow lane and into a little clearing where a small but cosily lit dry stone cottage sat, well out of the sight of any passing traveller; 'What will we do with him Cornelius?' asked the second good Samaritan, bearing the dizzy headed young rapparee's lower limbs. 'Put him up on the table beside her ladyship there.' replied a low gruff voice. Archie felt himself being placed gently upon a strong wooden bench or table, and a bag of hay being set behind his head as a pillow. The room continued to spin and vibrate for McClung who suspected that he might be suffering from the effects of extreme exhaustion, and palpitations of the heart. His vision was blurred and in the half darkness he was all but blind.

'Good sirs,' panted McClung; 'I must thank you most kindly for your hospitality, if by any chance I could trouble you for a drink of water, and perhaps a small piece of bread, I have but little money but I'd be more than happy to pay you back when I can.'

'Not at all young sir,' replied the first gruff voice, who Archie could just make out was hunched over, lighting an oil lamp on top of a rough wooden cabinet; 'consider it our pleasure.'

'Yes,' said the second; 'We'd be more than happy to have you for supper.'

As the oil lamp brightened the room and Archie's eyes came into focus, he was finally able to make out the two figures clearly. His gaze fell first on the man by the oil lamp. Being only about 5 foot 2 in height, he had the appearance of a man in his 60's, with a huge barrel torso but thin spindly arms and legs. His back was crooked and hunched and he stood with such a stoop that the apex of his back was above the crown of his head. He had but one bulging bloodshot eye and even the most charitable of observers could not help to notice his striking resemblance to - a toad! McClung's heart gave a jump but he tried to remain calm. Diverting his stare in order to avoid causing offence, he glanced at the second man. This fellow was of average height and stood as straight as any healthy person; his back was at first to Archie but as he turned slowly, his face was revealed to be horribly disfigured, with half his lip missing and his face ever fixed in a threatening snarl. He held a large, vicious looking knife in his hand, that appeared to be razor sharp and a foot long. But the greatest shock for Archie was yet to come; looking to his left, he found that he was not the only body on the heavy oak kitchen table. The body of a stout, grey haired woman in her early fifties lay face to face with him just inches away, her cold blue steely dead eyes fixing him in an unseeing stare. McClung instantly deduced that he had fallen into the lair of the toad people, and was about to become their latest meal unless he could make good his escape. Summoning his last reserves of energy, Archie rose from the table and dived for the door, pushing through the two murderous toad people and pelting down the narrow lane. He hadn't got far before two pairs of arms were around him from the front and struggle as he might, they were not letting him go. He fell to the ground sobbing and pleading and begging for it all to stop. Then a familiar voice said; 'Easy there Preacher! You are safe; we have you now.' McClung sat on the ground crying as Barra McCann rubbed his shoulder in consolation. 'I am undone!' he cried, shaking his head and blubbering like a baby. 'I have seen such horrors as no mortal man should. Devils and demons and ghosts and imps pursue me at every turn! What is to become of me!'

Barra stifled a giggle. Eugene O'Cahan spoke quietly and calmly; 'Archie, you may not understand what I am about to tell you, but after the – incident with Mrs O'Reilly, we discovered that you had helped yourself to a little midnight snack, did you not?'

McClung snivelled pathetically; 'Oh, please forgive me good sir. I was quite intolerably famished and took only a little handful of mushrooms.' Barra burst out laughing and was joined by Tomas who had just turned up with the four toad children in tow, his hands resting on the shoulder of two of them. Eugene smiled but resisted the temptation to mock his sergeant; 'Yes Archie, well we consulted with Mrs O'Reilly and it turns out the concoction which you helped yourself to, was shall we say- a potion put together by persons adept in certain practices in order to alter the perception of the senses.'

'It's the magic mushrooms Archie!' added Barra; 'You've been flying all night and we've been trying to catch you to tell you. Granny mixes that stuff up so she can talk with the people in the next world and tell the future; but it's not to be taken by the likes of us, you have to know what you're doing with it or you end up running about like a lunatic thinking all sorts!'

'I believe this sort of practise is typical of many shamanistic cultures in Africa and the new world,' added Eugene; 'The substances combine to confuse the senses and cause hallucinations. Fortunately the effects are temporary; you should be quite all right after a good night's sleep.'

'Aye Archie,' added Tomas; 'Sure young Barra there necked a ween of the mushrooms when he was a bairn and he's turned out all right.' Archie paused and looked up at Barra, then started sobbing again. 'But I lay with a subbuccus in the cottage! My willy is going to shrink away and drop off. '

'It can hardly shrink any smaller than it already is!' laughed Barra, joined approvingly by Tomas.

'I saw you dancing around like an idjit then you went behind the curtain, you didn't do anything though.' said Barra.

'Mrs O'Reilly says you only tried to lay down beside her,' continued Eugene reassuringly; 'you do understand that laying with a woman isn't just laying beside her don't you? You have to do things too.'

'I knew that!' sniffed Archie, lying.

Tomas laughed, and then Barra laughed too pretending to understand what Eugene meant. 'Well you don't have to worry about that then. Mrs O'Reilly was quite understanding once we'd established what was going on, she's fixing a tea for you at the minute which should help nullify the effects of the hallucinogen.' advised the Frenchman.

'Hello Ignatius! Hello Cornelius!' called Tomas to two approaching figures. 'Hello Tomas my boy!' called back one gruff voice. 'Is the wee lad all right?' Archie turned to see the two toad people from the cottage. 'There! See! Do my eyes deceive me now? Or are you going to deny the existence of these monstrous cannibals?' Tomas delivered a short sharp slap to the back of his head. 'You mind your manners young Archie, Sergeant or not. This here is Ignatius and Cornelius Toal, both of whom are good friends to the family.'

'I was just about to cut you a bit of bread and cheese when you ran out the door.' said Ignatius.

'Liar!' cried Archie, turning to Eugene and pointing to the two Toal brothers. 'He's lying sir. They have murdered a woman in that cottage and have laid out her body to eat on the table.'

'That woman there you mean?' said Ignatius, pointing. The boys looked to the door of the cottage to see a short plump woman in her early fifties waving to them. 'Katie has had to sleep on the table for some years past due to the pain in her back. She sleeps with her eyes open on account of having no eyelids.'

'Oh,' said Archie, quietly; 'I suppose that sounds plausible.'

'Hello Mrs Toal!' shouted Barra to Katie, waving.

'He's been on the magics Mr Toal, he's been running about mad all night and us after him too.' smiled Barra. 'And thesuns thought they'd join in on the hunt as well!' added Tomas, nodding to the Toad headed children. 'In the name of God, take those heads off boys you're scaring our guest here.' ordered Cornelius Toal. The boys duly removed their full head masks to reveal themselves to be quite normal, ginger headed freckle faced boys. 'And what do yousuns have to say for yourselves? You're old enough to know better than scaring a poor deluded imbecile like the Sergeant here young Connor' remarked Tomas, in mock judgement. Connor Toal shrugged; 'Sorry. It was only a bit of fun.'

'I would be inclined to agree. Just don't do it again.' said Eugene with a smile, stepping forward to examine the masks. 'These are very impressive. Did you make them yourselves?'

'Yes sir!' replied Connor; 'We made them with clay or mashed paper when we can get hold of any. We paint them ourselves. We have about a score of such masks, each one different.'

'Fascinating!' said Eugene, smiling; 'You have a great talent here, make sure you put it to good use.'

'Oh but we do sir!' replied the boy; 'We scare off nosey parkers and tithe collectors and the like. Keeps them from taking liberties with what was given us by God sir.'

'I should explain;' began Cornelius Toal; 'you have probably heard the rumours about toad headed people eating travellers on this side of the forest. Well as you can see, my brother and I are not exactly of a conventional appearance. We hailed originally from the townland of Edenderry, but were subject from a young age to all sorts of indignities at the hands of the general populace.

Our surname is Toal, but the jokers of the town thought it good sport to refer to us as the toad family.'

Ignatius nodded; 'Every person we met called us it and every one of them thought themselves the first one to have thought of the joke. People are utterly predictable in their spite.'

'Aye sure I used to know a fella called William Hearthen and everybody used to call him wee Willy Hardon. He didn't appreciate the humour one bit.' laughed Barra. Eugene raised an eyebrow then shook his head disparagingly.

Cornelius continued; 'We have learnt that people can be quite uncharitable to those of us who are unfortunately cast, so many years ago we made the decision that rather than enduring the cruel taunts of the uneducated, we would come here to live in splendid isolation.'

'I am sorry to hear that, as you are obviously both fine honest men. I personally am of the opinion that the good Lord loves us all in equal measure, regardless of the cut of our cloth or the situation at birth. Wouldn't you agree, Archie?' said Eugene, sympathetically. Archie nodded apologetically; 'I am sorry that I judged you so harshly when not in full possession of the facts. Please forgive me.'

'Ah never mind son, we are used to people keeking themselves when they first catch sight of us. Water off a duck's back to us.' replied Cornelius, generously.

'But you need fear no more; I shall speak with Shane and we shall ensure that everyone knows the Toal family are under our protection.' added Eugene.

'Oh no sir, there's no need!' replied Cornelius; 'You see over the years people have forgotten the origin of the story of the Toal family, and I suppose through the telling of drunken tales, have constructed such a myth that is sufficient enough to terrify them out of coming here. I suppose the boys' little japes with their masks have contributed to this. However, it serves us well that no one comes here and no one knows what we get up to- we have business here you see.' he tapped the side of his nose to emphasize the final sentence.

'Cornelius and Ignatius here are the finest manufacturers of poteen in the north of Ireland.' explained Tomas.

'Perhaps we could tempt you all with a wee dram?' asked Ignatius, hospitably.

'Oh that would be lovely!' said Tomas, rubbing his hands. 'I think,' said Eugene, 'we would be better advised to get young McClung back to Mrs O'Reilly's so he can sleep off the effects of the draught. Another time gentlemen.' Eugene gave a partial bow and tipped the peak of his hat. The boys said their goodbyes and ambled off back to Sadie O'Reilly's cottage, where after the necessary apologies had been made, Archie received a special brew to help neutralise the effects of the potion. The boys settled down to sleep once again, managing to get a few hours in before preparing for their journey back to Slieve Croob. Archie thought about the events of that night, and how it had been impossible to tell what was reality and what was an illusion; 'So the visions I saw;' he thought; 'The Fairy Queen, Seamus, the grey lady – were they all simply delusions caused by this little concoction created to baffle the mind? Or was there something else? Was the potion somehow allowing me to peer into a realm of existence which at other times is invisible to the eyes of mortal man?'

At length he proposed that it could only really be looked at as a matter of interpretation; some may choose to believe that what he had seen and heard that night was a mere trickery of the senses, others may choose to believe that there were other planes of reality which existed alongside our own, which on occasion, may overlap with the world of men. Perhaps one day science could offer a more satisfactory explanation of the events that took place that night, but for now, it was best to put it from one's mind and concentrate on the task of completing the mission. In the morning, the rapparees would treck the 16 odd miles to Slieve Croob in ones or twos to avoid suspicion. They would meet with Shane and deliver up the necklace as requested. Eugene would explain the killing of Seamus and the boys would vouch for him, Shane would understand and they would be able to put the past behind them. The worst of it was over. That was how it was supposed to happen anyway.

# 10. THE DUEL

The sun was just beginning to poke it's face above the horizon when Richard Pilkington, his adversary Viscount Wills Hill of Hillsborough, their seconds Colonel Roger Lambert and Sergeant Seymour Wilkes of the 37th North Hampshire Regiment, and spectators Lady Isabella Murray of Atholl and Mademoiselle Amelie Babineax took to the field, or rather the lawn outside the Viscount's country estate. 'A fine to do this is.' Thought a fearful Pilkers; 'Here I am, only hours after heroically defending the household from a murderous robber and uncovering a plot to kill the King at great danger to my own safety, about to be run through as reward for my actions! Where oh where is the justice in this world?'

'All fired up to go sir?' said Sergeant Wilkes cheerfully, rubbing his hands. Pilkers glanced over to where the Viscount stood, haughtily examining his blade. He watched as Wills picked up an apple from a silver platter being held aloft by Forbes, and after taking a bite, tossed it into the air. Isabella and Amelie gasped and clapped as the Viscount cut the fruit into 4 equal parts in mid air. He nodded to the girls with a self satisfied grin and then raised an eyebrow in the direction of the terrified Captain. Pilkington gulped nervously. 'It's probably all show sir, don't let it put you off your game.' said Wilkes, reassuringly; 'Just remember, block, counter, parry and strike, keep it simple. Oh and if he does turn out to be any good then surrender at the earliest possible opportunity.'

Pilkers wondered if perhaps the matter could be settled with a game of chess instead. 'Wilkes! A word please.' called the Colonel, walking over to where the two stood. 'Certainly sir.' replied Wilkes. 'Now listen carefully, by careful negotiation and with the kind assistance of the Lady Murray, I have been able to persuade the Viscount that given the sensitivity of the current situation, the potential termination of a young officer by duelling with a member of Parliament would be liable to shed an ill light both on the regiment and on the Viscount's good name. Therefore, this will not be a duel to the death.'

'Oh hooray!' sighed Pilkington, with massive relief. 'Thank you so much uncle Roger, I could kiss you!'

'Do you forget yourself sir?' replied Lambert angrily.

'Forgive me sir, I mean uncle, sir, Colonel uncle Roger sir.' replied the captain, shakily. Colonel Lambert sighed but decided to let the matter go as there were more important things to worry about. 'As I was saying, this is not to be a duel to the death, however, in order for honour to be satisfied, some blood must be spilled. A small nick to the hand should do the trick, so just stand still, let him do it, then you can both put up your swords and leave the field.'

'Blood spilled?' gasped Pilkers; 'A nick on the hand? Is that really necessary, I mean what if it turns septic?'

'Oh for Heaven's sake Richard, don't be such a crying little ginny! I've been stabbed 3 times and shot twice myself, one expects these things when one joins the King's army. Now you will go out on to the field sir, and acquit yourself like a true gentleman. Otherwise, when I've finished with you a nick on the hand will be the least of your worries!' with that, the Colonel stormed back over to the Viscount and the girls. 'There you are sir, not so bad then eh?' beamed Wilkes; 'and you don't even need to surrender! Don't worry about the hand, we'll get it bandaged up right away and you'll be as right as rain within a couple of days. Give us a brave smile now sir, here they come.'

The Viscount was impeccably dressed in a dark red velvet frock coat with matching breeches, yellow waist coat and dazzling white shirt and stockings. He removed his coat and held it out without a word to a waiting Forbes, who duly received it and folded it carefully. His gaze did not leave Pilkington's eyes the whole time, as if trying to intimidate his opponent, not that any further threat was necessary. Wills was well aware that Pilkington was terrified and although he had no desire to cause the Captain any great physical harm, he did want to teach him a lesson he would never forget. But the unanswered questions of the night before still persisted. Why did that rapparee fellow come to the house? Why did Isabella not scream instead of trying to reason with the knave? And what of her uncle in exile, had she communicated with him, could she possibly have sympathy with the Jacobite cause, even against the interests of her own father? These questions about his friend troubled him; he knew he should be addressing the issues himself, but he had tried to bury them for the love of Isabella. All Pilkington was in truth guilty of was forcing these unpleasant ideas to the surface, bringing them into the cold light of day for all to see. Wills was angry but he knew in truth that he was angrier with himself than he was with the Captain, and it was partly for this reason that he had agreed that the matter could be settled without the termination of either party.

'Now then sirs;' said Colonel Lambert; 'you will each withdraw five paces and thence unsheathe your blades when so bidden. Neither party may strike until I give the order.'

The Viscount remained staring into Pilkington's face while all this was said, the two men being of about equal height. Finally both turned back to back and advanced five paces. They turned and faced each other. 'On guard gentlemen.' called the Colonel. The Viscount drew his sword, but a trembling Captain stood unsurely. 'You need to draw your sword sir.' whispered a nearby Sergeant Wilkes. Pilkington shakily struggled to get the blade out before Wilkes stepped forward and assisted him with removing it from the scabbard. The Colonel rolled his eyes; 'and begin.' he said defeatedly, shaking his head. Pilkers held up his blade awkwardly as the Viscount edged expertly forward, on his guard. As the Viscount drew nearer, Pilkers edged back. 'Stand your ground sir!' called Wilkes, helpfully. Pilkington edged back more quickly and the Viscount picked up his pace to compensate. Feeling queasy at the sight of the Viscount's long slender blade, the

Captain turned around and bolted in a fit of panic. Unsure how to address this new situation, the Viscount chased after him, and was for several minutes pursuing the cowardly Captain as he dodged behind people, garden furnishings, and ornamental hedges. 'Pilkington!' shouted the enraged Colonel; 'I order you to stand your ground sir!' The order was duly ignored by the panic stricken Captain. Finally he ran behind Wilkes, who stood still as the two men paced around him.

'Come out from there you dashed coward!' called Wills.

'Perhaps we could resolve this with a game of cricket. Or golf! I'm quite good at golf. Handicap of four!' reasoned the Captain. 'You'll be bloody handicapped in a minute if you don't come out of there!' cried Wills, infuriated by Pilkington's time wasting. The Viscount finally made an ill judged, off balance lunge which connected his steel with soft human skin and bone, but not Pilkingtons; 'Aaaaaarrrggghh!! Me foot! Me foot!' cried Sergeant Wilkes, receiving his first wound in an army career spanning over 3 decades. The girls gasped and even Pilkington stopped thinking about himself for a few moments. 'Good grief! My dear fellow I really am terribly sorry. Forbes! Fetch the stretcher and summon the physician.' ordered the Viscount. Two footmen appeared and loaded the injured Wilkes onto a stretcher.

'That's enough swordplay for today gentlemen. I should never have agreed to this in the first place.' said a rueful Colonel Lambert. Wills and Pilkers duly complied. Lambert walked alongside the moving stretcher; 'I dare say at your age this will be the end of your career Wilkes. I'm very sorry as men of your calibre are hard to the come by. I shall ensure that you receive a letter of commendation and full pension rights.'

'Thank you most kindly sir.' said Wilkes weakly, struggling to contain his glee.

Betty Higginson was polishing the back room of the butcher's shop with a fanatical zest whilst every now and again cursing her husband under her breath for taking his absence on a working day. George had taken one of the horses just before the scrake of dawn to set out on his journey to Downpatrick, where he intended to lodge his highly questionable claim to the £20 reward money for the capture of the infamous rapparee Seamus McGrogan, whose enormous mouldering corpse was at that moment taking up half the main room. Betty had argued with him fruitlessly, pointing out that many people had borne witness to the fact that George was a relative latecomer to the death scene; and was he sure that this claim would not constitute fraud if he was found out? George had stated somewhat ambiguously that as he was the Captain of the militia who had captured the carcass he was legally entitled to the reward money, but could not quote line or verse where this was stated in law.

Betty's parting words to her husband had been; 'Well go get yourself put in jail then, tis little odds to me!' She regretted the harshness of this statement, the sentiment of which George had come to view as typical behaviour from his overly excitable wife. Though they cared for each other in an affectionate although not passionate way, they were a terrible mismatch as a married couple. Betty was grateful to George for having rescued her from dire circumstances and offering her a decent standard of living, far above the level that her own parents had aspired to as common field labourers. George was a good couple of decades her senior, already a widower with an 8 year old son when they met. A life of 14 hour days bent double in the fields can put decades on a woman, and Betty was keen to make her escape before she ended up broken before her time as her mother had done. She had caught George's eye on more than one occasion whilst out making deliveries and when his first wife lost her life in the typhoid epidemic, he needed to move fast to find a new mother for his boy.

Betty had thrown herself vigorously into the role of wife and mother and had driven George's career forward with constant hen pecking and hard work to match, but her devotion to the shop and to the boy John, who was in truth a bone idle shister whose sole aspiration in life seemed to be to cause irritation to others, were merely symptomatic of the crushing boredom she felt. Betty didn't really know what she wanted in life, but despite her reasonably comfortable situation she felt terribly unfulfilled. She thought about the events of the previous night; the madness that seemed to overtake her when she led the charge against the rapparees. She recalled how she had felt the blood flow and her heart pump as she charged into the fray. It was an insanely dangerous thing to do, she could have so easily been shot, or stabbed or trodden under the horses. So close to death, and yet – she could not recall a single time in her life when she felt more alive! She thought for a minute about men, boys, the likes of young John who lay upstairs snoring his head off. So many opportunities they were given to live exciting and fruitful lives, and yet most of them wasted theirs by settling for safety and mediocrity. Oh to be able to enlist with the army, the navy, anything other than the mind numbing monotony of everyday life. It wasn't fair; Betty scrubbed harder and cursed harder in her bitterness. Scrub scrub scrub, but you can't scrub clean an unquiet mind.

The bell above the door in the front of the shop tinkled, signalling that someone had entered. 'John, get that will you my love.' She said, before remembering John was still snoozing away peacefully upstairs. Tutting with annoyance she wiped her hands and forcing a smile, proceeded into the shop front. 'Mrs Clinton!' she said pleasantly; 'I'm afraid George isn't here at the moment, he's gone into Downpatrick on important militia business. I can call John down if you need some meat cutting.'

'That won't be necessary dear,' replied Ma Clinton;'It's actually militia business which I came to see George about. Do you know when he's likely to return?'

Betty shrugged; 'Early evening I would hope. Is it anything I could help you with? Or could I give George a message?'

Mrs Clinton shook her head with a smile; 'Not really a woman's affair Betty. I wanted to report the attempted theft of a horse from the farm.' Betty's eyes lit up; 'Really? Well I am sure that George would want me to take as many details as possible in order to assist his operations. Please do tell.'

'Well you see, it was yesterday evening, when Kenneth and Gareth were away, I heard a terrible commotion coming from the yard. Luckily I had my late husband's trusty flintlock at hand so I felt safe enough to go down and investigate. Anyway who should it be but some young ne'r do well making off with the grey mare! I shouted to him to stop but he took no notice, so having given him fair warning I let loose a barrel full of shot at him. And would you know, I hit the little bugger!'

Ma Clinton's wrinkled face beamed triumphantly with a toothless smile at the last sentence. 'Very well done, Mrs Clinton, so, did the thief escape with the horse?' queried Betty.

'No dear, that's the thing. A few hours later she wandered back to the farm of her own accord! Saddle and all. Kenneth found some spots of blood on the track in the morning, so he must have been too badly injured to ride further. The boys are looking around the fields to see if his body's about; would there be any reward if we were to bring him in?' said Ma Clinton, rubbing her hands expectantly. 'As far as I'm aware he would have to be a prescribed rapparee, and you need to bring him in dead or alive, just wounding him would avail you not. I am not sure if it would be advisable for members of the public to hunt for rapparees alone, they are very violent and desperate men.'

Ma Clinton nodded; 'Aye I thought as much. Well if you could mention it to your husband, perhaps he could send some of the men to keep an eye out? Also if George is looking for men to serve in the militia, Gareth and Kenneth can manage most evenings, between 6 and 10.' Betty nodded; 'I shall mention it to George when he returns from Downpatrick Mrs Clinton.'

'Thank you dear. Goodbye!'

'Goodbye!' waved Betty. She stood and waited, watching through the window as Mrs Clinton climbed aboard her pony trap and made for home. She walked through to the back room and took down her Grandfather's pistol again. 'John!' she called, to the slumbering apprentice upstairs. 'I'm just taking the horse and going out for a while. Don't bother opening up. Take the day off but don't go anywhere near the woods.'

'Mmmmmm.....' came the careless reply.

Archie had been allowed to sleep longer than what would normally be advisable given the potential danger of rapparee hunters, at the bequest of Sadie O'Reilly who had assured Eugene it was necessary to alleviate the effects of the potion. Archie had lain awake for a good portion of that time watching the flashing lights and strange visions in his head, resisting the urge to react to them by reciting the King James bible in his mind. He had eventually drifted off in the middle of a smiting and had then slept soundly for a couple of hours, before awakening to a dry tongue, groggy head and bits of straw stuck to his face. He had the good sense this time to ask for a drink of water before taking it and as he sat on the floor sipping from a large earthen beaker, his attention was taken by the sound of Barra and Eugene arguing outside. His raging paranoia had not quite extinguished and every sense felt raw to the bone; in his weakened mental state he worried that they might be arguing over him, either Eugene wanting to punish him for ruining the mission or Barra still wanting satisfaction for his Grandmother. Pressing his ear to the door he was relieved to hear that Tomas was the subject of the discussion.

'Honestly sir, I looked all along the river bank and he's not there. He left two hours ago to catch fish for our breakfast and what has become of him I know not. He wouldn't just go off a wandering at his leisure without telling us, something must have happened to him.' said Barra's voice. Archie walked to the door and peered out.

'He has the jewel Barra; the reason we set out on this mission in the first place. We must recover the jewel. I will ask you one more time;' said Eugene, pointing his gloved finger close Barra's face; 'Where is your cousin?'

'Hang on there sir,' said Archie, speaking in his friend's defence; 'I'm not sure exactly what has happened here, and I cannot vouch to Tomas. But I can assure you that I know Barra very well and would trust him with my last sixpence. If he says he knows not what became of Tomas, then he knows not.' Archie surprised both himself and his fellows with his forthright opinion. Eugene stood looking at him for a second, then glanced at Barra, then turned his back shaking his head.

'All I can think,' said Barra, 'is that he's been got by something or somebody. Maybe a bear, or a river dragon, or the shadow man!'

'No!' said Archie, sternly; 'No, no, no. No river dragons, no ghosts, no goblins, no fairies or toad people. No more of that shite do you understand? I do not want to hear another word about these fantastical creatures that you seem to think lurk behind every tree trunk in this horrible forest. No more, do you understand?'

'Ah frigg off!' said Barra, turning his back and kicking some stones. 'We need to think what really happened to Tomas, no more silly stories. There is too much at stake.' continued Archie. He turned to look at Eugene. 'Tomas was no coward, he wouldn't have deserted. But there's no denying he had a weakness for the liquor and for women and gambling.'

'Ha!' interrupted Barra, who marched up to McClung's face; 'You stand there talking about Tomas behind his back when he might well have been murdered. Weakness for women? You tried to ride my Granny last night you filthy devil!' with that he gave Archie a rather ineffectual push in the chest.

'I am trying to surmise what has become of Tomas you fool, you would be better served to assist me rather than taking up his part! What do you think Shane will do if we return to him empty handed, with one brother slain and God knows what has happened to the other?' shouted Archie angrily.

Gaining some composure, Eugene interjected; 'He spoke of the Americas last night. He said he never wanted to be a rapparee in the first place, and that he intended to blackmail the person whose letter he had to gain his fare and the price of a farm. Could he perhaps have gone to make use of this stratagem?'

Archie shook his head; 'There was no address on that letter, the old man must have been delivering it in person. Tomas isn't a great reader, I would be surprised if he hadn't have thrown it away already.' Everyone paused to think again. Eugene raised his index finger; 'Perhaps he went to gain his passage by other means! Could he be intending to sell the jewellery?'

'But sir, no one round here would have the means to buy such an item!' protested Barra. 'Not all of it,' countered Archie; 'but he did say that he could maybe sell some of the smaller stones at Roscoe the jewellers in Banbridge.'

'Surely he would not be so foolish as to wander into that pit of snakes!' replied Eugene, aghast; 'You saw the hatred on the faces of the mob last night, they would as like tear anyone they suspect of being a rapparee limb from limb were they to lay hold of them.'

Archie shrugged; 'Some of the lads go into the towns and villages all the time. It's quite safe unless you are seen by someone you've robbed, if anyone asks they just claim to be a tinker or salesman.'

Eugene nodded; 'So he may well have determined to sell some of the stones for his fare and keep the rest to make his life in the new world, the devious swine!'

'Houl on there, neither of you two know that. He might have headed straight back to Slieve Croob to meet with Shane!' argued

Barra. 'And he did so without leaving word with any of us?' countered Eugene. 'There is no option other than I shall have to go into Banbridge to look for Tomas and recover the jewel. You and Barra may make your way separately to Slieve Croob in order to avoid arousing further suspicion.'

'With all due respect sir, given your current apparel you would likely be of some note to the simple people of the town. It might be better if I were to go into the town and bring Tomas out.' replied Archie.

'But you are known to the townspeople are you not?' cautioned Eugene. 'I am aye, but I was but a boy when last there and my appearance has greatly altered over the past year.' replied Archie. He wasn't lying, the harsh mountain conditions could put decades on a man. 'Besides,' he continued; 'Given that I am responsible for Seamus' death, I am necessitated to make use of all available opportunities to ingratiate myself to Shane.'

Eugene nodded; 'Very well. Make your way into town and complete the mission, and do so with God's speed. We shall meet with you again on the mountain.'

Gareth Clinton was idly poking the thick end of his cudgel into a thick rowan hedge with as little enthusiasm as a man can muster for a task whilst actually doing it. 'I don't like this Kenneth,' he sighed; 'are you sure we won't upset the little people by poking around in their bushes?'

'Little people?' repeated Kenneth, raising his head from the stock of the flintlock he had trained on the bushes where Gareth was carrying out his investigations. 'The only place that's full of fairies round here is in between your ears Gareth. For a man who went to school anybody would think you were dragged up. This here is a rowan bush, no different from any other and just because you heard some oul biddies saying there were people living in it you take it as gospel. I despair of you Gareth, I really do.'

Gareth gritted his teeth at his brother's unnecessarily harsh reaction to a perfectly reasonable question. Sometimes Gareth could swing for him, there was no call for such rudeness. Kenneth was capable of being polite to other people, why not his own brother? 'Surely this is a waste of time anyway. The'on fella would have scarpered long ago, if he was still alive. We've been looking for a couple of hours now, I'm famished too.'

'What!' exclaimed Gareth;'You had breakfast not two hours ago, a giant bowl of porridge you had.'

It was actually a fairly medium sized bowl. 'I could well do with a lovely big plate of bacon and eggs, and a nice big cup of warm milk.' replied Kenneth.

'Bacon and eggs!' cried Kenneth, theatrically; 'I do beg your pardon your lordship, I had no idea I was in the presence of the Duke of York.' He punctuated his sarcasm with a low bow. 'You shall know your arse from your elbow my lad, when mother passes on. I'll soon put a stop to your extravagant ways whenever I am master of the farm.'

'Ha!' said Gareth; 'That's a snake's thinking and no mistake. Well you are sadly misled Kenneth, what makes you think that you're going to inherit the whole of the farm? It will be split between us, there's more than enough for both. And when I have my share, I shall be paying a visit to Arthur Henderson and asking him for Gracie's hand in marriage.'

'Half the farm? Gracie Henderson? Brother you do indeed live in a dream world. I am the elder brother you will find, albeit by 15 minutes. But Father left very specific instructions that I alone am to inherit the farm. He didn't want it split, especially not for you to let it go to wreck and ruin! Oh yes it's all in the will, I have seen it with my own two eyes. Of course you'll be more than welcome to stay on, but you shall have to get used to getting your back into a bit of work.' spat Kenneth, with a cruel glare.

Gareth stood open mouthed in disbelief, as his bullying brother turned his back contemptuously. Gareth gripped the cudgel hard and watched his knuckles turn white.

'Of course if you do want to marry, you would need to leave the farm as a house can have but one lady and one master. I can't imagine they'd be lining up to marry a man with no property though.' continued Kenneth, bending down to peer into another bush. 'Perhaps I myself shall call on Arthur Henderson and ask for Gracie's hand!' Gareth imagined himself raising the cudgel up above his unsuspecting brother's head, preparing to strike. At that moment a determined voice called out; 'You men! Put down your weapons and put up your hands!' Turning, the brothers saw a middle aged man in a broad brimmed hat, leather jerkin and riding boots with a 41 inch long Potzdam rifle, of the type used by frontiersmen in the American colonies, trained on Kenneth. 'Do it!' demanded the newcomer; 'I don't miss with this thing.' The brothers put their weapons on the ground and raised up slowly with their palms turned outward. Several other men appeared and picked up the weapons, before a large bald headed man with a huge moustache stepped forward and examined the flintlock.

'What's all this about?' asked Kenneth, nervously. 'If it's money you're after we haven't got any. You can keep the gun if you like.'

'Have our shoes too!' added Gareth; 'We heard you're looking for shoes.'

Daniel Phillips didn't answer at first, continuing to examine the gun. Finally he spoke; 'Are you Shane McGrogan's men?'

'Heaven's no!' said Kenneth; 'That's who we thought you were; we're just farmers, we came up here to see if we could find any sign of the hoodlum who tried to steal one of our horses last night.'

'You're up looking for rapparees eh? And what were you planning to do whenever you found them, tickle them to death?' barked Hawkins, dismissively. The men all laughed and Gareth laughed a bit too, pleased to see his brother being the one to be picked on for a change. 'We wounded him, we thought he might have come up here to find his companions and thereby expired. I didn't catch your name there sir-' explained Kenneth.

'He didn't give it.' said Phillips; 'We'll be needing proof of your identity though.'

'By what authority can you make such a demand of us?' demanded Kenneth. 'By this authority!' answered John Hawkins cocking the rifle. Gareth and Kenneth looked one to the other. 'Ask Captain George Higginson who we are! He's the captain of our militia, he swore us in last night.' blurted Gareth. Phillips sighed; 'Everybody wants to be in the militia. All up for setting light to the thatch of some oul doll's roof then they shite themselves when the balls start flying.'

'Bloody do-gooders are more of a danger to the public than the rapparees are!' added Hawkins. 'Right then your 'captain' would have given you a signed letter detailing your oath to the King and your permissions to carry out your duties. Let me see them please and you may be on your way.'

'I've mine here!' said Gareth, pulling the rolled up paper from his pocket and holding it out. Michael Darroch stepped forward and unrolled the note, then turned to Hawkins and nodded. 'Sorry for the inconvenience Mr Clinton.' said Michael to Gareth; 'you may be on your way.'

Michael turned to Kenneth Clinton, expectantly. 'I haven't mine with me.' said Kenneth. The men looked at each other suspiciously. 'When I get an important piece of paper, I take it home and put it in the box in my bedroom with my other important papers, like what normal people do. I don't roll it up in a ball and stick it in my pocket like some sort of idiot. My brother here will vouch for me.'

The men turned to Gareth, awaiting his confirmation. Gareth paused and thought, then declared; 'I've never seen this man before in my life.'

'What!' cried Kenneth. 'You shall have to accompany us until your identity can be made known sir.' said Michael, pulling Kenneth's hands down and attaching a rope to his wrists. 'Gareth! You come back here! I shall tell mother about this!' shouted Kenneth, as Gareth walked on down the road smiling to himself. Michael trussed Kenneth Clinton up good and tight and began marching him in the opposite direction. 'I shall put him in the camp with the rest of the suspects, we've over a dozen now so I'll need another man to help me keep an eye on them.'

'We need everyone out searching, I don't pay men to sit idle all day.' replied Phillips. 'Keep them all sitting in a line and if any of them move just shoot them. They're all well trussed up so they're going nowhere anyway.' added Hawkins. Michael sighed at this reckless plan but he knew there was no point in arguing. He would need to watch these boys like a hawk all day, no chance of sleeping off that hangover. In truth it wasn't a difficult task, if people knew that the first one to make a move would get a lead ball between the eyes they tended to wait and wait until someone else took the risk.

Phillips pointed to some track marks in the road; 'Look, that to me looks like it was made by two horses pulling a cart at full gallop. That must have been made by the militia...' he scanned around; 'and there! There was a lot of blood spilled right here. This is the place, without a doubt.' Several of the men started looking about the bushes. 'Be careful there boys, we don't want you destroying any leads we might have here.' cautioned Hawkins.

'I've found something Danny!' called one of the men. 'What is it Sam?' called Daniel Phillips into the bushes. 'A window pole!' called the man, holding his prize aloft with a smile. 'Well hold on to it. If it gets too hot later on we can open a window.' replied Phillips. The man shrugged and tossed Betty Higginson's pole back into the bushes where he found it. 'It appears to me,' said Hawkins, at length; 'that some of them escaped downhill here to the river, see where the grass is broken and the footprints in the mud down there.' Phillips peered over; 'Ah yes.'

'The others,' continued Hawkins; 'escaped up through these bushes and over yonder hill. The ones who went through the river acted correctly as those who went uphill would have had their route back to Slieve Croob cut off by the militia.'

Phillips nodded; 'So no doubt they would have had to make camp somewhere up there before making their way home again. It makes sense. Bring the trackers up, we shall discover their camp and with some luck maybe even take them unawares.'

Barra and Eugene had meanwhile set off separately to make their way back to Slieve Croob, well aware of the risk of capture and the possibility that the country between where they were now and their destination could well be infested by the army, militia, bounty hunters and nosey farmers. Barra for his part, had decided he would travel due east and then take a sharp turn southwards, whereas Eugene opted to take the South Eastern path. The two had parted awkwardly as Eugene was starting to show the first signs of annoyance following the loss of the necklace, and Barra resented both the insinuation that Tomas had stolen the jewel and the accusation that he himself was involved. He had climbed a steep hill with his usual goat like agility and was pleasantly surprised at how easy it was to traverse the rocky patches in his new shoes, although he preferred to remove them altogether on the easier stretches, enjoying the cool moisture of the grass between his toes that he had become accustomed to. Barra made no effort to conceal himself as having no weapon save for his butcher's hook, he was not in violation of any law and was doing nothing to draw suspicion to himself. 'This is the way to do it,' he thought to himself; 'The'on fancy drawers Frenchman will probably try to hide behind every bush and hedge from here to there, it will take him days to get home! Bloody stuck up know it all.' Barra smiled at the thought of Eugene with bits of twigs and leaves stuck in his hat to hide from the hunters. He imagined Eugene standing in shite with his fine shoes and giggled to himself. Sometimes the only way to stay sane is to laugh at your own jokes. McCann idled along the top of the hill kicking lazily at the grass and giving no great measure of thought to anything in particular. His ears pricked up at a faint crying on the wind. He stopped and listened. 'Where's that coming from?' he thought. He heard it again, and was this time able to discern the source. Scrambling over the brow of the hill he saw two small raggedly dressed children crying. He rushed up and knelt beside them. 'There now, everything's fine! Tell uncle Barra what's happened.' The children pointed over the edge of the ridge. Barra peered over the edge and was surprised to see Annie O'Hare, the woman he met last night before the ambush, perched precariously on a ledge some ten feet down. The ledge was some 2 or 3 feet wide and beneath that again was another 30 feet drop onto jagged rocks. 'Annie!' called Barra; 'What are you sitting there for?' Annie had been sitting with her arms crossed over her knees and her head buried in her lap. 'I'm laying an egg, what does it look like.' came the reply. Barra looked puzzled, having always struggled with the concept of sarcasm. She looked up at him with red eyes; 'I fell over the edge in the dark. I've been sitting here for hours but nobody came.'

'Are you hurt?' called Barra again. 'No but I don't know how I'm going to get off this ledge, there's nowhere to go but down.' replied Annie. 'Don't worry, leave this to me.' assured Barra, trying to hide his nervousness. He didn't know quite how he was going to do it but he knew he had to first get down there and help Annie up, then worry about getting himself out. It was quite a drop to the first ledge and landing suddenly would quite possibly send him off balance and tumbing into the ravine below. He pondered the problem for several seconds, then the solution came to him in a flash; the hook! He retrieved the large bill hook from his inside pocket and studied it with new eyes. The vicious looking iron hook was cast to support the weight of a cow's carcass, and would not be greatly troubled by either his own slight figure or by Annie's. He unfastened the coarse rope holding his coat together and after removing the coat and placing it on the ground, he fed the end of the rope through the eye of the hook and tied it tightly. He pulled it several times to reassure himself of its strength and searching around, thanked his good fortune to find a conveniently placed fracture in the rock face. Attaching his improvised apparatus firmly, he slid himself feet first over the edge of the cliff face and lowered himself down as far as possible, before dropping the final few feet. He turned carefully and stared over the precipice breathing a sigh of relief, before turning to Annie and smiling. 'Now,' He began; 'I shall lift you up so that you can grasp the end of the rope, and thereafter assist you as best I can to push yourself up over the edge.'

Annie looked up and then at Barra; 'And then how will you get off the ledge?' she asked, anxiously.

'Don't worry,' replied Barra; 'I have a plan for that.' He hadn't. Kneeling down Barra cupped his hands together to receive Annie's foot. He heaved her up quickly and she grabbed at the rope in a panic before gaining a firm grasp, slipping down slightly to find herself standing on Barra's face. Barra stood on his tip toes and pushed her up as far as possible before she was able to pull herself over the edge. 'Are you over?' called Barra. 'Yes but now how do we get you up?' answered Annie.

'I think I can climb up the side here a bit and make a jump for the rope.' came the reply. Barra was not at all confident of this plan but decided to try it for want of a better one. Clinging to the ledge face, he managed to draw his shoulder level to the end of the rope but some four feet away. 'Can you reach the hook?' he called. 'Yes,' replied Annie; 'I think so.'

'I require you to swing the rope back and forth so that I can make a grasp at it when it draws near. Do you think you can do that?'

'I'll try.' said Annie. As the rope toggled backwards and forwards, Barra timed its movements for when came close to him. Three, two, one, Barra launched himself the two feet across through the air and grasped the rope with both hands. He swung back hitting his side off the rock face painfully, but adrenalin prevented him from being winded as he scrambled upwards for his life, being hauled the final foot or so by a grateful and relieved Annie. The two lay silently staring skywards for a few minutes as the children crowded round Annie for comfort. Barra struggled to take in the magnitude of the undoubtedly heroic deed that he had just performed. Finally they both sat up. Barra retrieved his hook; 'No doubt about it, this here hook is the finest gift that providence ever sent my way. I shall treasure you for always, my old friend,' he said, planting a kiss on the iron hook. 'So what now?' said Annie, combing her hair back.

'Well I'll be honest with you. I am a wanted man with no money, no trade, no skills and less than half my teeth remaining. However, it is my intention to henceforth find my fortune in this world by hook or by crook, if you pardon the pun. I have a cousin who has an idea to escape to the Americas and there make his fortune, and I myself share in this ambition. I have not yet devised the means to achieve this goal, but I can assure you that it shall be so. I would desire nothing more than for you and the childer to enjoin me in this endeavour.' Barra knew not where this sudden inspiration sprang from, and was both shocked and embarrassed at his sudden outburst. Annie sat silently for several seconds before speaking. Her appearance was quite restored from the vision of destitution that had greeted him the night before, the light of hope restored to her eyes; 'Well then,' she answered; 'we'd better get started then!' They each picked up a child and started walking.

Phillips and Hawkins stood staring in dismay at the horrific scene before them, wondering if there was really any future for humanity at all. They had known the bodies were there before they set eyes on them, as even a lifetime of snorting snout and drinking whisky in every tavern between Dundalk and Ballycastle wasn't enough to dull the unmistakable odour of blood mixed with the smoke of the camp fire; that stale, irony, tangy feeling on the tongue that wrinkled the nose. The buzzing of a mass of blue bottles as they drew closer provided further warning of the undoubted presence of fresh carrion, but it wasn't the presence of a corpse that was so disturbing; these two men had seen, and made, plenty of them. It was the way that this man had been killed. His face was all but obliterated, not by shot, but by the huge heavy reddened boulder that lay at his side. 'Christ Danny,' said Hawkins quietly; 'Redmond O'Hanlon would turn in his grave if he had seen the like of that there done in the name of the rapparees. I'm glad we're getting out of this business.'

Phillips nodded; 'Sheer bloody evil that's what that is. Shooting somebody's one thing but bashing a man face in with a rock- dirty, filthy animals! I want these bastards caught. I'll string whoever done this up myself.'

'Another one down here boss!' called one of the men slightly down the hill. 'Appears to have been shot in the face at close range.' Hawkins looked round briefly. 'Bring that one in, we might get something for him.' He looked back at Rafferty's body. 'No point bringing him in, he could be anybody! That could be Shane McGrogan for all we know.' Phillips shrugged; 'You never know what any of them look like. We've found that out to our cost before.' Hawkins sighed and nodded. 'Are we ever going to tell young Michael about what happened to his family? I mean I know we've both done bad things in our time, there are a lot of things I regret and then there's a lot of things I'm proud of too, like whenever we bring in a real vicious one, the type that does this sort of thing. But the boy's whole family Danny, we made an orphan of him! Just because some idjit sent us to the wrong house and we didn't check our facts first.'

'We've been through all this before, what do you want me to say John? That we come clean and beg the lad for forgiveness? Would you forgive us if you were him? We made a mistake, yes, we'll regret it for the rest of our lives, yes. But we've looked after the boy like he was our own! He's grown up thinking it was rapparees who murdered his family, he's dedicated to fighting them as best he can, do you really want to turn round now and have him know that everything he's believed for the past 10 years is a lie? Let sleeping dogs lie will you.' Phillips hoked through his pockets and retrieved his snuff tin, eager to blot out the smell of blood so reminiscent of a night in Dublin ten years ago, when he and Hawkins and their men shot round after round through the front window of a house they erroneously believed to be crammed full of rapparees. 'I suppose you're right.' sighed Hawkins 'It keeps me awake at night that's all. I think that's why we need the drink, you and me, and I can see that rubbing off on the boy too.'

'We'll get him out of the business, get him a trade or something. I know a blacksmith who's looking an apprentice, that's a good job. I'll see what I can do and we'll put something aside from this job for him too. But Michael must never know what happened. Right, there's no way of telling where these blood thirsty curs went after the dirty deed was done here, the trail runs dry. I suggest we go back down and join the others sweeping towards Slieve Croob. What do you say?' said Phillips.

'Aye I suppose so. Let's take our leave of this unholy place, before the flies get us too.' agreed Hawkins. Eugene O'Cahan watched from the bushes as the two leaders trooped down the hill. He had returned to the camp briefly to say a prayer over the bodies of his fallen comrades; if he had been a hair's breadth slower the hunters would have had him- if

# 11. A Man About Town

It was early afternoon by the time Archie made his way into Banbridge town, having evaded several of the hunter parties and on one occasion strolling casually past them with a brief nod of a hello. He was slightly nervous when entering the town, wondering if his appearance had changed quite enough to prevent people recognising him. Luckily nobody was looking for him in particular, and with the tall tales sweeping the town of the rapparees being routed, and each man taking more than his fair share of the credit, the mood was generally pleasant. This scruffy, dirty stranger was not perceived as a threat to the women and children of the town. Archie kept his head down under his tri-corner just to be sure as he moved through the market place, puffing occasionally on his unlit pipe and glancing over his shoulder every now and then. He picked up little snippets of conversations as he moved along, not wanting to appear to be earwigging;

'They found two bodies up on the hill'

'They reckon one of them might be Shane McGrogan.'

'One of them had his face eaten off, they think the Toad people must have gotten him.'

'They've had to call in the boys who caught Naoise O'Haughan.'

'The rapparees were planning to steal everyone's shoes so they couldn't run away when they burn the town!'

These and 101 other silly statements could be heard, and as much as Archie wanted to step up and put them all straight, maintaining his anonymity took precedent over restoring the honour of those who scarcely deserved it anyway. He paused briefly beside each stall and glanced round in the hope of spying Tomas; inwardly, he considered his errand to be of a token nature by now, suspecting McCafferty to be way too clever to get himself caught at this stage. For just a second he thought he saw the flash of a navy blue cloak in the crowd, which disappeared quickly through the throng and down the High Street. Tomas sported such an article, as did many people, but it seemed about as good a lead as he was likely to get.

Sidestepping diplomatically through the assorted rabble, he observed his quarry to be a man of McCafferty's approximate height and build, who had ducked into an alleyway behind a row of two storey well-to-do whitewashed houses. Sneaking quietly along behind the fellow, down a squalid entry full of stray cats and rotting vegetables, he observed the man enter the premises of a place of business. 'That's got to be him,' thought Archie, 'but what's he up to?' Although the yard door had been locked behind the man, the wall presented no great challenge to Archie. The large white cart horse in the yard didn't stir at the arrival of this interloper, being thoroughly engrossed by the oats in his nosebag, and within seconds Archie had silently invaded the back room of the house. He heard a whispering as the man proceeded upstairs in the company of another. Archie looked around the pristine white washed room with its heavy benches and iron hooks. It was divided in two with the back of the room sectioned off with a heavy black curtain. Archie crept up to the curtain and peeped inside, and his heart jumped at the sight of the last person on earth he would ever want to see, alive or dead.

Barra, Annie and the children were making as good a progress as one would expect with two small children in tow as they negotiated the narrow winding country lanes towards Slieve Croob, and several hunter parties had passed them by without question. Barra was about to round yet another corner when the sight of a familiar face caused him to duck into the side, motioning the family in behind him as he went. 'What is it?' hissed Annie behind the crouching rapparee. 'There are two of the hunters up ahead.'

'Can't we just walk past them like we did with the other ones?' asked Annie, quizzically.

'No you don't understand, one of them knows me. That fellow there- that's wee Willy Hardon!'

Annie peered over Barra's shoulder to see at a distance of some 50 yards, a burly looking young man of about 6 foot in height with a paunchy stomach, dressed a grey shirt and brown leather waistcoat. He was leaning against a small wooden gate smoking a pipe with one hand, whilst holding his musket by the stock over his shoulder with the other. 'Obviously he's grown a bit since the last time you saw him.' said Annie; 'How do you know him?'

'Ach we used to knock about with him when he was younger, his real name is William Hearthen, but I thought of calling him wee

Willy Hardon and everybody else started calling him it too. He never liked me after that.'

'I'm not surprised!' said Annie; 'That's a horrible thing to do. I hope you're ashamed of yourself.'

'Well I didn't know it was going to stick did I?' protested Barra. 'I would say I'm sorry but he'd more than likely just blow my head off with that musket there. I wouldn't be surprised if he joined up with the hunters in the hope of getting his own back on me, the devious wee swine.'

'He must have taken it a bit thick I'd say' agreed Annie; 'If you treat people cruelly it always comes back to bite you, I hope this serves as a lesson to you!'

'If I live to tell the tale it will do aye!' replied Barra, affronted; 'and what about all the nice things I do for people all the time, does it not work in reverse as well?'

'Well you've got me and the children haven't you?' laughed Annie, quietly.

'I didn't mean that the way it came out.' said Barra, apologetically.

'Well we're going to have to get you past him somehow Barra. I mean me and the children could just walk past him but he could wait there all day for all we know, and we've only a few hours to get to Slieve Croob.'

Barra sighed and nodded, then thought for a few minutes. Suddenly his face lit up; 'Wait here, I've got an idea.' Annie pulled the children in tight and watched as Barra crawled down through the undergrowth to within 20 yards of where William

Hearthen stood chatting to his companion, a little man of about 5'3 in a tri-corner hat and a frock coat hanging down to near his ankles. The other man was perched on a tree stump at the other side of the road, removing a stone from his shoe. Their two horses were tied to a tree beside them. Barra listened intently to the men's conversation; 'You're from around this part of the world originally aren't you Hearthen? So what was it made you decide to move up to Belfast then?'

Hearthen tutted; 'I'm from round here but I don't like any of the ones who lives round here. They're all wee petty, small minded people, I can't stand any of the lot of them. I changed my religion and moved up to Belfast to get away from them and to make something of myself. I could probably buy and sell the lot of them with the small change in my pocket now, the shower of beggars they are!'

Barra was taken aback and quite hurt to hear Hearthen's harsh words; however he resolved that his plan was the best way to gain satisfaction from the treacherous rascal. Cupping his hand to his mouth, he threw his voice to the spot where the little man sat; 'I heard you left here because people used to call you wee Willy Hardon!'

Hearthen put his pipe down and stood bolt upright; 'What did you call me there?' he snarled to the little man. The other fellow looked at Hearthen in confusion and held out his palms; 'I didn't call you anything!'

'I heard what you said, I just want to see if you're man enough to repeat it!' shouted Hearthen, angrily. 'I didn't call you a name Bill honest I didn't. You've been out in the sun too long.' Hearthen scowled at his friend for a good half minute but eventually calmed himself. He picked his pipe up and started to puff again. 'Catch yourself on, wee Willy Hardon!' called the voice again. Hearthen slammed his clay pipe down angrily, smashing it to pieces. He stormed angrily over towards his diminutive accomplice; 'Call me that name again you wee bastard! Call me that name one more time, I friggin dare ya!'

'Call you what name, what are you talking about?' cried the little fellow, scared. 'Call me wee Willy Hardon! Go on, I want to hear you say it again, let me hear you say wee frigging Willy Hardon!'

The wee fellow looked up at his friend in bewilderment; 'Wee... Willy Hardon?'

'Aaarggh!!!' roared Hearthen as he launched himself at his mate. The little chap wasted no time in hot footing it up the road, with the demented William Hearthen in close pursuit. As they disappeared around the corner, Barra emerged from the bushes with a smile and waved for Annie to come forth. 'We can pinch their horses!' he grinned, gleefully.

Seamus McGrogan looked surprisingly at peace lying on the heavy oak table, and in fact was almost unrecognisable without his trademark scowl and the redness drained from his nose. In truth he looked better than he did in years. Archie stood in quiet contemplation for a minute, before gathering his thoughts to concentrate on the task at hand. Hearing the two pairs of footsteps descending the stairs again, he ducked behind the curtain and hopped up onto the table along with Seamus to prevent his feet from being seen.

Holding his breath, he listened as the pair entered the room. The woman spoke first; 'We will have to leave separately to avoid suspicion, I'll meet you on the road leading out towards Edenderry.'

'This is it then, our new life together starts today my love,' said Tomas's voice. Archie's eyebrow raised. There was a pause and the sound of a long slobbery kiss. Archie couldn't resist a peep through the curtain, to see what unfortunate woman Tomas had pulled the wool over this time. His jaw dropped- Betty Higginson! The events of the previous night were beginning to seem mundane by comparison. He closed the curtain again and waited. He heard the latch as the door opened, a brief pause as they held hands and smiled at each other in a very juvenile manner, then the motion in the yard as the horse was saddled and the gate opened. Hearing the clip clop of the departing horse from the yard, Archie peeped out the curtain to see Tomas smiling smugly to himself and waving meekly out the window.

'What is it with you and married women?' said Archie, loudly. Tomas spun round, clutching his heart. 'Frigg!' he gasped. 'I thought that was your man there come back to life! Hang on, what are you doing here anyway?'

'What am I doing here?' repeated Archie. 'What about you? Deserting your comrades so you can cuckold the captain of the militia? Have you taken leave of your senses?'

'Ah, wait a minute there preacher, it's not all as it may seem. I didn't desert I was taken prisoner, and the lady and I are in love, we intend to start a new life together in the Americas.'

'What!' said Archie, 'How can you be in love man, you've been gone but four hours!'

'Love doesn't care about time or common sense Archie, it's just something you feel. I've never met a woman like Betty before-come to think of it I've never met anyone like her before! She shares my sense of adventure and want of new experiences. Ireland is too small a place for two such as me and Betty, that's why we have to leave together. If you were any sort of a friend, you'd be happy for me!' spouted Tomas, in a hopelessly besotted manner. Archie was quite unaccustomed to hearing anyone talk so openly about love, least of all Tomas McCafferty. He wasn't quite sure how to reply to him.

'Well if you think that you will be escaping to the America's with Shane's jewels, I may only presume you've been out too long in the moonlight.' He said at length.

'Oh that!' said Tomas, with a smile; 'I've got that here in my pocket. No we were going to drop that off to Shane before we leave, we are making our way first of all to Slieve Croob to hand over the goods, but after that I'm finishing with life on the road. Betty has the means for us to purchase our fare to the Americas, and enough for a small plot of land or a fishing boat too.'

'So you wish to cuckold Mr Higginson and rob him too? Have you no soul, what did he ever do to you?'

Tomas hesitated, shaking a finger; 'now – I wouldn't go wasting any sympathy on that fellow Archie. Do you know where he is right now? He's taken himself off down to Downpatrick to claim the reward for killing Seamus! Blood money for the body of a man he didn't even kill! And that money has to be raised off the local population Preacher, twenty pounds out of the purses of the ordinary working people!' Tomas leaned against the workbench as he stuffed his pipe; 'Betty is only taking the worth of her share of the money which she herself generated for Higginson by her own labours. She did most of his work for him, so she's entitled to something.'

'And what of her child?' demanded Archie, incredulously.

'He's the child of Higginson's first wife, and he's almost a man now. Betty's not even old enough to be his mother. He's no need of a mother, he's more in want of his father's belt round his backside.' replied Tomas. The boys went quiet as the front door creaked open, Tomas slid over and secreted himself behind the curtain along with Archie and the deceased Seamus. Footsteps could be heard in the hallway, then at the base of the stairs. 'Ma! I'm home, is there anything for dinner?' The boy waited but no one answered. 'Ach! I'll have to fix it myself.' They heard the boy enter the kitchen and clatter around at the bread and cheese. Archie motioned to Tomas to pull his scarf up over his face, to which Tomas complied. They stepped out from behind the curtain to see John Higginson with his back to them. Archie cleared his throat to announce his presence.

'Shop's closed. Me Da's away into Downpatrick and me Ma's away out somewhere.' The rapparees made no answer as John continued to fix his snack. 'Are you deaf, I said-' John trailed off and turned white as he turned to see the two rough looking intruders in his home.

'You really do need to think about getting yourself a guard dog, John Higginson.' said Archie, in an intimidating manner.

John's breathing became heavy; 'Me Ma won't have one, she says they're dirty oul things.'

'I don't think you're going to have to worry about for much longer my boy.' said Tomas, ambiguously. John considered a dive for the door but Archie was there before him, in his face; 'Didn't I tell you what would happen if there was any more messing about out of you John? Didn't I tell you we would come down here and put manners on you all?'

'I- I had to tell me Ma and Da something! Coming home with no shoes like that!'

'Our captain's dead cos of you! two of our other men too!' snarled Archie. Tomas looked at his infuriated accomplice in puzzlement, failing to see how John's actions could be in any way connected with Seamus' death. John's eyes began to water; 'I'm sorry, I didn't mean-'

Archie grabbed John by the scruff and pulled him over to Seamus' corpse, forcing the lad's head down to look; 'this is your fault Higginson! Look at him! Look what you've done!' John started blubbering, then Archie felt a firm hand on the nape of his own neck. 'That's enough Preacher! Do you hear? Leave the lad alone!' Tomas pushed Archie's neck and he flew across the room, before spinning round, preparing to fight. He stopped. He looked at Tomas, he looked at John, he looked at Seamus.

Then he thought. He thought about how brutally Seamus had treated him, just because he could. He thought how vulnerable and terrified that had made him feel, and how he despised Seamus for it. He thought about the madness of the previous night, how Seamus' vision had said Archie would become like him, and how he had sworn he would never be like Seamus. Is this what it all meant? He breathed deeply. John sat on the floor snivelling. 'I'm sorry John Higginson, for the manner in which I have treated you. It is becoming neither of a Christian nor of a rapparee. Please forgive me.' John gave no answer. Tomas ladelled a tankard of water from the barrel and handed it to John. Archie gathered his thoughts, and then spoke again. 'I should never have taken your shoes, that was wrong. I should not have threatened you either. However, you had no right to be tormenting another person as you did with the carter. I have no further umbrage with you John, however as you were partly responsible for what has occurred here, I expect you to help us put it right. The people of the town are under the impression that we acted without provocation and that we intend to burn the town, neither of which are true. I would require that you set your father straight on this matter. Can you do that John?'

John Higginson nodded. 'Very well then,' said Archie; 'My friend and I will take our leave, do not speak of this meeting or seek to alert anyone of our presence. I swear on my oath there will be no further repercussion in this matter.'

With that, Archie and Tomas left number 26 Newry Street and made their way towards Edenderry.

Eugene continued his slow progress towards Slieve Croob, resisting the temptation to take to the open roads until he at least had the cover of darkness. He did however stay close to the roads in order to follow their direction. In this manner, he was able to monitor the toing and froing of the search parties and their captives, who seemed to be anybody unfortunate enough not to heed the warnings to keep out of the woods over the next few days. Some were allowed to go about their business, such as a courting couple and a school teacher out picking daisies. It was very much a case of whether a person had the right face or manner as to whether they were interned by the hunters or not, with little or no logic applied to the process over and above the sensibilities of the particular hunter that the person encountered. 'We're bringing far too many in, we'll not be able to hold them all,' came a voice from down the road. Eugene backed deeper into the cover of the bushes, discerning the grunting and groaning of a couple of manhandled unfortunates in the hands of the party. 'You can be sure these bastards here have a price on them.' Came another voice, and then again loudly; 'Or are you going to tell me you were just carrying this pistol for your Granny?' Several of the men laughed and there was also a grunt of pain from another. Eugene peered out of the bushes and was able to see 6 hunters with 2 bound young men, being forced along the road, roughly. He recognised the men to be Rhuiri O'Donnell and Fintan McDonagh, O'Donnell being of the McGrogan gang and McDonagh a member of another local rapparee gang. 'You boys are making a big mistake I can tell you, when our mates get word of what's going on here they'll flay the skin from your backs and feed you your own todgers for breakfast!' snarled O'Donnell. The outburst generated further mocking laughter from the men, followed by a heavy blow to the back with a musket butt for the defenceless rapparee. O'Donnell fell to the ground gasping, and his assailant followed through with a boot to the ribs. Suddenly, McDonagh made a break up the road at full pelt. As he passed Eugene, a shot rang out and he fell forward onto his face, quite dead. 'No need for that, we could have caught him!' said another of the men, not really that bothered about the shooting. 'We shall have to carry his corpse now, all the way back to the camp!'

'Ach, why should we bark when there's a dog? Untie this fellow's hands, he can carry him for us.' Eugene watched and waited, as the hunters forced O'Donnell to pick up the body of his friend and lump him up the road. He winced in disgust at the uncivil treatment of a captured enemy. 'Don't worry, there'll be plenty of your mates back at the camp you can sit and have a wee cry with, you're all bound for the end of the rope anyway so there'll be plenty for yous to talk about!'

Eugene resolved that he would follow the men to discover the location of the camp, and thereby effect the rescue of any captured rapparees. Following at a distance, he was able to observe as Rhuiri O'Donnell was lead through a gate into an open field, which had been cleared of cattle for the day. He was thereafter forced into a paddock with around two dozen other people, some rapparees, some just local unfortunates. Then he spied the pile of bodies at the other end of the field, some 8 men stacked unceremoniously on top of one another. Those who had put up but a little resistance had been brutally treated for their efforts. 'Throw that dead bastard over there with the others. There's plenty more where he came from.' Eugene spotted young Michael Darroch in the midst of the field, looking worried and confused. In truth Phillips and Hawkins would not have advocated this sort of behaviour at all amongst their men, but when you need to get 70 men at arms together at short notice it isn't always feasible to wait for references. 'The boss isn't going to like this,' protested Michael, nervously; 'We're supposed to be bringing them in alive, they've to be questioned about a letter that's missing. We don't know which ones are even guilty anyway.'

'Are you trying to tell me how to do my job?' growled one fat, unwashed brutish looking thug. 'No, but-'

'No nothing. You don't worry about what we're doing. Your job is to watch these bastards and make sure none of them escape.'

Michael looked around, unsure what to say; 'That fellow there for instance, you've beaten him too harshly, he can hardly stand.'

'You're all right, aren't you boy?' said the fat man, putting his arm round O'Donnell's shoulder. O'Donnell stood with his head down. 'See he's all right! On the other hand, if I do this!' the brute delivered a sharp blow to the boy's solar plexus, instigating another fit of laughter from his cronies. Michael watched in horror as the hunter pulled his hand out, holding a dagger covered in blood. O'Donnell fell dead to the ground. Wide eyed, Michael first looked down at the fallen rapparee and then into the eyes of the brutal hunter. 'You'll have no complaints from that one. Put him over there in the pile with the rest of the shite.' Eugene decided then and there that this man was going to die.

O'Cahan watched as the 6 hunters exited the field through the gate, 3 going to the left, the murderer and two others to the right. Measuring their dawdling pace, the Frenchman was able to overtake them through the bushes in complete silence as they neared a turning in the road partially hidden by low hanging branches. As Eugene stepped out into their path, the party of 3 were slightly taken aback by the sudden presentation of this unusual character; what Eugene said next threw them even further off balance.

'Good afternoon Gentlemen, my name is Captain Eugene O'Cahan and I am here on rapparee business. It is not my usual practise to announce a man's death prematurely, however given the surety of the present situation I can advise you with great accuracy that you will be quite positively dead in a few moments. I am therefore offering you the opportunity to make your peace with the Lord before I proceed to your dispensation.' The men looked one to the other in astonishment and then went for their weapons. The first fellow only got half of his pistol out of its holster before a thrown stiletto dagger hit him right between the eyes, killing him instantly. The next wrestled to shoulder his musket in a panic, a task he failed to complete before O'Cahan's rapier spilt his guts upon the road. The last, the great fat murdering brute, unsheathed his cutlass and swung incompetently at O'Cahan, who parried expertly before sending his opponent off balance. Sliding his blade down to the other's handguard, the Frenchman whipped round and delivered a sharp blow to the other's neck. As the murderer lay on the ground with the life bleeding out of him, he stared piteously up at O'Cahan, as if to beg for mercy. The Frenchman shook his head in mock sympathy, 'I gave you a chance to atone for your crimes in this world; now, you may atone for them in the next.' With that, he quickly despatched the hunter.

Tomas and Archie ambled casually along the road out towards Edenderry, still hoping that they could evade capture simply by looking like two normal travellers going about their business. Archie was somewhat on edge, reticent in quiet contemplation of his earlier behaviour towards John Higginson. He wondered at how the rapparee life had changed him as a person and if he could ever now find the true path to salvation. Tomas for his part seemed oblivious to his friend's inner turmoil, whistling merrily as he went along his way. 'So are you not going to ask me then?' asked McCafferty, with annoying cheeriness. 'Ask you what?' replied McClung, wearily. 'About what happened to me today!' replied Tomas.

'What happened to you today.' said Archie, resignedly.

'Well,' started Tomas; 'I went down to the river in the morning as I said, to catch some fish for our breakfast. I've pulled some enormous brown trout out of that river of the years, I don't even need a rod. There's a technique for tickling them that my father-'

'How did you end up with Mrs Higginson?' interrupted Archie irritably. 'I was just getting to that. I was coming back with the fish and I suddenly became aware of a presence behind, you know, that feeling you get? Well I thought to myself, yikes, that could be the shadow man, or the river dragon or even Terrence two heads, or maybe that chap from Dromore who goes down there to dress as a woman, and calls himself the Duchess of Dromore. There are all sorts in these woods. I started to walk faster and my pursuer picked up the pace to match. I glanced round and what did I see, but a dark, hooded figure in the trees on a great big white horse. So of course I broke into a run! No man can outrun a horse, even one of my athletic prowess, and wouldn't you know, the next thing is it's galloped up, the rider has stood up on the saddle and literally dived on top of me! Before I know it I was looking up at this terrific pair of- ' he cupped his hands in illustration; 'and I thought it was my lucky day. But then the next thing I've got a pistol shoved right between my eyes.'

Archie picked up his interest slightly; 'so then what happened?'

'Well she says she's taking me in and I'm going to hang for threatening her son! Oh by the way you might want to apologise for that when we meet her, she's still pissed off about that. She ties a rope around me and gets on the horse, orders me to march down to Banbridge. Of course I tried all the usual tricks, telling her she's got the wrong man and so forth, but it availed me not. I kept talking and talking hoping to put her off guard, so I can make good my escape, gave her a sad tale of how I came to be a rapparee and all that. She wouldn't let me go but her mood lightened when I made her laugh a few times.'

'And how did you come to seduce her then?' inquired Archie, now genuinely interested.

'Well as we continued on we came across one of those search parties, but we saw them before they saw us. I told Betty she might as well let me go because those fellows would just take me off her anyway. But she comes up with a plan where we should pretend to be a courting couple in the midst of a 'tryst', so to speak.' He illustrated his point with a raised fist. Archie was flabbergasted. 'Not actually doing it, you know, just kissing and that. Well it worked a treat, they walked right past us with nothing more than a boorish jeer, shouting give her one from us, that sort of thing. Some people have no decorum.'

'And then she fell for your charms?'

'Well we repeated the same scenario every time we encountered a party, and I jokingly asked if she was deliberately leading us into them, and then it all sort of- came out!' replied Tomas, with a shrug.

Archie stopped walking and looked at his friend in disbelief. 'What came out?'

'She craves adventure Archie! A cause! She can't be satisfied by the humdrum or the inane, and when she lead the charge on us the night before it aroused something in her that had lay dormant for years. That happens to people in the woods you see, something about them changes people, brings out their true selves. She can't be fulfilled by the domestic way of life anymore. She said at first she would let me go if I would let her join up with the rapparees, but I wouldn't have that, I mean, some of those lads of ours haven't seen what lies beneath a woman's skirts for four or five years. So then I told her of my plan for a new life in the Americas, where a man isn't bound forever into the circumstances of his birth. She shared my enthusiasm for the scheme and we contrived to make use of whatever means were necessary to secure our passage. There's a boat leaving tomorrow morning from Newry, Betty and I intend to be on it.'

Archie first folded his arms, then scratched his head and then cupped his chin with his index finger and thumb; 'So how can you two be married then, no court would grant a woman a divorce in those circumstances, much as like she'd be committed to jail.'

'Oh aye, well we thought we would go by an alias in the colonies, then marry over there by the first person who would perform the ceremony. How would anyone know? There is land beyond measure, and the chances of meeting someone who knows us from back home are slim.' replied Tomas.

'The Lord will know Tomas! What of her holy vows before God?'

'What of them?' shrugged McCafferty; 'Betty says she doesn't believe in God and I myself am ambivalent on the subject of religion, it seems to be more the cause of strive and division than of joy and unity, in this country, anyway.'

Archie was horrified; 'Doesn't believe in God? How could anyone not-'

'She has all sorts of funny ideas like that, she even said a woman should be allowed to do all things that a man is allowed to do.' replied Tomas, chuckling.

Archie was now of the opinion that there could be no situation which the fates could contrive that would come as a surprise to him. Very soon he would learn otherwise.

Victor Spratt sat cross legged in the tiny cage staring defiantly up at his long suffering wife Felicity, with not a hint of embarrassment or repentance. The rouge of his cheeks was smeared messily across his face, having put up a bit of a struggle as the hunters pushed him in along with Kenneth Clinton, who had been getting on everyone's nerves with his constant complaining. One of the carefully tied bows in his hair was straggling down his meticulously shaven chest, and the blackberry juice with which he had stained his lips had dyed his bushy moustache a dark purple. 'Yes, that's him all right,' said Felicity, resignedly as Michael opened the cage. Victor stepped out to stand upright and dusted himself down dramatically, bemoaning the state of his best daffodil yellow satin summer dress and his recently purchased white linen bloomers. He reached into his tiny matching silk bag and pulled out a delicate lace fan, before proceeding to fan himself indignantly.

'He told us he was the Duchess of Dromore.' explained Michael, holding his palms out. Mrs Spratt nodded knowingly; 'He tells everyone that, he's – you know.' she tapped her forehead descriptively. Felicity turned and grabbed her husband's arm, unceremoniously. 'Come on Victor, we're all getting sick of this!' she snapped, marching him away. 'I was enjoying myself in there!' complained the unconvincing cross dressing farmer. Michael shook his head as he watched the pair leave, before turning to lock the cage door again.

'You're going to find yourself in a lot of trouble my boy, locking me up with that pervert!' yapped Kenneth Clinton. 'Ah shut up you, or I'll tell everyone how you were planning to court him before you found out he was a man.' replied Michael. 'I did nothing of the sort! This is outrageous.' complained Clinton. Michael ignored him and locked the cage. By rights Kenneth should have counted himself lucky that Michael didn't put him in the other cage, there were some rough types in there.

Michael decided he had earned a break and went to his sack, retrieving a large floury bap, half of which he tore off and shoved in his mouth. He took out a bottle of water and settled down on the grass, putting his musket aside to enjoy his meal in comfort.

'On your guard! Look behind you, there's a dandy looking rapparee sneaking up on you!' cried Kenneth Clinton.

Michael frowned and tried to gulp down some bread so he could speak; 'Will you shut the frigg up! I'm trying to eat my breakfast here.' Glancing aside he discovered his musket had been lifted.

'Good afternoon young man. My name is Eugene O'Cahan and I believe you have some of my compatriots as your guests here. It is my intention to relieve you of their company. I have no argument with you personally, so I would advise that you desist from interfering in my business and thereby you shall come to no harm.'

Michael spat his bread out and jumped to his feet; 'You give me that musket back! These men are to be taken to Downpatrick to receive a fair trial.'

'And those men,' replied O'Cahan, nodding to the pile of bodies, 'Did they receive a fair trial? Oh don't worry, I have already dispensed justice to three of the murderers. You can be sure I shall show the other three the same measure if I cross their path again.'

Michael whipped round behind him and pulled a small pistol from the back of his breeches, pointing it shakily at Eugene. O'Cahan simultaneously drew his own pistol, resulting in stalemate. Eugene's hand did not shake as Michael's did; in truth, he could have dispensed the boy quite easily, but was assured of his ability to disarm the lad without violence. 'Get you into that cage there!' shouted Michael, motioning with the pistol. 'Why?' asked Eugene, calmly, lowering his voice and the speed of his breath. 'If I get into that cage I will either be hung as a rapparee or murdered by your colleagues, either way I'm dead. So why would I comply?' Michael shifted nervously, as O'Cahan continued;

'More to the point, why do you want me to? Why place any man in a cage, in the knowledge that the termination of such a venture would result in his demise? Do you enjoy this life Michael? These men here, rough as they might appear, are fighting against injustice and oppression, what are you fighting against Michael?'

'I'm fighting to protect the people of this country against murdering scum like you!' raged Michael Darroch. 'And how do you know my name anyway?'

'I heard your two employers discuss you on the hill, they talked about the tragedy of your life and their guilt at the killing of your family.' replied Eugene, edging closer.

Michael backstepped without even realising he was doing it.

'My parents were murdered by rapparees, Hawkins and Phillips took me in and raised me as their own.'

'No Michael, I heard them discuss the matter. They were looking to find rapparees but were sent to the wrong address. They shot into your house and all save yourself were killed. Oh, they intended no murder of innocents, but the outcome was just that.' O'Cahan put his pistol in his belt and moved closer. 'Just as you would be murdering these people without recourse to proper justice if you let Hawkins take them in.' Michael gave no resistance as Eugene took the pistol from his hand. Taking the keys, Eugene began to open the cages as rapparees, vagrants, hikers and farmers emerged to stretch their legs. 'What will I do now?' asked Darroch, glumly, sitting on the grass.

'I am returning soon to France, we would have use of a man such as yourself in my regiment if you have the will to fight for a true king.' replied O'Cahan. Darroch raised an eyebrow at the interesting proposition. 'Well there's not much here for me now, no family, no job, ah to hell with it, a new start is what I need!' he bounced to his feet.

As the assemblage gathered round, Eugene spoke to all; 'I am here to recover the men under Shane McGrogan's command, however given the urgency of the situation I would suggest that any of the rest of you who are rapparees or wanted men should fall in with me. As to those of you who are not wanted, you are free to return home henceforth. Have a care though, for whilst you have nothing to fear of the rapparees, the same cannot be said of the bounty hunters, as yonder pile of bodies would testify.'

In all, 6 of the 24 fell in with Eugene and Michael. 'There are many other camps dotted about the place,' advised Michael 'probably better guarded than this one. The aim is to take all those who have been captured to Downpatrick goal at sunset.' warned Michael. Eugene nodded; 'We shall firstways rendeavous with Shane and then consult on how to make good our friends' escape.' Eugene, Michael and the assorted rapparees headed off towards Slieve Croob whilst everyone else stood looking at each other, wondering what to do.

# 12. SLOW PROGRESS

Archie and Tomas were just about to round a bend in the road when they discerned a low muttering of voices hailing from the direction in which they wished to travel. Tomas signalled to Archie to hang back while he had a look. Edging cautiously round the corner, McCafferty was able to observe a party of some dozen hunters, having a break by the roadside, resting their feet and smoking their pipes. 'Bout twelve of those bastards round there,' remarked Tomas; 'don't know how we can get past them without going the whole way back into town. Any ideas?' Archie shrugged; 'We may just get into cover and hope they move on soon.' The boys moved into the cover of the bushes and long grass by the roadside. 'They'll never see us in here.' said Tomas, assuredly. 'Ssshhh! Somebody else is coming.' They ducked further in and waited to see who was passing through from the direction of Banbridge. Shortly, a horse drawn cart pulled past. 'Yousuns hiding in the bushes again then?' called a familiar voice. It was the carter who Archie and Angus had helped the day before. 'Keep it down will you, there are people round the corner looking for us!' hissed Archie. The carter nodded. Cupping his hand to his face and whispering, he said; 'Don't worry, climb up here and I'll get you past them.' A few minutes later, the cart rounded the corner.

As the carter passed through, some of the hunters eyed him suspiciously and eventually one of them hailed him to stop. 'Whoa there, friend, what are you carrying today?' Glancing round at the very visible large bales of hay in the back of the cart, the carter replied; 'I should have thought that to be apparent!'

The hunter frowned, unappreciative of the humour. 'I'm going to have to have a look back there, to make sure there is no one secreted in amongst the bails, you don't mind do you?'

'Well yes actually I don't want them all pulled out-'

'Oh that won't be necessary!' replied the hunter, taking a long pike from one of his companions. The carter looked on nervously as the hunter went to the back of the cart, and jammed the pike into the hay. Hearing no cry and feeling no hidden object, he moved round a little and jabbed the pike in again. The hunter repeated the process in gaps of a foot or so over the whole of the back of the cart, to no avail. Finally, he admitted defeat. 'You may go about your business sir, sorry to have troubled you.' The cart rumbled off up the road and the hunters, finishing their break, continued off in the opposite direction. Scanning round to make sure all was clear, the carter drew the cart to a halt once more. He dismounted the cart and opened the box which he had been sitting on, allowing a very cramped pair of rapparees to emerge. 'They never check the box.' said the carter, beaming. 'Lucky for us too!' replied Tomas. 'We are indebted to you sir,' said Archie; 'what was your name by the way?'

'My name is Hubert Toal, and you are indebted to me for nothing. One good turn deserves another.' replied the carter.

'Toal!' said Tomas, 'Any relation to our good friends Cornelius and Ignatius?'

'Cousins of mine they are, and in some ways my employers too, you see I am the distributor of their poteen about the district, the straw here is really just to keep the powers at be from prying into our affairs too closely. Normally I secrete the jars in the box where you were hiding, and they assume it to be nought but a seat. I am on my way up to the forest later today if you care to join us for a wee dram' replied Hubert.

'As much as we would love to sir, we really must be getting on. There are bounty hunters abroad and we are to meet with our captain before evening falls.' replied Archie. The boys and Hubert Toal shook hands and went their separate ways.

'Hubert's appearance there was timely was it not?' remarked Archie as the two strolled up the road; 'Perhaps the fates are smiling upon us at last!'

Tomas nodded; 'They've been smiling on us all along in truth. I've been living on the road as a proclaimed man for three or four years now Archie, in that time I've dwelt in the mountains in the harshest of winters, and I've half starved during the famine of 41, when thousands of better people met their ends in despair. I've dodged the ball of many a musket and I've put out the brains of three of the King's soldiers, not because I hated them, as I hate no man, but because I loved my own life enough to preserve it more than they did. But every day I consider myself to be fortunate to be alive and to have hope for the future. I have found that if you consider yourself to be lucky, then that is the blessing that befalls you. If on the other hand you allow your heart to be mired with tragedy and regret, such as Seamus and Rafferty did, then you will be drawn to the path of sorrow just as the salmon is drawn to swim up a river to meet its end. Look always for a reason to be happy and grateful for your life Archie, and happy is what you always will be.'

Archie was quite surprised to hear his friend speak so deeply and sincerely on philosophical matters, his usual subjects of conversation being limited to fishing, cards, and women. Perhaps he really had found true love after all. He became quite intrigued to meet with Betty Higginson, to see for himself what she was like. He didn't have to wait very long for as they rounded the next corner they espied the lady herself, idling impatiently beside the great white cart horse and kicking her heels at the ground. Tomas broke into a smile as he and Archie grew close to her, and McCafferty drew in for an embrace; 'My love this is my friend who we call the preacher who-'

Bang!

Before Tomas had finished sentence Archie felt a red flash of pain across his eyes as Betty's forehead connected at high speed with the bridge of his nose. 'No one frigging threatens my family, Preacher do you understand me?' barked the enraged Betty, glaring down at the prone McClung. She removed her foot from his chest as he groggily nodded his compliance. She reached down for his hand and jerked him up roughly, slapping him on the shoulder. 'Good, well now that that's out of the way hopefully we can all be friends. Onward to Slieve Croob then, you two try to keep pace with the horse.' Without looking back, Betty hopped on to the horse with impressive agility. Tomas turned to Archie and gave a silent shrug as McClung nursed his bloodied but thankfully unbroken nose. He moved in closely to whisper to Tomas out of Betty's earshot; 'Are you sure that isn't the Duchess of Dromore?'

Eugene, Michael and his group were now tramping warily along a leafy country lane, trying to make reasonable progress towards Slieve Croob whilst erring on the side of caution. The tactic of travelling in ones and twos was abandoned due to the fact that anyone and everyone without means of identification was now being rounded up regardless of who they were or what numbers they travelled in. Michael went ahead first as it was reasoned that any hunters espying him would assume him to be a friend, giving the others time to make good their escape. With 5 guns between the 8 rapparees they made a legitimate challenge to any travelling bands who might cross their path anyway, and despite his usual pragmatic approach to military matters, the earlier episodes of brutality committed by the hunters had wetted Eugene's appetite for the dispensation of some righteous vengeance. Michael pointed his gun as a vibrantly coloured figure burst forth from a hedge, but he quickly motioned to the others to hold fire; 'At ease boys, it's just the Duchess, don't hurt him he's quite harmless.' Victor Spratt lifted his skirts and ran excitedly towards Michael and Eugene; 'Whoa, there Duchess! What are you doing here?'

'I've been looking all over for you fellows!' he bellowed, animatedly; 'I've run away from home and have come to join you!' Eugene and Michael looked at each other awkwardly; 'I'm not sure that life on the road would be quite suitable to a gentleman of your – peculiarities, if you pardon my directness,' explained Eugene; 'It really isn't anywhere near as thrilling as what people make it out to be.'

'All your fine dresses would be ruined Victor!' added Michael; 'You'd have holes in your stockings before you know it. It's very difficult to maintain an acceptable standard of social apparel from halfway up a mountain.' Nodded Eugene in agreement. 'But I want to live wild and free where a man or a woman may dress as they please and answer to no one. I can cook and clean for the rest of the gang.' protested the Duchess. 'That's a very appealing offer I am sure,' agreed Eugene, 'however, the gang are not recruiting at the moment, we are presently full to capacity and I am sure you are not a proclaimed man, or woman, although you soon might be if you keep running around the countryside dressed like that.'

Victor's heart sank. 'You'd be best to go home now,' said Michael, placing a consolatory hand on the Duchess' shoulder; 'look here's your wife coming down the road now!' He pointed to Felicity approaching in the distance, with a furious scowl on her face. She grabbed Victor's arm and hauled him back along the road again. 'You'll let me know if there's any openings in the gang will you?' called the Duchess, over his shoulder. 'You'll be the first name on the list my good lady.' called back Eugene. 'If you're looking for me my farm is the third on the right coming from Dromore, about 2 miles from the town.'

'Right you be, safe home!' called back Michael.

Angus McGrogan had made a surprisingly good recovery thanks mainly to Mary Cayley's devoted attention, and now fancied himself well enough to travel. Although still bruised and sore, the fever had long since passed and the initial fear of sepsis had proved to be unfounded. Mary was anxious that the wound may still be tender and had persuaded him to wait until her father returned to give his professional opinion, which Angus was just about to request of the newly returned Doctor before checking the grave look of concern on Cayley's face. 'Something troubles you Jacob, have you heard news of how Shane has fared? Did the Frenchman and the others complete the mission yet?' enquired Angus, with great concern.

Cayley hung up his hat and ladelled a tankard of water from the bucket. 'I am afraid what little news I have for you bodes badly for us all. Firstly, whilst doing my rounds today it transpires that a band of unchecked bounty hunters are pillaging the countryside, locking up or murdering anyone they may come across on the road. Several people have reported to me of relatives being beaten or imprisoned. Some who I have encountered have advised me that they were liberated from captivity by a mysterious gentleman with a strange accent who had some sympathy with the rapparees- I would assume that this would be the mysterious Frenchman whom we have heard so much of.'

Angus sat up on one arm and struggled to put his shirt on. Mary spoke first; 'But Father, how can these bounty hunters be murdering the people and neither the militia nor the army raising arms in their defence?'

Jacob Cayley sighed gravely; 'This is the manner of things I have found since arriving in this country, the law is both blind and impotent on behalf of the common man, and on behalf of catholics in particular. I would not be in the least surprised to find that the blame for these acts of barbarism is laid at the door of the rapparees themselves.'

'I must go.' grunted Angus; 'Shane will need to be warned of what is happening, and we will need to decide what- if anything, can be done to remedy the situation.' He awkwardly pulled on his overcoat and lifted his hat, ignoring Mary's advice to the contrary. 'Under any other circumstances Angus, I would insist that you rest on here for at least another day. But I am needed myself by the people of the district and there is no one else I can send in your stead. I can lend you a horse though, try not to fall off it this time!'

'Thank you sir it is much appreciated.' replied Angus. 'But Angus there is more news that I need you to relay to Shane.' continued Cayley, with a cautionary tone; 'When out on my rounds I encountered a colleague to whom I got chatting on medical matters affecting the people of the district; we Doctors like to keep each other informed of any prevailing fevers or the like. He mentioned to me that he had of late been brought to the Viscount of Hillsbrough's residence to treat a man whose foot had been injured during a duel. He said that whilst he was there he was asked to look at the dressings of a young lady with an injured hand. The servants informed the Doctor that this lady was under some sort of house arrest, and if she attempted to leave the estate she would be committed to goal. It would appear she is accused of consorting with a rapparee and of being involved in some sort of treacherous endeavour, the exact nature of which is unclear.'

Angus stopped and thought. Could that be the lady who was injured by Seamus? It seemed a logical conclusion, as the carriage was heading towards Hillsborough. What was her connection to all of this, and who was the rapparee that she was accused of consorting with? Angus didn't quite have all the facts but it appeared that this person must have somehow been involved in Shane's mission and was therefore an ally who had taken a considerable risk. That being the case, the rapparees were obliged to help her. 'Thank you for that Doctor. I am sure that Shane will be able to explain to us what exactly is going on and how we can set matters to rights.' Angus wasn't sure though; he wasn't one bit sure at all.

'Michael!' called Phillips.

'Michael!' called Hawkins.

They sighed and looked around the field hopelessly again. 'I don't know,' said Phillips, pessimistically; 'what do you think happened to him then?'

'How should I know?' snapped Hawkins; 'I knew this was too big a job for him.'

'Michael!'

'Oh so it's my fault then is it? We're going to start pointing the finger at each other now are we?' retaliated Phillips. He paused to tap his pipe out; 'He said there were too many for him to guard on his own, what if they broke out and overpowered him?'

'Michael!'

Hawkins grimaced; 'most of the ones we gave him were just under minor suspicion, probably none of them were the ones we were looking for anyway.'

'Aye but if you lock a fella in a cage all day for frigg all he tends to be a wee bit peeved when he makes good his escape. Maybe they all got out and decided to level the score.' worried Phillips.

'There are no signs of the locks being broken, whoever did this had the key.'

'Somebody could have came up and hit him on the head or something, look there are pieces of bread lying about there.'

'And then what, did they eat him too? There's no body, except for that pile of mouldering corpses over there, and I would like to know who was responsible for that; not to mention those three frigging ne'r do wells lying out on the round there!' spat Hawkins, irately.

'Michael!' called Phillips, again.

Hawkins put his hand to his forehead; 'I knew we shouldn't have took this job, it's too big and there's not enough trusted men to keep the rest of them in order. We let the money go to our heads Danny. These jobs take weeks to plan, months even. If you try to cut corners, try to rush things overnight, this is what happens!'

'There will be time enough for remonstrations once we've sorted this all out John.' replied Phillips; ' The way I see it, Michael has either been murdered or kidnapped by the rapparees, which I would find unlikely, or, as like he has lost his prisoners and fearing the consequences, has absconded in the belief that we would be angry with him.'

'Michael!'

'Either way we're not leaving here without him,' nodded Hawkins; 'we will continue to search up until an hour before sunset if we haven't located him by that time, we'll just have to send the lads on down to Downpatrick and we can follow on later. Their journey will be slow with the prisoners so we will be easily able to catch up with them once we've located the boy.'

'That sounds like a plausible plan. Hopefully he's not too far. Knowing Michael he's cadged a drink off somebody and is sleeping it off under a hedge somewhere.'

'You two need to pick your pace up a bit, we're still a long way from Slieve Croob' called Betty without looking behind, as the horse trotted along. 'That's all right for you to say, sitting up there,' puffed Tomas as he and McClung jogged along behind; 'could I not come up there behind you?'

'And leave your friend to run along on his own? That's not very nice is it? Lightning here can't carry all of us, he's not a colt anymore.' replied Betty. 'Me neither,' called Tomas; '28 at my next birthday if I live to see it.'

'Shush, there's someone coming, you two get into the bushes there.' The boys ducked and Betty drew the horse to a halt. 'Can you see who it is?' hissed Archie from the bushes.

'A man dressed in black on a trap with two ponies.' whispered Betty.

'Problem solved!' beamed Tomas, drawing his pistol; 'We'll borrow the horses and trap from this fellow, he's only a few miles from Banbridge so it won't be any great hardship to him.' Archie nodded in agreement, pulling his scarf over his face.

'No you can't, he's a minis-' started Betty.

'You wanted to be a rapparee, well this is what we do, fear not we shall do the fellow no harm.' interrupted Tomas. 'But you don't understand he a man of the clo-'

'Pull up your reins and dismount!' cried Tomas, bouncing into the middle of the road.

'These horses and trap are being commandeered for rapparee purposes!' shouted Archie. Then his eyes widened, his heart jumped into his throat and his face drained of colour. The old man in the cart leaned forward and squinted into McClung's face. 'Archibald McClung! Where in Heavens have you been my boy?' Archie's arms went limp and his pistol fell to the ground. He looked at the man before him, turned to Tomas and pointed at the man but said nothing.

He wanted to ask Tomas if he could see the vision too, but his tongue would not work.

In truth no confirmation was needed.

This was real.

His own father, whom he had thought dead by his own hands for over a year,

the reason he ran from home and became a rapparee,

for whom he had carried an enormous weight of guilt and grief and regret for over a year,

was right there before him in the flesh.

'Why didn't you tell me he was Reverend McClung's boy, maybe I wouldn't have stuck the head into him!' said Betty to Tomas, not fully sensing the enormity of the situation.

'He toul us his Da was dead!' exclaimed Tomas, eyebrows raised.

'Dead? Why are you telling people that I'm dead boy? And what on Earth are you doing jumping out on people like that? Look at the state of your breeches! Have you been living in a hedge this past twelve months?'

Sandy McClung reamed out these and a dozen other questions as his son stood open mouthed, before finally speaking; 'But I hit you with the toby jug! You were lying dead when I left!'

Sandy sighed; 'It would take a lot more than a sly blow from the likes of you to put an end to me, young sir. I was out cold for a minute or so yes but if you had waited I would have given you a thrashing hitherto undreamt of.'

It was true; as his father lay motionless and his mother jumped up and down screaming, Archie had just grabbed his hat and coat and ran. As he pelted the 200 yards down the lane blubbering inanely and contemplating the stricture of the hangman's noose around his pencil thin neck, he had never heard his father cry 'Come back here til I show you God's mercy ye ungrateful wee blaggard!'

'So you mean to say,' said Tomas to Archie, smiling and pointing; 'That you have been living rough and running from the army for over a year for no reason at all? Ha! Wait til I tell the lads about this, they'll piss themselves!'

'Watch your language in front of the Minister there.' scolded Betty.

'But- but there was a search party looking for me, I hid from them! And there was an article in the Belfast Newsletter asking about my whereabouts!' protested Archie. Sandy McClung rolled his eyes; 'I asked the militia to help me to look for you to bring you home. Some of the men were angry at you for failing to honour your father, but their chief intention was to bring you home to safety. As to the article in the newspaper, I commissioned that myself, and Mr Higginson kindly agreed to act as my agent, his shop being located in the centre of the town. How is George and young John by the way Betty?'

'He's er- fine, gone down to Downpatrick on militia business. Things are a bit complex at the minute, I can't really say too much.' replied Betty, evasively.

'Well I hope none of you young people had anything to do with this!' Sandy tossed a rolled up copy of the Belfast Newsletter which Tomas caught. Opening the paper up, he read aloud;

'News has reached us of a notorious incident which took place on the road from the town of Banbridge to the village of Dromore, whereby on the evening of the 29th of April a coach carrying passengers from Newry to Hillsborough was set upon by a mob of up to 200 rapparees. The valiant Captain Richard Pilkington of the 37th North Hampshire Regiment of Foot, is to be commended for his stirling efforts in defending the coach almost single handed, killing the leader of the rapparees, whose men took to flight on the arrival of the militia, obviously lacking the appetite for a fair fight.' Tomas looked at Archie somewhat indignantly before continuing; 'Captain Pilkington will be rewarded for his bravery by a new commission to India.'

'That's that wee fella who shit himself,' added Betty; 'excuse the language, Reverend.'

'I've heard worse.' sighed Sandy McClung.

'So there's no one looking for young Archie here then Father?' inquired Tomas, mischieviously.

'No sir! No one is looking for Archibald save myself and his mother and his sister, who will be overjoyed to see him when we return. Mount up here boy, we are going straight ways home, and you are going to knuckle down to your studies to attend the Theological College in Ayr in the summer.'

Archie breathed and thought and tried to take it all in. It was true! He had been running for over a year for no reason. He had never been a wanted man. He had never used his real name on a job, and was referred to the 'the Preacher' almost constantly by the group. He had always kept his face covered. There was no good reason why he couldn't return as a prodigal son right this instant to the warmth and safety of his loving and forgiving family.

But there's always a but. He might not be a wanted man, but he had still been sworn in as a rapparee, and was still in Shane's service.

'I can't.' He said, looking up into his father's eyes with a wet face and red eyes. 'I have sworn a solemn oath to my Captain and my companions and they are in dire need of my help at this moment. I must continue on to Slieve Croob and complete my mission before I return home.'

'He's right there Father,' agreed Tomas; 'If you want out of the gang you've to speak to Shane McGrogan first and get his permission, sometimes a payment is demanded. If you just go off without by or leave, then the boys assume you've gone over to the other side and it's Huuuukkk!!' he drew a finger across his throat as illustration; 'the next time they see you.'

'Well then,' said the Reverend McClung. We will all go to Slieve Croob and I shall speak to this Shane McGrogan fellow myself. Now hop up here boy and no more blubbering.'

Archie mounted the trap beside his father and Tomas climbed onto Lightning behind Betty. Without further ado, the unlikely band of travellers continued on their way.

Gareth Clinton gave out a loud satisfying belch as he stretched back in his chair, patting his bloated stomach. He pushed his empty plate aside, smiling at the thought of the huge mountain of bacon and eggs he had just devoured. It was nice to be able to eat a meal without Kenneth's incessant whining about putting too much butter on the bread. He lifted the document on the table and read it again for his own amusement, chortling and shaking his head at the hilarious prank he had played on his brother earlier that day. Just then, Gareth's brother Kenneth burst through the door and he was fit to be tied. 'You devious little swine! I suppose you find your conduct amusing, have you any idea of the indignities I have been subjected to this day?'

'I haven't Kenneth no, but I would be quite interested to hear about it!' replied Gareth, cheerfully.

'You- just wait til I tell mother! What did you do it for anyway?' barked Kenneth.

'Well,' said Gareth; 'To be honest I firstways was weary of your constant sniping like an old woman.'

Kenneth's mouth fell open at this comment. 'So I thought I would let them lock you up for a few hours whilst I got a little rest from you. However on returning home I decided I should fetch your papers from the box in your room, thereby to prove your identity.' continued Gareth.

'Have you been poking around in my room while I was locked up with the Duchess?'

'For your own benefit, brother, to prove your innocence! But then I stumbled across this here in your box- Daddy's will.'

Kenneth paused; 'Oh now here, wait a minute-'

'Yes it appears you've a wee secret of your own haven't you Kenneth? Because Daddy's will doesn't name you as the sole benefactor at all, merely as the executor. In actual fact, the will states that the first of the two of us to marry will inherit the whole of the farm, save for the sum of fifty pounds which will be the given to the other to make his way in the world. I think we both know the farm is worth a great deal more than fifty pounds.'

'Now just listen a minute Gareth!' reasoned Kenneth; 'Let's not do anything hasty. I put it to you that I shall offer the sum of one hundred pounds if I retain the farm. All you have to do is allow me to marry first.'

'I could make you the same offer,' replied Gareth; 'But I won't. Daddy's will is Daddy's will. Besides I am generally considered the better looking of the twins, which is probably the source of your resentment towards me. I am confident of my ability to secure a wife for myself before you can do the same.'

'I am minded to take my belt to your backside!' shouted Kenneth, lurching forward. 'Try it brother, but rest assured such an endeavour shall terminate in your humiliation!' roared back Gareth, as he jumped to his feet. Kenneth desisted from further threats as they heard the front door creak open. Ma Clinton shuffled into the kitchen; 'Ah there you are Kenneth, both my boys together!' she smiled. 'Hello mother!' chimed the boys in unison, smiling through gritted teeth. 'Hello my boys. Gareth, I went over to Mr Henderson and sought his permission for you to call on Gracie, he said he would be delighted to receive you so you may wash your face and put your Sunday clothes on.'

'Yes mother.' said Gareth, casting a gloating smile at Kenneth.

'Kenneth, you may bring the cows in yourself this evening, your brother has courting to do!'

'Yes mother.' said Kenneth, glaring at Gareth.

Mrs Clinton went over to the stove and heated the kettle with her back to the brothers. 'You boys are so lucky to have each other. Your father and his own brother used to fight like cat and dog!'

# 13. THE PLOT UNRAVELS

In their separate groups and as individuals, the travelling rapparees and their entourages were all converging on Slieve Croob to meet with Shane McGrogan. Angus Og McGrogan arrived first, being possessed of a far superior mode of transport to the others. Shane was greatly relieved to see his brother in reasonable health although this peace of mind was short lived, as he learned of the perilous position which Lady Isabella and her maid now found themselves in. It was whilst these matters were being discussed that Barra, Annie and the children arrived, much to Shane's consternation, as this was no time to be taking on any new mouths to feed. It was in many ways a relief when Barra announced his intentions to leave the gang, as although he was a popular fellow he was by no means useful. Shane had more pressing matters to attend to than the loss of Barra's services, and he made little effort to spare McCann's feelings as he waved him away dismissively. Barra now regretted his politeness in going all the way to Slieve Croob to give Shane fair notice, but at least he was in the right place to await Tomas's return. Eugene and his party arrived next.

'Good to see you my friend,' said Eugene gravely; 'although we have met under better circumstances.'

'It warms my heart to see in good health my friend,' replied Shane; 'I understand you were forced to take charge of the mission, and I apologise for this imposition given that it was not your intention to involve yourself in our business at this stage. Angus has told me of what occurred- I chose badly to allow Seamus to command the men.'

'We have all played our part in this comedy of errors,' nodded Eugene; 'Perhaps I could have handled things better myself. But he struck a lady, and more importantly a Frenchwoman- I had no choice but to act. Young McClung is innocent of any crime by the way, his pistol discharged in error.'

'Yes I certainly wouldn't have him down for a murderer, although he carries a heavy weight on his shoulders for the loss of his father; I forgive him. But we have urgent matters to attend to here, news has reached me that the lady you spoke of is in grave danger. Hillsborough is holding her against her will and it is highly probable she may be tried and executed for treason! She risked her life to bring us the items we need, I will stop at nothing to secure her safe release. It would also appear that many of our men have fallen prey to bounty hunters, we have scarcely a score here and many are deserting as we speak. Have you any news of the men?'

Eugene sighed; 'I liberated one of the enclosures and put an end to three of the marauders, but the countryside was awash with them! My friend here can advise us of the full capacity of the bounty hunter's party.' Eugene gestured to Michael, who nodded; 'That's right sir, threescore and ten men all with muskets and horses from Belfast, not to mention another 30 or 40 who we recruited on the way. They are lead by Daniel Phillips and John Hawkins, famous for-'

'Bringing Naoise O'Haughan and his gang to the gallows.' nodded Shane. 'So as you can see Shane the situation is quite ominous, we are outnumbered 4 to 1 and most of our men are poorly equipped and ill disciplined,' said Eugene, pessimistically. 'And what of the quarry, were you able to recover it for me?' asked Shane.

'Tomas McCafferty had possession of it when last I saw it, although we are unsure as to what has become of him. McClung went into Banbridge to look for him, but they did not cross our path on the road.'

'Tomas is arriving Shane,' called Angus; 'and the Preacher with him. They appear to have taken prisioners too, a woman and a Scottish priest!'

'What!' exclaimed Shane. He didn't wait for an explanation as the group approached; 'What the hell are yous taking prisoners for, you're going to bring the whole army down on us now!'

'Don't threat Captain, she's not my prisoner, as a matter of fact I'm her prisoner!' replied Tomas smiling.

'What?'

'And this here gentleman is Archie's deceased father!'

Shane sighed; 'I really can't be thinking on your riddles at this moment McCafferty, release these people and send them home. No more nonsense.'

'We're here to ask you to let Tomas leave your gang,' interrupted Betty; 'or more precisely we're telling you he's leaving.'

'Oh are you now?' replied Shane, affronted, glancing from Tomas to Betty. Tomas dropped his gaze but Betty didn't. 'My son will also be resigning forthwith sir,' added Reverend McClung 'I intend for him to attend the theological college in Ayr and I would expect that-'

'I don't give hoot what you're intending him to do Father, he can go when I say and not before.' replied Shane. 'He will be leaving forthwith I'm afraid, although I am prepared to recompense you for any losses incurred. And you don't call me Father by the way.' replied the Reverend.

'Shane is quite right father I have obligations which I must fulfil before I retire from the road.' chipped in Archie.

'You called him father!' declared Tomas.

'I am supposed to call him father, he is my father.' replied Archie.

'As usual one law for you lot and another one for the rest of us eh?' said Tomas, with misplaced joviality. Betty jabbed him hard in the arm. 'Err... yes as I was saying Captain I'd like to be leaving the gang if you please, Betty here and I are bound for the Americas and a new start in life so if you please...'

'Mrs Higginson!' interrupted the Reverend, aghast; 'have you taken leave of your senses madam, what of your husband and child?'

The group burst into an incoherent babble, with all and sundry putting forth their opinions and being heard by no one save themselves. 'Ach stuff this. I'm away for a shite.' said Barra, meandering off towards the bushes. Shane drew his pistol and fired it in the air, silencing all. 'Enough of this nonsense! McCafferty, you have the prize which I sought, hand it over to me and not another word!'

Tomas rummaged in his pocket and tossed the necklace to Shane with the satisfied smile of a man who had just done a good job. Shane caught the jewellery in his left hand and graced it with only the swiftest of glances. Without a word of thanks, he looked up at Tomas and said; 'Where's the box?'

'What?' said Tomas, confused.

'Don't what me, where's the box Tomas?' said Shane threateningly. 'We haven't got the box, we've brought you the jewellery like Seamus said, what more do you want?' declared McCafferty, defensively. 'I want the frigging box Tomas, what have you done with the box?' roared Shane.

'We burnt the box,' admitted Eugene, reluctantly; 'we thought it was just the necklace you needed.'

'Aaaaaarrrrggghhh!!!!!' screamed McGrogan, sinking to his knees and clutching at his hair with his fingers. Everyone jumped back a little and looked at each other nervously.

'I've got a jewellery box at home if that would help.' said Betty at length, before being quietly shushed by Eugene. Shane sat cross legged on the grass, eventually letting his hands drop to his lap and looking up at Eugene in dismay.

'It's all been for nothing. My great plan! Lady Isabella held and no doubt to be executed, Seamus dead, the men hunted and captured, but still, all of that would have been worthwhile if we'd only had the box. The means to the liberation of Ireland within our grasp- and we burnt it!' He threw up his hands, shook his head and sat quietly. 'You really shouldn't let the men see you like this Shane, I mean, they're looking to you for leadership.' advised Eugene. 'All is lost, Eugene, it's over! No box, no plan, no gang, we're undone!'

'What was so important about the box if you don't mind me asking sir?' asked Archie, quietly.

'That box,' sighed Shane, 'was as valuable to the people of Ireland as the Ark of the Covenant was to the people of Israel.

When I was in France, I met with a group of powerful people, including Lady Isabella's uncle, the true Duke of Atholl. There are many amongst the Scots people who still have some fight left in them, perhaps more than the present generation of Irishmen do. These men harboured a great and noble ambition, to restore the true King of Scotland to the throne. They revealed to me that the son of the true King will make an attempt to reclaim his rightful throne within the next few years, and they assured me that if the men of Ireland were to rise with their Scottish brothers, then the freedom of both lands will be brought out from under the yoke of the Hanoverian oppressor. What they required was a man in Ireland to lead the rebellion, who could muster a force strong enough if not to defeat the English outright, at least to hold as many here as possible while Scotland fought for its freedom. It's a great ambitious plan and it could work, Eugene, I know it could.'

O'Cahan nodded in a non-commital way; 'But the box, how-'

'Information needed to be relayed to Ireland as to the names of people who should lead the rebellion in each part of the Kingdom, and there were details of where landing parties could safely arrive in order to assist us against the English. It was not considered safe to trust any one man with this information. We couldn't send a letter because a letter would be intercepted. And so an ingenius plan was formulated, whereby the information was carved into the lid of the box using an ancient cipher of letters, used here in Ireland in the old days but now long forgotten. Only myself and a few others were able to translate these symbols. And so the plan was that Lady Isabella would carry the box into Ireland for us. In order to avoid drawing suspicion to the lady, we were to contrive the ambush and seem to take the object by force, and the English would suspect that nothing more than a robbery had occurred.'

Everyone looked at each other again, each one with a different question they would like to ask but none of them daring to do so. 'So there you have it then friends,' said Shane resignedly; 'We had the ticket to a golden future right there in our hands, and we might as well have wiped our arses on it.'

A light lit up in Archie's eyes and he took off like a shot towards the crapping bush were Barra McCann had recently headed. For his part, McCann was crouched in a moment of quiet contemplation, enjoying one of the few pleasures which a man living rough in 1740s Ireland could still look forward to. His peace was broken by his friend descending on him violently almost knocking him over, tearing his coat from his back and turning it inside out in the process. Rifling through the pockets, he let out a yelp of triumph as he located the object of his desires, a piece of paper which McCann had secreted in his pocket the previous night. 'Hey, get your own paper!' protested McCann, grabbing clumsily with his breeches round his ankles; he was ill timed however as McClung took off back up the hill, coat and all. Returning to the group who were standing in either complete bafflement or defeated ambivelance, he held the paper aloft in front of his beleaguered Captain; 'I have here a copy of the writing on the top of the box sir, courtesy of Barra McCann.'

Shane snatched the paper and gazed it over intently, as McCann lumbered up, somewhat indignantly; 'Give me that coat back you!' he demanded, snatching the article.

'Barra – you – genius!' proclaimed Shane, shaking the confused rapparee's shoulder. Grinning at the others, McGrogan declared; 'the day is saved! McCann here has preserved the information needed to liberate the nation of Ireland from under the repressive boot of the Saxon hoards. There will be singing and dancing in the green fields once more!'

'Oh give it a rest will you,' said Betty, pouring water on the fire of McGrogan dreams; 'You lot were living in mud huts before we came here and put knickers on your arses. Right, our job is done then. Say goodbye to your friends Tomas, we've a boat to catch in the morning.'

'Here take this Barra, with my blessing,' said Shane, tossing the necklace to McCann; 'It's not as valuable as I may have lead you all to believe but it should be enough to get you and your family to the Americas.'

'Aww, thanks boss, that's the best thing anybody's ever given me!' said Barra, delighted. Archie interjected with a question to Barra; 'Is that a British officer's coat you're wearing?'

'Aye it is!' replied McCann proudly; 'this is the one I got proclaimed for. I wear it inside out so the boys don't think I'm an Englishman and shoot me.' Archie could think of at least a dozen scenarios over the past year where such an item could have helped get the boys out of a scrape. Given the urgency of the current situation, he let the matter drop for the time being.

'Were that it were so simple.' said Eugene; 'no great work has been done here today I'm afraid.'

'What do you mean?' asked Shane his smile fading. 'Well,' started Eugene, uncomfortably; 'You will recall that when you invited me here some months ago I agreed to observe, assess and report to you on the potentiality of your gang as a military force. It is my observation Shane, that despite having organised this gang for several years now, you have assembled a force of, at best, 40 men? Of that number, I would say that no more than a dozen hold any ambition further than evading capture and nourishing their base wants. As it is, you can seldom address even these simple demands. My assessment is that your men are poorly disciplined, have no military training, and their equipment leaves little to be desired. You equipped this man here for instance, with something resembling a musket which later blew the face off the man who was wielding it.'

Shane nodded, his feelings hurt; 'Aye. Well it isn't easy you know, coming across food and shelter with the enemy breathing down your neck, and guns are hard to come by too, because of the repressive laws of the land; but I am hoping we can draw more men to our cause when the Scotsmen rally. From many raindrops, a mighty torrent is born!'

 'Madame Higginson,' said Eugene, turning to Betty; 'How long did it take the people of Banbridge to assemble the force which harried us on the road?' Betty shrugged; 'It was timely in that the main body of the men were at our house for a celebration anyway. But I imagine under normal circumstances we could group about 200 men within an hour, most with muskets and horses. All of the farmers have guns of some description.'

'Thank you.' said Eugene, bowing; 'And Michael,' he continued; 'How long did it take your employers to recruit the hundred odd bounty hunters who are interning our comrades as we speak?'

'I was lying drunk sir but Hawkins and Phillips were able to send out runners and have that body of men assembled within a matter of hours. All of the men have their own arms and all have some degree of military experience. Rapparee hunting is highly sought after work sir, but it requires a fair amount of capital to finance such a venture. The gentleman seemed quite anxious to recover his property at any cost.'

Eugene turned to Shane with a raised eyebrow and a sympathetic half smile; 'and that's before we even count the regular army, famed as one of the best in the world, how many, 10 perhaps 12 thousand in all Ireland?' Shane sighed; 'Very well maybe our band is not currently sufficient to liberate the island however there are raparree bands from here to county Cork who..'

'Who are probably even bigger bullshitters than you are.' interrupted Betty; 'Give it up McGrogan, the only place you're leading your men is onto the point of a pike. Let everyone go and find their own fortune, instead of satisfying your own selfish ambition.'

'Or...' said Eugene, hoping to divert his friend from Betty's inflammatory rhetoric; 'You could take those men who actually wish to be of service to their country, and return with me to France where you and I, my friend, will grind and remold them into the finest of soldiers. We can then return here in a few years time with a battalion of men every bit the equal of their enemies.' Shane turned and looked down the hill at the land sweeping down before him into the green fields. He knew there was no other alternative to what Eugene had suggested, and that the advice had come from one of the finest military minds he had ever encountered. The men needed discipline, they needed respect. You can teach a man neither of these things if you can't put food in his belly. Turning once again he addressed all;

'You people seem to have it all worked out then. Very well, all may do as he wishes. I myself intend to do what I can to liberate the Lady Isabella, who may I remind you has sacrificed her own safety for the good of all, and also to recover our friends who have fallen prey to the greedy clutches of the bounty hunters.'

'You're not alone in that venture Shane, *Semper et ubique Fidelis*' declared O'Cahan; 'We shall all do whatever is necessary to extricate our fellows before they reach the goal at Downpatrick. Michael, do you know what it is that the hunters are seeking? Perhaps it may give us some clue.'

'A letter sir!' replied Michael; 'This fellow called Reverend Threader offered us all sorts of money to recover his letter with all haste.'

'Threader!' repeated Tomas; 'that's the fellow we took the satchel off, I have his letter here.'

'Let me see that a minute Tomas,' said Reverend McClung; 'I know of that person, a devious fellow indeed he is, perhaps by discovering his secret we can use it against him.'

Sandy and Archie McClung took the letter and stood at a distance, having a brief but animate discussion. Suddenly, a look of surprise came over Sandy's face, as he pointed at the letter and explained something to his son. Returning, Archie declared; 'We have the means to secure the freedom of a great many of our men here, however we must first affect the rescue of those currently held, and Lady Isabella of course. I have a few ideas as to how we might use the assets at our disposal to overcome the superior odds. But we need to put our heads together to perfect the plan, and must then act with all due haste. Time is of the essence.' The gang gathered round and with each contributing their ideas, a plan was hatched.

Hubert Toal was quietly driving his cart along the Castlewellan to Banbridge road just outside of Katesbridge, humming along to the gentle trundling of the wheels and the swishing of the horses' tails without a care in the world. His peace was broken by an approaching rabble of mounted bounty hunters, prodding a line of bound and blindfolded rapparees along the road in a very unkind manner. One of the men eyed Hubert suspiciously as he passed; 'Here you're that fella we searched earlier on aren't you? Pull that wagon over, I want to search it again.'

'What!' said Hubert, dismayed; 'You already searched me and found nought. What exactly do you think you're going to find in a cart load of hay?'

'You're hiding something you sleeked devil, no doubt about it! Look at how those two big horses labour, they're carrying something more than hay. Pull up your reins and not another word about it.' Hubert tutted with annoyance and pulled his cart over to the side. After a brief rummage, the bounty hunter held aloft a jar of poteen. 'Arrah you oul rascal!' laughed the hunter; 'this looks like a fine wee dram. How many jars have you in here?'

'Only sixty or so sir, please don't take all of them.' replied Hubert, humbly. 'Ah go on with you, about half of them will do us, a third of a jar each will get us all just a little tipsy and no more.' replied the bounty hunter, condescendingly. He beckoned the men come forward and help themselves to jars. They continued on their way, each one making sure he got his fair sup of the booze. As they moved off, none saw the flaming arrow shot into the air by a hidden archer, as a signal to his comrades just over a mile away. On the other side of Katesbridge heading towards Castlewellan a small party of rapparees lay in wait. 'They've taken the bait!' said Tomas McCafferty, seeing the signal; 'Granny's potion should have well and truly manifested by the time they get here, they'll be seeing all sorts of things.'

'Excellent.' said Betty; 'Right everyone into your positions, hold fast and no one move until I give the signal. Preacher, you know what to do.'

'I'm supposed to be leading this miss-'

'You can lead the next one.' interrupted Betty, knowing there wouldn't be a next one.

The captive rapparees for their part were baffled and somewhat disturbed at the drastic change in tone and conversation of their captors, who were now laughing and babbling incoherently as they went along the road. They pointed and laughed at trees and bushes, waved to imaginary little people and broke into convulsions over nonsensical jokes and anecdotes. As the skies grew darker and the trees seemed to reach in overhead, their mirth turned to anxiety, and then to fear. They were alarmed to hear strange calls and a woman's scream from somewhere in the darkness. They proceeded cautiously and shakily, a silent erriness pervading their mood. The group gave a collective jump as a loud cry was heard in the road ahead, and an officer of the 37th North Hampshire regiment burst forth from the bushes. 'Flee! All is lost!' cried the terrified officer, as the startled bounty hunters looked on in confusion; 'Hold there! What is occurring?' called the leader.

'The Toad people! They've infested the forest, they've wiped out my whole company and eaten my men alive! Bullets cannot harm them, they are of the Devil himself!'

Terror and panic spread like wildfire through the group, despite their leader's efforts to rally them; 'Stand firm! We are ninety armed men here, what harm can befall us?' The question was answered as two horrific toad monsters pounced from the bushes, ripping the arms from the young officer who fell to his knees in a mass of blood. The men dropped their weapons and took to flight like startled sheep as another dozen of the hideous creatures emerged from the bushes, leaving the bound and blindfolded prisoners in terror and ignorance, to the mercy of the creatures of the forest. As the hunters disappeared from sight, the band of rapparees removed their masks and set about freeing their companions. Archie McClung stood up and extracted his own arms from the inside of his coat, before lifting up the two false arms and inspecting them with pleasure. 'That young Connor Toal really does have a talent for making these gruesome artefacts.'

'Yes.' agreed Eugene O'Cahan, removing his false toad head; 'I told him to put his talent to good use and he's certainly done that. Our mission could not have gone better my friend, let's hope that Shane and your father fare as well as we did!'

The guard on duty at the Hillsborough estate were quietly vigilant, carrying out their regular perimeter searches in order to deter any further incursions by rapparees, but not overly visible in order to prevent the ball guests being unduly alarmed. The ball was actually a glorified dinner party by the standards of the day, with less than 30 guests attending, the immediate area not being greatly over populace with aristocrats to invite to such an event. A judge and his wife here or a physician there would arrive. Colonel Lambert himself only got an invite to make up the numbers, not being the most popular person with the Viscount at the present time. Richard Pilkington was sulkily going about the task of overseeing the sentries, a duty which he considered to be beneath him, as an officer and a gentleman. The job had been allotted to him by Colonel Lambert, who had ordered the young Captain to take over all of Sergeant Wilkes' responsibilities until his transfer to India came through. This was both a punishment and a practicality given the unexpected loss of an experienced Sergeant. Lambert had not at all been impressed with his nephew's shenanigans at the duel and his expressions of relief at having got off the hook by another man being injured. Pilkers threw himself into the job with his usual gusto by ordering the sentries to search only the front portion of the house, allowing him to slope about idly on the veranda under Lady Isabella's bedroom. His plan, if he was discovered, was to claim that he had taken personal charge of the most vulnerable part of the mansion which was also the most likely to be attacked, a strategy which was about as likely to get him out of hot water as his little scheme of riding inside the carriage had done the previous day. It is true what they say, the definition of an idiot is someone who makes the same mistake over and over again.

Pilkington however thought himself an immensely clever fellow to come up with such a plan, and fancied the idea that he might he even espy the lady or her handmaid in a state of partial undress from the window. He thought himself all the more fortunate to find that an elegant figure clad in a daffodil yellow summer dress, the lower part of her face hidden behind a delicate lace fan approached, giving him the eye in a suggestive manner. 'Good evening milady,' said the Captain, bowing gallantly. 'Such a pleasure to see such a vision of loveliness on this fine night, I'm afraid you've strayed quite far from the main party though, might I escort you?'

'Oh no, no need for that at all young man,' came the flirtatious reply; 'just popped out for a breath of fresh air. Am I to presume that you are the famous Captain Pilkington, hero of the battle of Banbridge?'

Pilkers blushed with false modesty; 'You compliment me far too much miss-?'

'Victoria. The Duchess of Dromore.'

'Your servant Ma'am' said the Captain bowing low to kiss the lady's gloved white hand. 'Why you do have a tight grip.' He said nervously, struggling to release his hand; 'And hairy arms!'

Biff!

A swift uppercut with a right knocked the hapless Captain Pilkington out cold. 'Good work Victor.' said Shane, sneaking up stealthily. 'Ok Barra, you know what to do,' Barra McCann stepped forward out of the darkness and threw his hook up onto the balcony of Lady Isabella's room, where it caught on to the railings. After testing the rope to make sure it could take his weight, Shane climbed quickly up and tapped on the window, to be answered by Amelie. Despite Amelie's protestations, Shane clambered awkwardly through the window and landed with a clump onto the thick piled carpet. Isabella, who had been attended by Amelie, gasped in surprise at the sight of the dark raparree entering her boudoir; 'Shane! What are doing here?'

'No time to explain, where are your clothes?'

'They're in the wardrobe there but-'

Shane marched over to the wardrobe and flung the door open. Scooping up a half dozen dresses in one arm, he strode back over to the window and stuck his head out; 'Here you are Duchess, as agreed!' He threw the clothes down to Victor Spratt below, who scooped them up greedily; 'Thank you sir, a pleasure doing business with you!' hissed the delighted farmer as he disappeared into the night.

'What the- did you just give away all my clothes?' demanded Isabella, shocked. 'Well I had to give him something didn't I, the man just risked his life to rescue you! He knocked out 3 guards with his bare hands.' replied Shane.

'But you don't understand, I don't need rescuing, Wills has-'

'We've no time to jabber here woman, be still. Mademoiselle Babineux, you climb down the rope first. I will assist your lady with her injured hand. My friend Barra will help you at the bottom.'

Amelie looked to Isabella, confused.

'Go will you! Time is of the essence here.' snapped Shane, with frantic shoo-ing motions.

Amelie climbed out the window and lowered herself down the rope.

'Shane, will you listen please, we don't need rescuing, Wills has persuaded the Colonel there is no cause for concern! Shane, what are you looking for?' Shane was over at the writing bureau poking around as if he'd never seen one before and didn't know how to open it. 'I am looking for some paper and ink, I intend to leave an insulting message to the Viscount!'

'What on earth for? Shane will you please just leave!'

'Ah stuff it, I'll just shit on the bed!'

'You will do nothing of the sort!' protested Isabella; 'get down from there at once!'

Just then the door flew open and Viscount Hills burst in with his sword drawn, to be faced with the sight of Shane McGrogan squatting on the grand four poster bed with his breeches round his ankles. Shane pulled his bags up and drew his own sword, but Isabella threw herself in between the two men. 'Wills, please, no!' she pleaded. The Viscount was quick to put two and two together and his face dropped as he realised that his dearest friend was indeed a traitor. 'So I see. It's true then. You plot to dethrone the King. Isabella can you not see this is madness?'

'He may be your king he is not my king, Wills. To me, keeping the rightful King of Scotland in exile whilst a foreigner rules in his stead is the true injustice. Please try to see this from my point of view.'

Wills sighed, fell silent momentarily and then spoke; 'I cannot and will not condone anything so contrary to the wellbeing of my country or its people, what you speak of is treachery pure and simple. However I cannot find it in my heart to see you lose your life prematurely at the end of a rope, so I suggest you leave now and never return.' Glancing over at Shane, he added; 'The next time I lay eyes on you sir, only one of us shall live to tell of it,'

'Oh, you can depend on that.' nodded Shane. With that, the Viscount turned, walked out and closed the door behind him. As he walked down the corridor he reached into his pocket and took out the ring he had intended to give to Isabella that night. He gave a fleeting half smile and placed it back in his pocket.

Joseph Threader was arched over the writing table in his study in the rectory of his little church in Killeavey when Mrs Jacobs the house keeper rapped politely on the door. 'Come.' He said, with his usual dryness, not deigning to look up from the incredibly dull sermon he was writing to blight the Sabbath of his parishioners, or the best two hours of it anyway. Mrs Jacobs entered with slight nervousness given her employer's unpredictable temperament; 'I beg your pardon sir, there's a gentleman of the Presbyterian church here wishing to speak to you.'

Threader tutted dismissively; 'Come to beg alms no doubt. Send him in then, but keep an eye on the silverware if you will.' Mrs Jacobs curtsied and asked the Minister to enter. Threader glanced up and was surprised to see his old adversary Sandy McClung come to visit. 'What do you want McClung I'm a busy man.'

'Got a lot of old women to burn then have you Joe?' replied Sandy, facetiously.

'That's Reverend Threader to you. What is it you're after? Say what you have to say and get out.'

'It's not so much a matter of what I'm after Joe, it's more about what I can give you.'

'There is nothing that you could possibly possess McClung, that I would be interested in acquiring. I'm surprised they didn't pull down that ramshackle little outbuilding you call a church years ago.'

'So you wouldn't be interested in acquiring certain papers then, or to be more precise, a love letter from James Cardwell, Bishop of Newry, to Simonus Castellum; Simonus, being Simon, as in the disciple Simon who was called Peter, and Castellum as in Castle, just like- oh, I don't know, Peter Castle, Bishop of Down and Connor?' said Sandy, with a raised eyebrow. 'Those are scurrilous accusations Sir!' barked Threader, standing up. 'They are indeed my dear Threader, fortunately the good Bishop, whilst possessing the wherewithal to sign his name with an alias, albeit an ineffectual one, did not have the foresight to omit the bishop's seal from his correspondence! All is not well in the house of the not-so established church, were that Jenny Geddes were alive to see this day!'

'McClung- listen to me- this could be disastrous not just for the church but for the stability of the entire kingdom! If you have the letter you must hand it over at once, I will see that you are suitably rewarded.' begged Threader, desperately.

'The letter is in a safe place Threader, that's all I'm prepared to say for now. Here you can see I have made a copy as proof to your masters that I am in possession of the letter. Now, we get down to the business of the trade off.'

Threader sat back in his chair, white faced. Sandy McClung took his hat off and placed it on the desk, before perching on the corner and glaring down at the powerless Threader. 'So what is it your looking for then?' said Joseph Threader at length. 'Well firstly, I would like you to call off the search for rapparees. Pay your men off and tell them to quit the job. They will then release any remaining captives without further harm.'

Threader nodded; 'I can do that. I will ride to Banbridge in the morning and-'

'No Joseph, you will ride to Banbridge tonight. My second condition is a bit more difficult to acquiesce, however I am sure that where there's a will there's a way. You will instruct your Bishops to petition the powers that be, to see that everyone named on this list is a given a free and unconditional pardon.' Sandy drew the list of proclaimed persons from his inside pocket and pushed it across the polished dark oak writing desk to Threader. Examining the document, the cleric declared; 'But there must be over a hundred names on this list! The church doesn't have the power to-'

'Oh come on, Threader, use your imagination! There are plenty of backs to be scratched and palms to be greased in the corridors of power are there not? The church must either use its power to meet my demands, or it will lose its power altogether when the contents of the letter become public, the choice is yours.'

Threader sighed as he looked over the list. 143 names, many of them rapparees but more often than not harmless vagrants and people who had absconded without paying their rent. The Bishops would not be overjoyed with this news, but it was just about achievable, and infinitely preferable to the alternative. Eventually he spoke; 'Christ Sandy you Scotsmen drive a hard bargain.'

'That's Reverend McClung to you.' replied McClung, grinning smugly; 'and I will take that as a compliment.' Threader nodded. 'I dare say it will take a few weeks to sort all these pardons out, I must confess I am no great student of the law however as you say, the Bishops' influence is considerable.'

McClung nodded; 'Well as soon as the pardons have been posted I shall ensure that the letter is received into the hands of its rightful owner. I'll let you get on with finishing your sermon then, something on Matthew 7:5 might I suggest? Goodnight Joe.'

With that, Reverend McClung put on his hat and left Threader to his thoughts.

## 14. Breaking Even

The gang met up again at Slieve Croob shortly before dawn and the various parties all reported on the success of their respective missions with great pride. After consulting with Reverend McClung, Shane addressed the assembled rapparees; 'The past few days have been strenuous for us all; we have lost some good men, my brother and Owen McClatchy included, both of whom died valiantly in the service of Ireland whilst engaging the enemy.'

Betty and Isabella who were stood quietly at the back, exchanged incredulous glances and raised eyebrows at this blatantly untrue statement. Isabella stifled a giggle as Betty mouthed the words 'lying bastard.' Shane continued unawares; 'Many of you have been pursued, imprisoned, beaten, and given reason to fear for your life. This is the way of the rapparee, this is the life we choose. We tread the perilous ground so that others may hope to sow flowers in our wake. Many of you here have joined with me to help rid this country of the twin plagues of privilege and injustice, others I am aware took to the road when these very forces which we rail against deprived us of any alternative means of making a living, or harried us for trivial offences. When Seamus and I founded the gang we envisioned that many others would follow our lead and in time a mighty army would be born, however in truth we may never be in a position to offer a legitimate challenge to the tyranny of the Saxons. It is therefore with regret, that I have decided to disband the gang forthwith.'

A muttered ripple of concern spread across the assembled group as the men considered the consequences of Shane's decision; 'However, I am not abandoning you to the elements or to the mercy of our foes, far from it. Our friend here Reverend McClung has secured an agreement for us whereby the hunters have ceased to seek out our people forthwith, and furthermore a pardon will be issued for each of you within the coming weeks. By the end of the month you shall all be free men again.' The mood of the assembly lightened noticeably as the group groaned in relief. 'But there's more. I am sure that like me, there are plenty of you here who still have the stomach to take the fight to the English. To those of you who don't you are free to leave now, and no disgrace will be served upon you. You have already done more than most men in the fight for Ireland's freedom, and may hold your heads high in any company. To those of you who do, Eugene and I leave this morning to return to France, where I shall renew my commission in the service of the King of that great nation. Make no mistake my friends, Ireland has no greater ally against the English than King Louis of France. We would urge you to join us in this venture, and in due time we shall return to our mother country as a force to be reckoned with, and claim it once more as our own. The choice is yours my friends, and whatever you decide to do you may do so with my eternal blessing, respect and friendship.'

Shane was greatly relieved to find that his speech was well received by the gang who gave a spontaneous round of applause, and one by one each of the gang came forward to shake his hand and offer their thanks for all he had done for them. His elation faded gradually as it became apparent that most of the men were saying goodbye, with all but half a dozen electing to follow him to France. When all had said their goodbyes Betty stepped forwards and slapped him on the shoulder with mock affection; 'Wonderful speech there Shane, a pity that there's not too many save yourself who share your enthusiasm for a free Ireland. Do you ever wonder if you are, in fact, something of a latter day Don Quixote with your pointless quest?'

Shane turned and looked quietly down at Betty before replying with a mischievous grin; 'Or a bit like your husband with his wedding vows even!' Betty stood with her arms crossed and fixed a withering glare on the rapparee leader as he marched happily down the hill. 'She walked right into that one,' whispered Sandy McClung to his son; 'Matthew 7:5 seems to apply to a whole host of situations. We should be getting back now my son, your mother and your sister will be getting anxious to see you after all this time.'

'And I them, father.' replied Archie, happily. 'I must say my goodbyes to everyone before I leave.'

He went first of all to Eugene, who removed his thick leather glove and shook McClung's hand firmly. 'I am indebted to you for my life my friend, should you ever tire of the clergy there will always be a place for you in the regiment.'

'I appreciate the offer sir but I feel that I am done the harsh realities of life, I crave now more than anything a soft bed and a warm hearth.' replied Archie.

'We shall see,' replied Eugene, grinning; 'there may be more of the high life which you miss than you now realise.' Turning to Tomas and Barra, he embraced both warmly; 'The two of you have become like brothers to me over the past year, I am honoured to have counted the both of you as my friends. Look out for each other in the colonies, I know that you will prosper.'

'Come with us Archie!' implored Barra; 'What adventures we will have in the new world! What treasures we will discover!' Archie shook his head; 'I have only just found my family again I cannot run from them now. God has given me a second chance to live in his will and I am called to his service. I will never forget you my friend.' Saying goodbye to Angus was more awkward as although his friend had accepted that his elder brother's death was an accident, Angus had still not fully came to terms with what had happened. A hand was offered and refused due to the injury to Angus' shoulder, however a nod was returned. Archie wasn't quite sure if the handshake would have taken place if there had been no injury, however he resolved not to grieve over something that was beyond his control anyway. Finally McClung turned to his Captain Shane McGrogan; 'I am forever in your debt Shane,' said Archie, humbly; 'When you took me in last year I had nothing save the clothes on my back, and I believed myself to be a wanted man. Were it not for you I would surely have perished in the wilds.'

'I am sure you would have prospered no matter what befell you Archie,' replied Shane, amiably; 'you have proven yourself to be a most resourceful fellow, and have met all adversity with zest and resolution. If you commit yourself to your studies with the same determination as you have done to serving your companions, you will make a fine clergyman, albeit of an errant religion.'

Archie chuckled at the last part of the sentence. 'However,' continued Shane; 'I cannot allow the death of my brother to go unpunished, I have a reputation to uphold.'

'But-' protested Archie, surprised.

'Sergeant Archibald McClung, for the crime of mutinying against your Captain, Seamus McGrogan, deceased, I hereby expel you from my company. Have you anything to say in your defence?'

'No,' said Archie, relieved; 'No that's quite all right by me Captain.'

'I thought it would be,' said Shane, holding his hand out with a faint grin; 'good luck my friend.'

Archie and his father climbed into their pony trap and waved to all as they headed back down towards Ballyvally. His heart was heavy at the thought of never seeing his friends again, given everything they had been through together, but he knew that a much brighter future was beginning to dawn for him. He thought of his bed, his home and his mother and sister waiting for him, and a single tear rolled down his cheek. His father glanced sideways but said nothing. Inwardly, he gave his heartfelt thanks to his God for the return of his prodigal son. The rest of the group travelled part of the ways together, with Barra, Annie, Tomas and Betty and Annie's children heading to Newry and Shane, Eugene, Michael, Isabella, Amelie and the others bound for a secret location somewhere along the coast, where a small boat had been chartered to spirit the group back to France via Scotland. This was expected to be quite an arduous journey even by the standards of the time and not at all the sort of thing that Isabella and Amelie were accustomed to. Everyone was however quite relieved when the two groups finally parted, as Shane and Betty's constant bickering had long since exceeded its capacity to entertain.

There was someone else however with a much longer, much more unpleasant journey ahead of him. Captain Richard Pilkington of the 37th North Hamsphire Regiment was by no means overjoyed with the commission he had earned for his acts of bravery against the rapparees, jacobites and conspirators as he leant over the guide ropes of the East India Company's Clipper the Salty Witch, trying to be sick. 'Finding our sea legs are we young fellow?' said the bluff captain, slapping him affectionately on the back. 'Please be careful sir, one is feeling a little green around the gills.' replied Pilkers, miserably. The Captain chuckled; 'We haven't even hauled anchor yet! Still with a good wind at our backs, we should be there by this evening.'

'What, India?' asked Pilkington, leaning up. 'Heavens no sir, Portsmouth! Tis from Portsmouth we shall sail for India. It takes months and months to get to India sir, round the cape and through the roughest of seas. Plenty of time for you to savour life on the ocean wave.' Pilkers sobbed gently in a manner most unbecoming of an officer and an Englishman. 'Cheer up sir!' beamed the Captain, slapping Pilkers on the back again. 'It's not all doom and gloom. Tonight you shall dine with me at my table, cook is making a special celebration dinner. Mutton pie I think.' The Captain wandered off licking his lips as Pilkington heaved his breakfast into the deep blue sea.

Shane's accomplices had wasted no time in getting under sail in the hope of evading any Royal Navy patrols, and the small group huddled together above deck as they braced themselves against a strong, penetrating wind. Shane looked out to the sea and then to the disappearing shores of Ireland. 'Farewell my sweet green fields, I shall return to you again ere too long,' he said poetically. 'Well friends, I am sure you will agree that this mission did not go as smoothly as we would have hoped it to. However, we have striven in the face of adversity and live to fight another day. I feel we should congratulate ourselves on a job well done.'

'Oh do you now sir,' replied Isabella, who had maintained an uncomfortable silence for quite long enough. 'Yes, well, we got you out alive and well didn't we? Right from out of the jaws of the lion, so to speak!' explained Shane, cheerfully.

'Jaws of the lion? I would have been in no danger whatsoever had you and your men shown even the slightest bit of common sense or competency. First of all, you made a complete hash of the ambush, resulting in poor Amelie here receiving a broken nose and I myself almost having a finger ripped off-'

'Well there are always dangers associated with-' interjected Shane

'Then,' continued Isabella, 'for reasons unbeknownst to anyone save yourself, you exposed us to further danger by visiting me at Wills' house, who by the way will probably never speak to me again!'

'No loss there eh?' replied Shane with an uncomfortable half grin, scanning the group for some sign of support. There was none. 'But that's not all, no. Betty informs me that your men actually managed to burn the box? The object which Amelie and I risked our lives to bring here to you, and they just threw it on the fire! And why Shane? Because YOU never told them what it was they were supposed to be looking for!'

'Now hang on! The reason for that was that if they'd been captured and interrogated-'

'And then of course, your so called 'rescue'. Oh, what an episode of daring do that was, worthy of Robin Hood himself. Except that I didn't need rescued Shane, as it was I was about to attend a very pleasant ball in my honour, and would have been travelling home tomorrow in the lap of luxury. However, you weren't to be outdone in your quest to bring misery into my life were you Sir? Not only did you manage to give away all of my finest clothes to a madman wearing a dress, not only did you ruin my friendship with one of my oldest and dearest companions, thanks to you I am now underway on a two to three day journey on this glorified barge!'

'Admittedly there are certain aspects of this mission which on reflection-'

'Don't! Just don't Shane, I do not want to hear another word of your excuses, boasts or delusions. This whole situation has been a laughable farce from start to finish. I am going below deck now, and I would be grateful if you refrained from speaking with me for the rest of the journey, and for some time after that also.'

With that, Isabella, turned, lifted her skirts and stormed off down the steps to the boat's single cabin. Amelie curtsied and followed. Shane and his group stood silently for several seconds. 'Sorry how that worked out for you Shane, I thought you had rather a soft spot for the Lady Isabella.' said Eugene, at length. 'Who that one?' said Shane, casually; 'Nah, not me, I like a bit of meat on the bones if you know what I mean. Besides, she's a refined Lady used to soft living. She would never be able to adapt to our Irish ways and customs.' A pained expression came over Shane's face and he stood for several seconds staring into the middle distance. The gang looked at each other in bewilderment. The rapparee Captain let out a long lingering fart and a satisfied smile came over his face. He wandered off down the deck, leaving his friends to enjoy the smell.

# Epilogue

George Higginson dandered idly down the stairs of 26 Newry Street Banbidge, a broad grin of satisfaction spread across his pleasantly plump face as he re-read the note that Betty left him on the dressing table the night before. He had got back relatively late and after a quick supper had retired to bed without the aid of a candle, as was his custom. He had assumed Betty to be grinding away at some seemingly pointless task somewhere in the yard or another part of the house, and it was only the breaking dawn illuminating the lace bedroom curtains with disparate shards of light which eventually roused him from his slumber. He had unfolded the letter curiously and held it at arms length to decipher Betty's spiky handwriting;

'My Dearest George,

You may be aware that I have of late, grown increasingly restless and frustrated with both our home life and your general attitude towards the business. I feel that our differences have become irreconcilable and it is with great regret that I must inform you that I am leaving you forthwith and shall not be returning. I have taken what funds are necessary for my immediate sustenance and no more. Please do not attempt to pursue me or to change my mind. Give John my love.

PS I shall put Lightning into stables at the Kings Arms Newry, you can collect him there.

PPS You MUST wash out the store and the front shop from top to bottom at least 3 times a week, the tiny creatures I told you about which bring disease DO exist, I am sure of it.

Betty.'

Sitting down at the table, the master butcher gave a wry smile and shook his head as he read the last sentence. 'Tiny creatures indeed. There's wiser locked up.' John Higginson entered and scanned round the room. 'Where's me Ma?' he asked, bluntly. 'Your Ma has left us son!' replied George, leaning back in his chair and making no effort to disguise his glee; 'she's run off to join the circus or something, God alone knows.'

'What!' replied John, more annoyed than shocked; 'Who's going to run the shop? Who's going to make the tea? Who's going to clean out the stables?'

'Well son,' said George, pouring himself a cup of tea, 'obviously things are going to have to change a bit around here. I'm 53 with a bad back, and I certainly don't intend to work myself into an early grave with my big lump of a son idling about the countryside getting himself into trouble. You will be 16 next month and a man in the eyes of the law, as it is there are lads younger than you serving in the army and navy, so I'm offering you a choice my son.'

John stood open mouthed in shock at his father's bold words, the years of Betty's mollycoddling having sheltered him from taking responsibility for his own behaviour. 'Your choice is this John; either you can knuckle down under me, do your fair share of the work, learn the trade, and stop disrespecting your fellows in the frightfully childish manner in which you have been doing. I in return will allow you to take over joint running of the business when you attain the age of 18 and full mastery of said business at the age of 21. Alternatively, I will award you sum of £100 on your 16th birthday, and you may leave here to make your own way in the world, although I must caution that young men availing of such an option invariably gamble away their fortunes within a few months and end their short lives in the gutter, with little to show for themselves save for sad stories and regrets. The choice is yours son.'

John stared at his father wide-eyed for a long silent minute while the wheels and cogs whirred in his head. This was probably the first serious decision the boy had made in his short and indolent life. He cast his mind back to the events of the past few days, the consequences of his foolishness. Finally he spoke; 'I would very much like to learn the butchery trade sir.'

George beamed and slapped his son's shoulder; 'Good lad, I'm proud of you! Right let's get down to work. They're coming to pick your man up and take him to Downpatrick later today' George nodded to Seamus McGrogan's prone corpse; 'They're going to hang draw and quarter his corpse would you believe! Utterly pointless but I'm sure some fool will gain amusement from it. Then they will pay me the twenty pounds. There's to be no more of the incessant scrubbing your mother insisted on. I suggest instead we shut up shop early this Saturday and you and I shall go fishing together- we haven't been fishing in years!'

John nodded and grinned at this suggestion. 'Right my boy, I'm off out to the yard to fetch in some water. Why don't you light the fire there, we'll have sausages and eggs for breakfast.'

'Very good father.' agreed John. George picked up the bucket and went out into the yard as John pulled the curtain over, which was separating Seamus' carcass from the rest of the room. He struck the flint and lit the sticks under the stove and watched as they began to crackle, before carefully adding some coal. He stared up at the high window and wondered how to open it without the window pole. The room could get very warm with the fire lit and no window open. He resolved to leave it as is and get on with some other work. The bell rang in the front of the shop and John went in to greet the customer; 'Morning sir, what can I get for you?' Back in the store room the temperature was rising quickly. No one was there to see as Seamus McGrogan's eyes flicked open.


THE END?